Misty Lake in Focus

Margaret Standafer

MISTY LAKE IN FOCUS

By Margaret Standafer

Copyright © 2016 by Margaret Standafer

All rights reserved.

ISBN-13: 978-1537394060

This book is a work of fiction. Names, characters, places, and incidents are either the product of the author's imagination or are used fictitiously. Any resemblance to actual persons, living or dead, business establishments or locales is entirely coincidental.

For the other four of the Original Five.
We make quite a team.

A very special thank you to those who helped make this book possible.

To my beta readers, Joan, Jan, and Jen:
Triple J, your feedback, as always, was invaluable.

To Kim, who was so patient with all my newbie yoga questions and who made Shauna an expert.

To my cover designer, Kristin Bryant, who always seems to know what I want even when I don't.
Contact her at kristindesign100@gmail.com

And to Phil, my brainstorming partner, my sounding board, my first test audience…my everything.

1

Cassie gave one final wave goodbye and then closed the door softly behind the last guests when what she really wanted to do was slam it. Hard. The Johanssons had been the stuff of innkeepers' nightmares. They'd shown up on Friday a full two hours before check-in time demanding their room. When Cassie had politely told them it wasn't quite ready, they had staked out a spot in the parlor and had spent the next ninety minutes alternately badgering her regarding the status of the room and sending her to fetch everything from magazines to cocktails. And it had only gotten worse.

Oh well, she told herself, they were the exception. For the most part, the guests they'd had over the past six months had been a joy…thrilled with the bed and breakfast, with the lake and surroundings, and, for those who had taken advantage of it, with the ambiance and functionality of the barn-turned-event center. The Inn at

Misty Lake was a huge success.

It was some sort of teacher workshop day, so Cassie got Jennica and Jordyn—the sisters she and Susan had hired to help out with cleaning on the weekends and over their school breaks—started on the guest rooms. She then sat down to go over the upcoming reservations and to check email.

She was going to owe Susan another drink soon.

Back in August, when Cassie had come to Misty Lake from Chicago to start working at the inn, she'd tried to convince Susan to close after the holidays and reopen in the spring. They could use the time to tackle the small details they knew they wouldn't get to before their grand opening in September. And Cassie had assured Susan she'd be okay with a reduced salary during their down time. Everything she knew about the hotel business—and it was a lot considering she'd been working at it since the age of sixteen—had told her it was the right thing to do. A bed and breakfast in Minnesota's lake country, and a relatively unknown one at that, simply wasn't going to fill up during the dead of winter. She'd argued long and hard, trying to explain to Susan they'd be losing money keeping the place open, but Susan had dug her heels in and had insisted she knew what she was doing.

Cassie'd had to make good on her bet when the reservations had started coming in months in advance for January and February. Apparently she had underestimated the strange appeal of ice fishing and snow shoeing as well as the popularity of the town's annual Snow Daze celebration. All that, combined with Valentine's Day, had added up to them being booked solid every weekend and with a more than respectable occupancy rate on weekdays.

Cassie had taken Susan out for margaritas back in November when they'd filled the rooms through Valentine's Day. Now, as she looked at the new emails and confirmed reservations into March and April, she figured she'd be doing it again soon. It was definitely a good thing to have to think about. Cassie never doubted the inn would be successful, she just hadn't guessed it would be so successful so quickly. Looking back, she should never have doubted Susan Taylor…correction, Susan McCabe. The woman was as hard-working and determined as anyone she'd ever met. When Susan had decided to convert the old farmhouse into a bed and breakfast, she'd given it her all. And it showed, Cassie thought, looking around her.

The parlor was a cozy step back in time with many of the house's original features including a huge stone fireplace, a glowing, refinished wood floor, and even a few antique pieces of furniture and knick-knacks left behind by previous owners. What wasn't original had been carefully selected with the help of Shauna McCabe, Susan's sister-in-law and admitted antique nut, to match the Rococo Revival style. Cassie remembered how Shauna had succinctly informed them that 'Victorian' was really just a catchall category and encompassed several separate and distinct styles. Cassie had stopped listening about ten minutes in, hedging her bets that her guests wouldn't ask too many questions. In truth, Cassie hadn't ever given antiques much thought, preferring the new and modern, but she had fallen in love with the room.

Susan's cousin, Sam, had worked hard to repair and refinish some of the pieces that Shauna had insisted were well worth the effort. One of Cassie's favorites was an ornate chair made from dark walnut with intricate carvings on the arm rests, a plush red velvet seat cushion, and cabriole legs—a term she'd learned from Shauna and that still made her feel like something of a fraud when she used it in conversation with a curious guest. The red cushion worked well with the exposed brick wall in varying shades of red that had been covered with plaster and hidden for years, but discovered during renovation. The writing desk she sat behind and that was tucked into the corner of the parlor to serve as their registration area, was another of Cassie's favorites. Its marble top had just the smallest chip on one corner, but otherwise the piece had been restored to its original glory and provided the perfect work surface.

Cassie was glad Susan had kept the fussy accessories in the room to a minimum. Shauna had shown them countless examples of lace doilies, glass table lamps, ruffled throw pillows, and ceramic figurines that would fit with the time period of the furniture they'd salvaged. And, it seemed, everything had been pink. Susan had selected just a few things to scatter around the parlor, but had tempered the look with some updated, even some lake-themed, items. Somehow it worked, and the room was a favorite gathering spot for their guests.

Cassie managed to busy herself for a few hours answering emails, checking inventory and placing orders, following up with the linen supply company on changes to their standing order, and taking a little time to search the web for interesting brunch recipes. After Jennica and Jordyn finished the cleaning and said their goodbyes, Cassie checked the rooms, but like usual, everything was neat, clean, and in place. The two had been a very lucky find.

Today, however, she wished she could have found some fault with their work because she was running out of things to keep her busy and she knew once she slowed down, she'd have to start thinking about the coming evening.

She restlessly clicked the pen she was holding and tried to keep her nerves from getting the better of her as she made a few notes for Susan. They needed to finalize plans for the bridal shower group that had booked both the inn and the event center for early April. The budget for the shower appeared to be somewhere around infinity so Cassie and Susan had been dreaming up all sorts of elaborate ideas for food, decorations, and entertainment. It would be the grandest event, outside of Sam's and Susan's weddings, that they had hosted. The caterer and the decorating company needed final decisions soon. The mother of the bride who had contacted them to arrange for the shower had given them carte blanche with regard to the event....and with her credit card. Her only stipulations had been that it be fabulous, fun...and purple.

Initially, Susan had balked at the idea of hosting a shower with so few parameters. The guests were supposed to take care of planning, she and Cassie would just make sure it happened like they wanted.

Cassie, however, had embraced the challenge. She'd had experience handling some fairly fancy affairs during her stint at a resort in the Catskills and had convinced Susan they'd have fun with the shower. And the amount they were charging would make it all worthwhile.

They had already ordered personalized champagne flutes and had booked a country band to perform on Saturday evening. Keeping with the theme, they'd gotten shirt sizes from all the band members and had ordered purple cowboy shirts for them to wear during their performance. It would be a nice touch with the purple cowboy hats all the attendees would be receiving.

Cassie reviewed the options they had considered for party favors and then had to laugh to herself at the term. The items they were considering weren't like any party favors she'd ever received. She studied the information for the plush, monogrammed robes and matching slippers they had been considering and, knowing Susan had liked them just as much as she had, went ahead and placed the order so she could be sure they would arrive in time. The robes and slippers were only part of the swag the guests would be taking home with them, but she was certain they would be favorites. She could picture all twenty women sitting in the parlor in their matching robes, sipping champagne, laughing, and thinking what a perfect choice the Inn at Misty Lake was for their celebration.

After another thirty minutes focusing on details for the shower, Cassie couldn't find anything else to occupy her mind. She glanced at the clock. Susan and Riley would be on their way back from the airport by now. Her stomach flipped at the thought. Other than the long weekend in September when he'd come home for Sam and Jake's wedding, and then the ten days he'd been back for Christmas and for Susan and Riley's New Year's Eve wedding, Cassie hadn't seen Frank since the previous April. That day, having no idea what was headed her way, she'd been shocked to her core to find out he was the twin brother of Susan's then boyfriend, now husband, Riley.

Frank had left on a cross-country assignment for a prestigious magazine photographing historic farmhouses and barns before Cassie had started her position in Misty Lake. Cassie couldn't help but wonder if he would have accepted the job if the situation had been different and she hadn't been on her way to town. Now he was back to stay, and she knew she'd have to come up with some answers as to what happened between them years ago.

And figure out how she was supposed to deal with the fact they'd be living together.

2

Cassie almost turned her car around before she got to Sean and Anna McCabe's house, but knew it would just be postponing the inevitable. It was a small town, he was the twin brother of Susan's husband, and, most importantly, Cassie was living in his house. She wasn't going to avoid him for long.

She cursed herself again for her decision months ago agreeing to the living arrangements. When she'd arrived in Misty Lake Frank was already gone and Riley was living alone in the house he and Frank shared, but was so busy with the finishing touches on the inn and with spending time with Susan, he was hardly ever there. Everyone had told her moving in to the McCabe brothers' house was the perfect solution. A few months later, after Riley and Susan had gotten married, Cassie'd had the house to herself. That was fine because she had been certain Riley would quickly tire of living at the inn and that he would convince Susan the two of them should move back to town. Then Cassie would move into Susan's room at the inn since one of them would need to live on site, and she would be far away from Frank's house well before he finished his assignment. But that hadn't happened, she was still living in Frank's house, and what had all made so much sense a few months ago, now seemed like a colossal mistake.

She smoothed her jeans, applied a quick touch of lip gloss, and ran a hand over her wild mass of black curls. It was a move she knew was an exercise in futility as the hair simply had a mind of its own, but it ate up a few more seconds and delayed her walk to the door.

Cassie knew the whole family would be there to welcome Frank home. She and Susan had argued about the evening. Cassie had said she shouldn't be included, she wasn't family and she'd be intruding, but Susan had just brushed Cassie's arguments aside. Now Cassie wished she'd argued harder.

Susan had marked the date on their calendar months ago, once Frank had decided he'd be coming home to Misty Lake after he finished his assignment, and hadn't taken any reservations for the day so both Susan and Cassie would have the night free to celebrate. That had been Susan's word. Celebrate. Cassie wondered what she was supposed to be celebrating. The next few days, or weeks, or months, or however long it took, were going to be unpleasant, there was just no way around it. Frank had questions and Cassie figured his patience with her avoiding them had most likely run out.

She was the last to arrive, so the house was crowded and noisy. Chalk one up on the plus side. She wanted to go as unnoticed as possible. Shauna greeted Cassie with a smile and a wave while chasing her toddling nephew, Dylan, around the room as he squealed in delight. Susan, Sam, and Karen were seated on the sofa, glancing across the room at their husbands, and laughing. The men were eyeing them suspiciously. Cassie didn't spot Frank right away and figured he was probably in the kitchen catching up with his parents.

Cassie had gotten to know Anna McCabe over the past months and guessed the woman had likely settled her son into a chair where she could keep him close and where she could pepper him with questions. She had given Riley and Susan strict instructions to bring Frank straight to her house from the airport. She wasn't going to take the chance that he spend too much time with anyone else before she had her Frank time. Cassie figured Sean was there, too…to catch up with his son but, more likely, to pour Frank a glass of Irish whiskey and to temper Anna's loving onslaught.

"Did you finally get the Johannsons out of there today or did they refuse to leave?" Susan asked after she left Karen and Sam on the sofa and made her way to Cassie.

"They left. They were the last to leave, but they did finally leave. As I was waiting for them to come down from their room, I was dreaming up inventive ways to get them out. By the end, it got quite violent."

Susan smiled as she shook her head. "Weren't they just the worst? I haven't come across anyone so demanding since we hosted that political gathering at the Billingsley. Remember that disaster?"

"I'll never forget it. I almost quit over it. Trying to

placate bored wives, trying to keep tabs on philandering husbands, trying to keep the media at bay…it was a circus. And don't forget Avery Scoop." Cassie laughed at the memory of the young, clueless reporter trying to sneak into the hotel and make her way into closed meetings. "She dreamed up every possible angle to get herself inside. I still wonder how much she paid Isabelle for the waitress uniform."

"Well, Isabelle lost her job, Avery Scoop was arrested after being caught planting bugs in the conference room, and The Billingsley has never been asked to host another function for a political party. Quite a week. I still think the best part, though, was learning Avery Scoop was really Thelma Foote. I wonder where she is now and what new name she's dreamed up."

Cassie didn't answer because at that moment Frank came out of the kitchen. She watched him glance around the room before spotting her and freezing her with his stare. Her pulse raced and she felt her face heat. He'd always had that effect on her.

His wavy hair was the color of the finest brandy but looked somewhat lighter today, sun streaked, and she guessed he must have come from some place much warmer than Misty Lake. His strong, chiseled features and intense, nearly navy blue eyes fit well with his tall, athletic frame. Cassie's eyes were drawn to the fingers wrapped around the glass he held. Long and slender, an artist's fingers she'd always thought, and she remembered how they'd felt on her skin. She closed her eyes for a long moment and ordered herself to get a grip.

Frank studied Cassie as he crossed the room and

couldn't miss the blush rising up her neck to her cheeks. Selfishly, it pleased him. He'd spent the past ten months thinking about her. No, that wasn't true. He'd spent the past seven years thinking about her. No one had ever come close to affecting him the way she had, and he'd told himself he was done waiting for her to decide if it was time to discuss their past. He was going to get some answers. Soon. And if it made her a little uncomfortable, well, it was her turn to be uncomfortable.

"Cassie, how have you been?" he asked with forced nonchalance as he locked his eyes with her deep brown ones. He'd never seen eyes darker than hers. So dark it was, at times, difficult to detect the black of her pupils. Huge and wide-set under perfectly arched brows, they gave her an exotic look. Her straight nose and olive skin spoke to her Greek heritage. Hers was a face meant to be photographed, he thought, as he remembered how the camera had loved her. How he'd loved her. When her black curls began dancing on her shoulders as she fidgeted under his stare, he forced his attention away from their days in Chicago and back to the here and now.

"Oh, fine, busy, you know, same old thing..." She bit her lip and looked desperately around the room.

Frank nodded slowly as he looked from Cassie to Susan. "So, business is good? We didn't get a chance to talk too much about the inn on the drive."

When Cassie didn't answer, just stared at Frank, Susan picked up the conversation. "Business is excellent. We've been booked solid every weekend since we opened. It's incredible, really. We blocked off those couple of weeks after Christmas and into January for the wedding and honeymoon," with that she unconsciously gazed toward Riley and her face softened, "where we didn't take any reservations, but aside from that, we've been full every weekend."

"Congratulations. I know how hard you worked. I'm proud of you, Susan." He reached an arm out and wrapped it around his sister-in-law's shoulders, drawing her in for a hug.

"Cassie was a huge help. I don't know how I would have been ready to open on time without her."

Cassie felt Susan's elbow in her ribs and threw Susan a scowl. While Cassie felt foolish standing there silently, she couldn't seem to find the right words. Or any words, for that matter.

Thankfully, she was saved any further embarrassment when Anna popped out of the kitchen and, after recruiting a couple of her sons to help her carry serving bowls and platters, directed everyone else to the dining room. Cassie stayed a few steps behind Frank and made sure she knew where he planned to sit. Then she chose a seat as far away as possible.

Dinner was pleasant with delicious food, casual conversation, and, much to Cassie's relief, no questions from Frank. She was busy trying to come up with a plausible reason to leave early when Jake, the oldest of the McCabe sons, leaned back in his chair and eyed his brother.

"So, Frank, tell us about your adventures on the road. Six months is a long time to be gone, something interesting must have happened. It's been a long winter in Misty Lake. We're bored. Entertain us."

Frank gave a quick laugh and scratched his head.

"I don't know that there's too much that's entertaining. Mostly, it was a lot of boring flights, car rides, and hotel stays. Some shoots were so hot the sweat blurred my vision. Some were so cold my equipment quit working. Most were somewhere in between. There was one shoot you would have appreciated, Joe, just for the way we got there."

Joe set down his fork and looked at Frank with interest. "Oh?"

"Yeah, there was a barn we heard about out on an island off the coast of Washington. It was supposed to have been carefully renovated and something we needed to take a look at. When I checked into getting there, it looked like a ferry was the best option. I mentioned it to someone at the office, he knew someone who knew someone, and the next thing I knew, he had arranged for a guy named Philippe to get me out there."

"On a boat? Or did he have a helicopter?" Frank had Joe's attention.

"It was a boat, but not like any boat I'd ever seen. Just imagine the fancy yachts you've seen in movies and go from there. It was incredible."

Joe, owner of a new boat and fan of all things boat-related, leaned forward in his chair.

"There was a pool, hot tub, game room, movie theater, spa, helicopter pad, several bars and dining areas, I think six guest rooms plus the owner's quarters and captain's quarters, a full staff, an out-of-this-world French chef…I don't know, you'd have to see it to believe it."

"Wow, I wish I would have," Joe answered in awe. "But you must have taken pictures? Please tell me you took pictures."

Frank laughed. "I took pictures."

Then it was Shauna's turn to question her brother. "So you were on this fabulous yacht and all you did was ride back and forth to some island? Seems like a waste."

"I don't think I ever said that's all I did," Frank answered with a sly grin.

Shauna's eyes grew huge. "You mean you got to stay on there? For how long?"

"Yeah, I got to stay on there. For about four days."

There were envious looks and sighs from everyone seated around the table as they all imagined, for a moment, what it would have been like to be invited along. It was Jake who spoke up first.

"Who is this Philippe and how did you end up on his yacht for four days? Just some friend of a friend who didn't have anything better to do than give you a ride to an island?"

"Not exactly. He's a big shot in the publishing business in Paris so he knows people at the magazine's offices in New York. From what I gathered, he doesn't work much anymore, just spends most of his time on his yacht. He has a fancy office on board, but I didn't see him spend much time in it."

"So it was just the two of you, along with the staff, on this little adventure?" Jake asked.

"No, he had a few, ah, acquaintances on board."

Now it was Riley's turn to laugh. "I don't suppose these happened to be female acquaintances?"

Cassie had been doing her best to stay out of the conversation, but at Riley's innuendo she wasn't able to stop herself. Her head jerked up and she looked at Frank.

She immediately regretted her actions and averted her eyes, hoping no one had noticed. She was saved by Frank's mother's admonition.

"Oh, Frank," Anna scolded.

"Geez, Mom, it was no big deal. It was a big boat."

Riley couldn't help himself. "Back to these women…how did Philippe know them?"

"Um, I don't know that he really *knew* them, I think he just sort of…" Frank looked over at his mother who had her lips pursed and her eyes narrowed at her son. Frank rubbed his chin between his finger and thumb and whispered in Riley's direction. "They were models."

"Of course they were models!" Riley slapped his hand down on the table and gazed into the distance. He mumbled, more to himself than anyone else. "I can just picture it…swimsuit models, no doubt…"

A punch in the shoulder from Susan had him clearing his throat and changing the subject. "Didn't I see a pie in the kitchen, Mom?"

Sam got up to help Anna with dessert while Susan dragged Riley to his feet and put him to work helping her clear the dishes. From his look, it was apparent Riley knew better than to complain. The crowd thinned more when Dylan started fussing in his high chair and Karen and Joe took him into the living room.

Cassie dared a peek at Frank and found him studying her. Probably saw that look she gave him. Just ignore it, she told herself. Just like she'd been ignoring so many other things.

Once dessert was over, the kitchen cleaned up, and she'd spent a little more time chatting and trying to keep her eyes anywhere but on Frank, Cassie figured she'd been there long enough and could make a reasonably tactful exit. Just as she was getting up from her spot on the sofa, Frank stopped her.

"Hang on a minute, Cassie, I think this might interest you, too."

He was concentrating on his phone, scrolling through something on the screen, but after a minute turned a wide grin on the room.

"I just checked my email. I got a final decision from the editor regarding which photos they're going to include for the Midwest section of the story. It appears The Inn at Misty Lake is going to be busier than ever."

For a moment, Cassie was confused. She looked at Susan who seemed equally puzzled. Then it hit them both at the same time.

Susan leapt to her feet, hands on her cheeks in shock. "You mean a picture of the inn is going to be in your magazine?"

"Country Chic is going to feature the inn?" Cassie asked at the same time.

The room erupted around them with congratulations and questions flying. Susan spoke over them all.

"I didn't even know you were using any photos of the inn. You never told me."

"I didn't want to get your hopes up," Frank answered with a shrug.

Susan danced across the room to wrap Frank in a hug. "I don't know how to thank you. It's just amazing to think that my inn will be seen by millions of people. I mean, people all over the country read that magazine."

"What you've done there is pretty incredible. It's just the sort of thing that this feature is about. I saw dozens upon dozens of refurbished barns and farm houses. Yours was right up there with the best of them."

"I've got Riley to thank for that," Susan said proudly. "He worked miracles with the place. Ooh, will his name be in the article?"

Frank held up his hands. "Slow down. I don't know too many details yet, just that at least one of the photos of your place will be included. I'll hear more as the editing process moves along."

Susan looked concerned. "There must be copyright rules or something that apply. Are there pictures I need to take down from the website or make sure I don't add? I don't want to do anything wrong and get you, or myself, in trouble."

"You haven't even seen the photos I submitted so no, you don't have to worry about that. Anything that's on your website is fine, as are any other pictures I gave you."

Cassie watched the exchange from a safe distance. She was thrilled for Susan…heck, she was thrilled for herself, but wasn't ready to rush across the room to thank Frank the way Susan had done. But she couldn't just stand there, either. She wound her way around Riley and Jake and came up behind Susan. Putting her hands on Susan's shoulders, she said, "Pretty amazing news. Thanks, Frank, it will definitely help business." She tried to sound casual, but knew she failed.

"I'd like to think so, but from the way it sounds, you're going to have to add on if you're going to be able to accommodate any more people." He sounded almost as tense as Cassie.

Not knowing what else to say, Cassie turned to look at the group. They were a close family, celebrating one another's successes and rallying when someone faced adversity. They'd supported Riley and Susan when circumstances had almost torn them apart the previous spring. They'd welcomed Sam, first to Misty Lake and then to the family, when she'd come searching for a fresh start, and they had swooped in and protected when her property and her life had been threatened.

Cassie continued to scan the room, but then turned her attention back to Sam and Jake. The two were huddled in the corner and apparently disagreeing about something. She watched as Sam shook her head and pleaded with her eyes. Jake just put an arm around her and turned her to face the room. Cassie was curious. Sam seemed to try once more to stop Jake, but he gave a loud whistle that stopped everyone mid-sentence.

"Frank, that's incredible news. I'm happy for you and I'm thrilled for Susan and Cassie. We're going to be famous here in Misty Lake which may make my job a little harder, but I'll take one for the team."

"Maybe you'll finally get to hire that extra deputy you've been begging for," Sean said.

"Maybe, Dad, I sure could use one. But as long as I have everyone's attention, and as long as we're sharing news…"

At this, Sam turned her back to the room and whispered something to Jake who just grinned and continued.

"Where's Dylan?" Jake asked Karen.

"He's sleeping in the other room," she answered slowly. "Why?"

"Oh, I just thought he might like to know he's going to have a cousin."

There was the briefest moment of stunned silence before the room exploded for the second time that night. Sam blushed and leaned against Jake.

Joe was the first to pound Jake on the back and offer his congratulations, followed quickly by his brothers. Susan was next to Sam in a flash, taking her by the arms and turning her to study her from every angle.

"You didn't tell me. Why didn't you tell me?" she demanded.

"I'm sorry, Suze, we wanted to tell everyone at the same time. Although, I didn't think it was going to be tonight. This was supposed to be Frank's night…I told Jake it could wait."

"Wait? Are you kidding? This is news that needs to be shared! It's fantastic! When?"

"In about six-and-a-half months," Sam said.

Anna appeared at Sam's side. She put a hand on Sam's arm, her eyes brimming with tears, and said, "I hope you know how happy this makes me, Samantha. Another grandchild, that's…that's the best news. Are you feeling okay? Is there anything you need? Anything I can do?"

As Cassie watched the exchange, she detected the slightest hesitation in Anna. It was to be expected, Cassie figured, after the heartache Anna and Sean had endured just a few months earlier. Thinking they had another grandchild only to find out it was nothing but a lie had dealt them, and the entire family, a blow. Cassie understood Anna's need to hold back, understood that fear of being hurt.

Sam reassured, and Anna seemed to relax before

she pulled both Sam and Jake into a hug and before the tears started to flow.

Sean took his turn congratulating his son and daughter-in-law while doing his best to blink back tears of his own. He then whispered something to Joe who slipped from the room and returned a few minutes later with a tray of glasses and a bottle of Sean's Irish whiskey.

When all the hugging, back slapping, teasing, and celebrating started to quiet, it was Sean's turn to ask for everyone's attention.

"I remember when Jacob was born. I never dreamed it would be possible to love someone the way I loved that little baby. And even though I never admitted it, I feared I wouldn't be able to love another child as much as I loved Jacob."

"Hah!" Jake said with a fist in the air. "I told you guys I've always been the favorite."

Sean gave Jake a slight head shake before continuing. "*But*, I quickly learned that just wasn't the case. With each one of our children, I learned that no matter how many children you have, your heart makes room for all of them. There are no favorites, just blessings that you are thankful for every day and that you would lay down your life for."

At this, he took a moment to look at each of his children, his tears making his eyes glisten. Anna snuggled closer.

"Then, just over a year ago, I became a grandfather and everything I thought I knew about love suddenly changed. Nothing prepared me for the feelings I had when I looked at Dylan for the first time. My child's child." Sean gave his head a slow shake. "Incredible. Love is an amazing thing…you never run out. Now, we are going to be blessed again and there's nothing in this world that could make me happier. There's an old Irish saying, 'Children are the rainbow of life and grandchildren are the pot of gold.' It's one way of saying you all have made me a very wealthy man, indeed."

He turned to Jake and Sam and raised his glass. "Congratulations. May God bless you both and bless this baby, and may this family continue to grow both in size and in love. *Sláinte*!"

3

He stared at the computer screen. It was so much easier now than it had been years ago when he'd had to rely on phone books, binoculars, and his own two feet. Today, even if someone tried to keep a low profile, the information was there. A person just had to know how to search. And he did. He'd made himself an expert.

His gaze lingered on his favorite picture of her…the one he kept not only as his screen saver, but in his wallet and next to his bed, as well. It had been taken years ago when he'd first met her. She'd been so beautiful, the most beautiful woman he'd ever seen. And the camera adored her, plain and simple.

He'd loved the way her shiny black hair cascaded down her back. He'd loved the musical sound of her voice, the way it made him feel as though everything was going to be okay, no matter what problems stood in his way. And her eyes. He'd never forget the first time she'd turned those dark eyes on him. She'd tried to stay aloof, tried to hide her feelings, but her eyes had spoken to him. 'Well, there you are. Finally. I've been waiting for you.'

Next he clicked on the most recent picture he had of her, the one he'd taken with the fancy zoom lens he'd purchased before—No. He wouldn't dwell on that, wouldn't let his thoughts go there. Instead, he focused on the picture as it filled the screen. She hadn't changed in the least. Her hair was still black and wavy, flowing over her shoulders. Her face was smooth, unlined, and he knew it would feel like the finest silk under his fingers. Her eyes were the same…dark and alive with the secrets that made them twinkle.

He allowed himself a few minutes to imagine what their life would be like when she finally came to him. He'd waited so long, but he'd learned how to be patient. He'd give her time. In the end, she would be his. It was meant to be. It had always been meant to be.

With a contented smile on his face, he turned his attention back to the computer and ran searches. He knew where she was now—just as he always knew where she was—and he was curious. He'd have to pay a visit soon. He clicked and learned more about the area and some of the town's more prominent residents. He studied options for lodging and dining nearby. He calculated the time it would take to get there and tried to figure out how long he could stay without having to answer too many questions.

He pulled out his calendar and began planning.

4

Frank still hadn't gotten used to coming home to a dog. Especially one that nearly did backflips she was so excited to see him. As he watched, Trixie jumped up and down, ran in circles around his feet, and quivered with excitement when he leaned down to pet her. Then, since he knew he was alone, he couldn't resist. He sang a few words in a forced, high-pitched voice and was rewarded with Trixie joining in and howling right along with him. It never failed to make him laugh.

He hadn't gotten used to coming home to girl things around his house either. He'd hardly seen Cassie in the few days he'd been back, but he couldn't miss her presence in his house. There was a home décor magazine on the coffee table, a pair of pink running shoes by the front door, and food he couldn't identify in the refrigerator.

He still didn't know what to make of the

arrangement. It had all made sense months ago when he'd left on his assignment and Cassie had been looking for a place to live. Frank had thought Susan might balk at Cassie moving in with Riley, but Susan hadn't minded, Riley was fine with it, and Cassie had agreed. Now, Frank was back, Riley was married and living at the bed and breakfast with Susan, and it left Cassie and Frank together in the house. Strange how life worked out.

Frank glanced at the clock and wondered if Cassie would find an excuse to stay away again, but guessed since the dog was there, it most likely meant she'd be home before long. It wasn't hard to figure out she was avoiding him. What was hard to figure out was how to get to some sort of normal. If she was going to stay, they'd have to reach an understanding.

He sat and turned on the TV. At once, Trixie was at his feet, cocking her head and looking at him with big, hopeful eyes. He actually looked around self-consciously as if someone might be watching before he patted the cushion on the leather sectional and invited the dog to join him.

When he'd first spoken with Cassie about the possibility of her moving into his house, she'd been clear that she came with a dog. A small dog, she'd clarified, and a well-behaved dog, but a dog nonetheless. She'd said she would understand if Frank preferred no dogs in his house, but he hadn't really cared. Cassie had assured him she'd keep the yard cleaned up and the dog off the furniture. Well, it was his furniture, he reasoned, as he stroked the dog's silky gray coat.

It was good to be home. He tuned into a hockey game, opened a beer, and put his feet up. Six months was a long time to be away. He'd missed Misty Lake and his family. He'd seen a good part of the country, but hadn't found any place he liked better than the town he'd called home his entire life.

Years ago, when he'd been set to graduate from high school and to begin studying photography, he'd been full of fantasies of living on one coast or the other, surrounded by successful photographers and models, and living an action-packed, fast-paced life. Lately he'd suspected, and the last six months had confirmed, that it wasn't the lifestyle for him. Sure, it had been fun attending fancy parties in New York, a movie premiere in Los Angeles, and, of course, there were those four days on the yacht, but it wasn't him. He was comfortable in Misty Lake where he had a successful business, where he was surrounded by people he'd known his entire life and whose motives he didn't need to constantly second-guess, and, if he were being honest with himself, where Cassie now was.

He'd tried to forget about her while he'd been away, but since he hadn't really forgotten about her for seven years, he'd quickly learned a few months wasn't going to do the trick. He'd had some long, lonely hours to think, but he still hadn't come to any sort of conclusion as to what could have happened all those years ago.

Frank had started to doze off when the dog jumped off the sofa and he heard the door open. He rubbed a hand over his eyes and looked up to greet Cassie before she could sneak by him.

"Hi there. Have a good day?"

"Oh, it was fine. Busy, but that's a good thing. We have a pretty full house for a weekday, but they all seem to be self-sufficient so Susan should have an easy night."

Rambling. Clearly nervous. It made him sad. Granted, they hadn't known each other long, but during the time they'd had together, Frank had felt more comfortable with Cassie than he had ever felt before with another person, except for, perhaps, his twin brother. He hadn't come close to matching that feeling since.

"Hungry? I've got a pan of lasagna that Mom sent home with me ready to go in the oven. I think she's trying to make up for all the family dinners I missed. The freezer is full with everything I've ever told her I like."

"I noticed. She missed you. Everyone did."

"Everyone?"

She flinched. "Six months is a long time to be away. And, since you're offering, I could go for some of your mom's lasagna. She's a fantastic cook."

He hadn't expected her to fall in his arms and admit she'd thought of him every minute since she'd last seen him, but the way she was doing her best to ignore almost everything about him hurt a little. He told himself he needed to be patient.

"How about a glass of wine while the lasagna cooks?" he asked as he headed into the kitchen.

"Um, okay. I'm going to change, be right there."

They lingered over a second glass of wine after the lasagna. They'd both determinedly kept the conversation light, discussing the inn, Frank's assignment, and easy current events.

"Are you glad to be home?"

"I am. It was an incredible opportunity, and I'm glad I took it, but before it was half done, I knew I wanted to come back to Misty Lake."

"Because of your family? Or you didn't like the travel?"

"Some of both. This is home, I missed it. The travel got old. And there were other reasons…"

Cassie quickly changed the subject. "Was there a lot of downtime between shoots?"

Frank accepted. "Some, but I stayed busy. There's a lot of work besides just taking the pictures. I had to weed through thousands of photos to choose the best shots, edit them, that sort of thing. And I spent a lot of time on shots to submit for stock photos. I spent two days inside a refurbished but working barn and got some incredible stuff. A baby calf, the farmer's young son milking by hand, a sunbeam through a dusty barn window, a pitchfork in a bale of hay, hundreds of pictures. Everyday things, but captured in a way that makes them usable for a wide variety of applications. I started seeing downloads on those photos within hours of posting them."

Cassie was surprised. "I didn't know you did that. I guess I thought you just focused on advertising photography."

"I've been selling stock photos for years. I kind of lucked out. Back when I was in school and needed to earn money, an instructor mentioned some relatively new websites that were breaking into the stock photo business. I started submitting photos, started making money, and I've kept on doing it. It's harder now for someone to start out, but there wasn't nearly as much competition years ago and I developed something of a following. I still post some on those sites, some I just have available on my website."

"Interesting. I had no idea it was such a big

business. What else? Do you take other kinds of photos as well?"

"I've done some things here and there…some calendars and postcards for the gift shop in town, I sell prints sometimes at the gallery, even did an album cover once."

"An album cover? Really?"

"Yeah. Local band, a friend of a friend. They had put out a couple of CDs with generic covers, but wanted something a little different, a little better. It was a lot of fun. Got some cool shots, some things I talked them into trying, and they were happy with the end result."

"Huh. I guess there's a lot I don't know about you."

"I could say the same. We've never had much of a chance to talk since that day last spring. I still don't know if I'm completely over the shock of seeing you sitting at the table with my family."

Cassie's mouth turned up slightly in a wistful sort of smile at the memory. "It was a shock, that's for sure." She looked off over Frank's shoulder. "When Susan introduced me to Riley I think I sort of froze. I knew it wasn't you, but…well, you know, it was almost you. I remembered then you were a twin…I didn't know what to do and I have no idea what I said. Actually, I don't know if I said anything. I was still trying to pull myself together when you walked up to the table…"

She paused, and for a moment she was back at the restaurant and feeling that sense of shock that had engulfed her when she'd caught sight of Frank. But then, just as quickly, she snapped out of her daydream and faced him with a forced smile.

"Of all the gin joints, in all the towns, in all the world…"

"Yeah, I know what you mean. I don't remember what I said to you when I first saw you either. We must have made for quite the sight."

"I know everyone was curious. Did you face the third degree from your family?"

"Surprisingly, no. But I'm pretty certain my mom doesn't know anything about our past so that could go a long way toward explaining the lack of questioning. How about you?"

"Susan wanted to talk the next morning, but I told her there really wasn't anything to talk about. We knew each other years ago, hadn't seen each other since, end of story."

"So that's it for you then? End of story? It's that easy?"

It wasn't hard to pick up on the hurt in his voice, but Cassie did her best to block it out. It had never been her intention to hurt him, and it wasn't now. She had loved him with everything she had and it had almost killed her to ignore his calls and emails. But she'd had to, just as she now had to try to get him to let it all go.

"It was a long time ago, Frank. I guess I've moved past it. I'm sure you have, too."

"It's hard to move past something when I have no idea what happened. I tried to contact you for a long time, thought about you even longer, but eventually I tried to forget. Now, with you here, it's hard to forget. It's hard to forget that you disappeared from my life and I never knew why."

"Frank, I never meant to hurt you, I hope you can

believe that."

"Fine. You didn't mean to, but you have to know you did."

Cassie closed her eyes and willed the tightness in her throat to ease. "I know," she mumbled.

"I need something, Cassie, some explanation, some reason. Can't you give me that?"

"There isn't much to tell. I had some trouble, personal stuff." It wasn't really a lie, she reasoned. More of an omission. "I had to take care of that and then I...I needed to get away. I went to New York. I needed to start over."

"You couldn't call? Couldn't let me know where you were? I was going crazy, Cassandra. I couldn't work, I couldn't concentrate. I went back to Chicago to find you."

That, she hadn't known. It hurt her heart, hurt as if someone had reached inside her, grabbed hold, and squeezed. Hearing him call her Cassandra made the pain even more real. She sipped at her wine in the hope it would buy her some time, but it stuck in her throat.

"I never wanted any of that, never wanted you to worry, and certainly never wanted to disrupt your life."

"You had to know you would." His voice rose with the anger, and the hurt.

"I'm sorry. I'm so sorry. All I can tell you is that it wasn't you, it was never you."

"That doesn't tell me anything."

"No, I guess it doesn't." She sighed. "I was a mess, Frank. I had to fix myself. I was no good to anyone, myself included, the way I was."

"How could things change so quickly? And why couldn't you talk to me? I could have helped, would have done anything in my power to fix whatever it was that needed fixing."

"But that's just it, don't you see? *I* needed to fix it. Leaning on you, or anyone else, wouldn't have solved anything."

"I guess I don't see," he answered helplessly. "I'm having a hard time understanding. We made promises to each other before I left. For me, at least, they meant something. I left Chicago certain we'd have a future. I never dreamed things would turn out the way they did."

The promises had meant something to her, too. More than she knew how to explain. She remembered back to the time when she thought, for the first time in her life, she had someone she could trust, someone she could count on. But that feeling had lasted such a short time.

She needed to get away, needed to be alone. "I'm sorry, Frank, it's all I can say. I don't like to think back to that time, it was very difficult for me, and like I asked you last spring, I hope you can respect my privacy."

Frank was quiet for a long time. Cassie had to fight the urge to run to her room and lock the door. When Frank spoke, it was with resignation.

"If that's what you want, then I'll let it go. But if you ever want to talk about it—about any of it—I'm here."

"Thank you."

"You're welcome to stay here as long as you want, but if you decide to look for someplace else, I'll understand."

Cassie bit her lip so hard in an attempt to keep her emotions in check, she tasted blood. "Let's give it a try. I'd like to be friends, if we can be."

Frank nodded and looked like he wanted to say more, but Cassie jumped from her chair, mumbled a quick good night, and bolted for her room. The coward's way out, she knew, but the memories were too close to the surface. She needed space.

5

Susan had known all morning that something was up with Cassie. Not that Cassie would ever admit anything, or ask for advice, or talk about anything even close to personal. Now, though, that the last of their guests were gone and they had some downtime before afternoon check-in, Susan couldn't resist.

"You look tired, Cass, is everything okay?"

"Sure, fine. We should spend some time this week going over details for the shower. I've ordered a few things, but we still have decisions to make."

Susan frowned at Cassie's back. "We'll do that. Oh, and Frank's stopping by one day this week to take a few pictures. Now that he's a famous photographer, I wasn't sure he'd want to bother with taking pictures of my little inn just for a photo credit on my website, but he's so sweet, don't you think? I mean, I'm sure he's got better things to do, but I just casually mentioned that I was thinking about updating some of the photos of the inn and he said he'd be happy to do it. He's got an intern working with him for a while, he thinks this will be a good introduction, good practice."

Susan watched Cassie tense at the mention of Frank's name. Just as she'd suspected.

"Hmmm, yeah, that's nice," Cassie mumbled without turning around.

"What do you think…should we have him take pictures of the empty rooms or have people in the pictures? I was thinking people might make it look more homey. Maybe we could have a couple sitting in front of the fireplace. We could take one when there are people in the dining room. Or someone using that scrumptious whirlpool tub in The Igloo."

"Maybe. Advertising is usually more effective with a human touch, people relate better." Cassie recited automatically as if it were something she'd heard hundreds of times and had come to accept as fact.

Then Susan had the perfect idea. Trying to keep her excitement in check, she asked, "Maybe you'd be willing to help? If Frank photographed you, it would probably save him a lot of time. I can't expect him to hire models, and if you helped out, he wouldn't have to try to work with people who know nothing about modeling. With you, he'd have the shots done in no time."

Now Cassie did turn around. Her face was stony. "No. I don't model anymore." With that, she walked out of the room.

"Well, that could have gone better," Susan muttered to herself. While she wasn't ready to give up on her plan, she knew she definitely needed a more tactful approach.

Later, as Cassie and Susan went over details for the upcoming bridal shower extravaganza, things were back to normal between the friends. They laughed and joked as they dreamed up crazy ideas.

"Well, I don't know about giving everyone a purple-dyed kitten to take home, but I do like the idea of the mobile spa." Cassie sighed. "Do you think they'd mind if I sneak in line for a massage?" she asked rubbing at her neck.

"It sounds heavenly, doesn't it? We should plan a spa day. Maybe we can block off a couple of days and take a girls' trip."

"Maybe, but right now what I really need is to get back to yoga. Aside from the little I try to squeeze in with a video here and there, I've hardly practiced since leaving Chicago. I miss it."

"I asked around when I got here, there's nothing close. Shauna told me there was a woman teaching for a while, but she got married and moved away. It's quite a drive to the nearest studio."

Cassie sighed again as she focused on her notes. "Okay, so no to the purple kittens but yes to the spa?"

"I vote yes. We've already ordered the bathrobes and slippers so the ladies will be set to be pampered. And the make-your-own perfume and bath products? I think that sounds like fun."

"I agree, and I can help facilitate that. We ran a promotion at the resort one summer and I got roped into handling something similar. It turned out to be a lot of fun, the guests loved it, and it was fairly easy to operate.

It's expensive, but since that's not a factor, I say we get the supplies ordered."

"Good." Susan pulled up a spreadsheet on her laptop. "Then here's what we have as far as a schedule for the weekend. Arrival Friday evening and once everyone is settled, move to the barn for hors d'oeuvres, drinks, a light meal…catered and already ordered. Then Sandy comes and runs her wine and canvas class for them."

"Sip wine and learn how to paint. I'm going to have to try that one of these days. I'm glad Sandy agreed to do it outside of her studio. She wasn't crazy about the idea when I first approached her, but when I told her what we're willing to pay, she changed her mind pretty quickly. We will need to get back to her soon with the design we want. What do you think?"

"She has a lot of nice choices, but I'm leaning toward Northern Lights. Call me sentimental, but I'll never forget the night I looked out the window and saw the Northern Lights for the first time. I named the first room then and there. It just feels like the right choice."

"Then Northern Lights it is." Cassie smiled. "Saturday?"

"Saturday they'll have brunch here before heading across to the barn for the actual shower complete with a few silly shower games, cake, and gifts, then they'll move on to the perfume and bath products. The mobile spa will arrive and set up in the barn while the ladies have a light lunch back here. Again, the lunch will be catered and the order is already in place. Then it will be massages, facials, manicures, and pedicures for everyone before heading back to the inn for a little rest before dinner."

"Perfect. We should see about ordering aprons

they can wear for painting and perfume-making so they don't get their clothes messy. I'll look into it." Cassie wrote herself a note.

"That brings us to Saturday night. The band is booked…you're sure about country music?"

"I'm sure. I checked with Angela's mother…and with her sister just in case Mrs. Whittington isn't up on the latest preferences. Both assured me it's Angela's favorite."

"Okay, then we'll go with the barbeque theme for food. The caterer is ready, just needs the final go-ahead from us. That means we have to make a decision on the guys."

Cassie pursed her lips and considered. "I just can't quite decide. I've got a list with names, phone numbers, and email addresses for all of the husbands and boyfriends—and, of course, the fiancé—and Angela's mother assures me everyone would be thrilled with the idea. She also confirmed that the bachelor party is scheduled for a different weekend, but I'm torn. It would be a surprise, that's for sure, but what if the girls want to keep it just girls? That's what they're expecting."

"I know what you mean, but with a band and dancing and the party I know it'll be, don't you think they'd have more fun with the guys joining them?"

Cassie tapped her nails on the table. What would she want? Honestly, it was hard for her to picture herself surrounded by girlfriends. If she had a shower tomorrow, who would even come? Susan, probably Sam. After that, she didn't know. While it didn't come as a surprise to her that she didn't have any girlfriends, it did seem a little sad. But she'd made her decision years ago and she knew she'd made the right one. Girls liked to talk and ask questions…and expected answers. No, it just wasn't possible.

"What would you want if it were your shower?" Cassie decided Susan had a lot more experience to base a decision on than she did.

Susan got the dreamy look in her eyes that happened whenever she thought of Riley. Cassie couldn't help but smile.

"You know, when something fun or exciting happens, I want Riley there right beside me to share in it. The same was true before we were married and when we were planning the wedding. I wanted him to be a part of everything. He may not have always been quite as excited as I was about choosing music and linen colors, but I still wanted him there. So, yes, I say we invite the guys. I would have loved it. If Angela is half as crazy about her fiancé as I was about mine, she'll love it, too."

"Okay, then it's decided. I'll start contacting the guys. That's a lot of guys to expect to keep a secret, though. What do you think the chances are that it actually remains a surprise?"

"We need to promise them something really great if they can keep it a secret. What's a good gift for a bunch of guys?"

Cassie thought, turned ideas over in her mind, then slowly smiled. "I have an idea. Let me do some checking and I'll get back to you."

Susan nodded. "Perfect. Then there's the matter of getting the guys here on time and without the girls seeing them. I still have the hotel in Summer Haven tentatively holding rooms for us, so I'll get back to them and tell them it's a go. What do you think? We hire limos to transport them here from the hotel? I almost think we have to. I don't want anyone driving."

"Yes, I think we have to. We have a little more control over the time they arrive that way, as well. In case the ladies are running late, we can just tell the limo drivers to give the guys a ride before bringing them here."

Susan gave Cassie a satisfied smile as she closed her laptop. "I think we did it. It sounds like an incredible weekend. Angela is going to love it."

"You know, I can't help but wonder…if all this just for the shower, what do you think the wedding is going to cost?"

6

Ten o'clock was much later than Cassie had planned on getting home, but with finalizing shower plans, a trip into town for a grocery run and a vet visit for Trixie, and then dealing with the day's guests, it had been a very long day. Trixie was at Cassie's heels as she pushed the door open. The dog bounded in ahead of her.

"I thought those shots were supposed to make you tired," Cassie said on a yawn. She watched the dog race around the living room with her nose to the floor before freezing in place for a moment then dashing into the kitchen. Cassie ignored her. Trixie had been fed and had spent ample time outside. It was time for bed.

Cassie was hanging up her coat in the closet and tucking her boots neatly on the boot mat next to the door when she heard Trixie growl. Shaking her head, she called to the dog as she made her way to her room. When Trixie's growling got louder, Cassie relented and headed to the kitchen to try to placate the dog.

"What's the matter? You were just outside."

She found Trixie growling at the refrigerator.

"If you think I'm feeding you again, you're sadly mistaken. You had your dinner and you had enough treats at the vet to last you a week so…"

When the dog stopped growling and cocked her head at Cassie, clearly indicating that Cassie had better figure things out, and quickly, Cassie sighed and bent down to give the dog a pat. That's when she heard the hissing.

Standing up again, it was her turn to cock her head. Looking at her dog, she asked, "Well, what in the world is that?"

Cassie couldn't quite place the sound, but it definitely wasn't a usual kitchen noise. "Hmmm," she mumbled as she opened the refrigerator door.

Determining it was nothing inside, she tried to peek behind the heavy appliance. The noise seemed louder, and it took only a moment for Cassie to realize what she was hearing.

"Oh, crap!" She tried to maneuver the fridge away from the wall. She had only moved it a few inches when her fears were confirmed. The floor was wet and she could see water spraying from the hose leading to the freezer.

"Crap, crap, crap!" She managed to move the refrigerator out farther and was rewarded with the hose dousing her. Wiping water from her eyes, she turned and ran for the basement where she remembered Riley showing her the water main valve. As she turned the corner, she ran smack into Frank.

"Why are you all wet?" he asked as he moved her

away from his chest.

"Turn off the water! Downstairs. It's spraying all over the kitchen."

Frank paused only a second before bolting for the basement. "It's off. Turn on the faucet in the kitchen," Frank called.

Cassie did as she was told and watched as the water ran, then turned to a trickle before stopping completely.

Frank joined her in the kitchen. "What happened?"

Cassie pushed her damp hair out of her face. "I don't know. We just got home. Trixie started acting weird and growling at the refrigerator. I could hear a noise and when I pulled the fridge away from the wall, there was water. Obviously," she added as she waved a hand toward her wet hair.

Frank moved the refrigerator farther from the wall. "Well, crap," he muttered.

Cassie grinned at his back. Unknowingly, he had just echoed her sentiment.

"The hose that brings water to the ice maker is split. It must have just happened, things don't seem too wet."

Frank grabbed rags and began soaking up the water. Cassie got down on the floor to help. Once it was fairly dry, she got the mop and gave the floor another swipe.

"How did you notice the leak? You just heard it?"

"Actually Trixie heard it first. Like I said, we came in and she started running around and acting kind of funny then made a beeline for the fridge and started growling. I could hardly hear it…it was probably the high-pitched whistling that got to her."

"It's a good thing she heard it. If it had run all night, we'd have a disaster on our hands." Frank leaned down and patted the dog who was standing at his feet. "Thanks, Trixie, you saved me a huge headache and a lot of money." The dog melted against his legs and soaked up the attention.

"It sure didn't take long for her to decide she likes you. Sometimes she's a little skittish around men. She tends to bark if she doesn't know them. Unless, of course, they bribe her with popcorn. She'd do anything for popcorn."

"She just knows a good guy when he's rubbing her belly. How long have you had her?"

"Almost four years. I got her as soon as I moved back to Chicago. I didn't like the idea of being alone in—" She caught herself, but it was too late. Frank studied her through narrowed eyes.

"Why were you afraid to be alone?"

She tried for carefree. "I didn't say I was afraid," although she had been terrified, "I just didn't want to be alone. I got used to being around a lot of people when I worked in the Catskills. I shared an apartment with three other girls. I needed some company, that's all."

Frank looked doubtful. "And why a Lhasa Apso?"

"It wasn't planned. I didn't even know what a Lhasa Apso was when I went to adoption day at the shelter. I just knew I needed a small dog since she'd be in an apartment. And she was about a year old, so I was able to leave her alone for longer stretches than I would have been able to do with a puppy."

"She seems to be a good dog. Any problems when you first brought her home? I have a buddy who adopted a dog and it took almost a year for the dog to finally trust him and to stop hiding from him."

"That's so sad, the dog must have had a rough start. Trixie was with a family until some serious health problems had the family relocating to another state to be near a specialized hospital. At least that's the story I got. But no, no real problems with her. Like I said, she doesn't always trust men right away and she'll bark her head off if someone comes around who she doesn't know, but for the most part, it's been easy with her."

The conversation stalled and they both fidgeted, uncomfortable with the silence.

"So what about the fridge? Is it something you can fix or will it take a plumber?"

Frank turned his attention back to the broken hose. "I'll ask Riley to take a look at it or to get his plumber out here. There could be damage I can't see. That would suck," he added with a scowl. "And you know we can't turn the water back on until it's fixed, right?"

She hadn't thought that far ahead. "Then I guess my shower is out." She put a hand on her hip and tilted her head as she considered her options. "Maybe I'll head back to the inn. There are a couple of vacant rooms tonight." She quickly warmed to the idea. "One of them is The Igloo…I've been wanting to try that Jacuzzi tub. What about you?"

Normally a night without water wouldn't be that big of an inconvenience, but he had a meeting first thing in the morning with a client. He'd need a shower and a shave. "I could head over to Mom and Dad's but," he glanced at the clock, "I'm sure they're asleep already. I'll just spend the night here then go over in the morning for a shower."

"Come out to the inn, there's a room for you. You know, you're the only one who hasn't spent a night there."

When Susan had insisted on having family members stay at the inn before Sam and Jake's wedding, saying she wanted to use the weekend as a trial run for the inn, Frank had wormed his way out saying he'd take responsibility for Jake, keeping him away from his bride until the decided-upon time and keeping him calm the night before his wedding. Frank and Jake had stayed at Frank's house while most everyone else had spent the night at the B&B.

Frank had carved a few days out of his schedule to come home for his brother's wedding, and it was the first time he'd seen Cassie since coming face-to-face with her the previous spring. He hadn't wanted Jake and Sam's wedding to be marred in any way by tension between Cassie and himself, so had wanted to keep as much distance as possible between them for the duration of the wedding weekend.

He was going to refuse the offer of a room at the B&B, but decided if they were ever going to come to a reasonable middle ground, he'd have to start treating Cassie as he would any other friend.

"I guess I could do that. You're sure Susan won't mind? They're probably settled in for the night."

"She won't mind. I'll just text her and let her know we're coming so she doesn't worry when she hears the door opening."

Cassie headed to her room to pack an overnight

bag. Frank watched her go, her dark curls bouncing on her back. He admired her tall, slender figure and couldn't help but remember the first time he'd seen her.

He had been nervous heading into the photo shoot. He had just started interning with Keith and had almost no experience under his belt. Walking into an empty warehouse where an entire shoot needed to be set and lighted had been intimidating, to say the least. And then he'd seen Cassandra. Cassie, he reminded himself. She was Cassie now. She'd been sitting in a make-up chair, chatting with the model seated next to her, and had just thrown her head back and laughed at something he'd said…and had received a swift reprimand from the make-up artist. Cassie had politely nodded her apology, but the glint in her eye had told Frank it likely wouldn't be the last scolding she'd receive.

Frank cringed as he remembered how he'd actually walked into the wall when Keith had told him where to start setting lights and he hadn't been able to tear his eyes away from Cassie. He couldn't recall if he'd believed in love at first sight before then, but once he'd gotten a look at Cassie, he'd never doubted its existence again.

They'd worked with a green screen for most of that shoot, he recalled. Cassie had been much more comfortable with it than he had. Aside from getting a brief introduction during his time in school, he hadn't done much work that way, preferring to shoot on location. It had given him an opening as he worked up the nerve to start a conversation with Cassie. From there, they'd had plenty chance to talk during that first day as Frank had quickly learned there was a lot of downtime while props were reset, lighting adjusted, and models retouched again and again.

After a day that was by most standards nearly interminable but to Frank had seemed to go by in a snap, he had convinced a somewhat reluctant Cassie to go to dinner with him. She had succinctly stated her policy against any personal involvement with photographers, models, or anyone else related to the business, but had relented when she'd been unable to resist his charm. Or so he'd liked to think. From there, they'd spent every moment they could together for the next two weeks. It had been the best two weeks of his life.

He was still standing in the same spot reminiscing on their time together and wondering what could have happened to change Cassie's feelings so drastically, when she reappeared from her room and looked at him questioningly.

"Did you decide not to go to the inn?"

Frank struggled to come up with some sort of plausible explanation but after stammering for a moment without saying anything that made any sense, he just turned and headed for his room. "I'll be ready in a minute."

7

Cassie settled Trixie into the crate she kept behind the reception desk. After reassuring the dog she'd be back bright and early to free her, Cassie led Frank up the stairs to the attic. When they reached the hallway, Cassie pointed to the door with the plaque reading The Hideaway.

"That's you." She smiled as she fit the key into the lock and swung the door open for Frank.

Frank poked his head in and flipped on the light. He'd watched the early stages of construction and had been treated to a tour of the inn when he'd been back for Sam and Jake's wedding. He'd taken pictures for the inn's website then, but hadn't looked around the inside since. He realized he was curious. This room had a cozy feel with knotty pine on the walls and ceiling, log furniture, a comfy-looking recliner beside a reading lamp, and an electric wood stove. Definitely not girly. He was pleased.

"Nice."

"Yes, it is, isn't it? You'll find towels, extra blankets, toiletries…everything you need, I hope. But let me know if I can get you anything else. Oh, and we have running water," she added with a wink.

"Sold. Where are you staying?"

"Right across the hall in The Igloo."

"Oh, yes, the hot tub."

"Do you want to see the room? It's really quite something."

"Sure." Frank dropped his bag on the floor and followed Cassie across the hall.

This room had an entirely different feel than the one he'd just left. The walls were painted a whitish-gray color with just the faintest hint of lines forming blocks to actually look like an igloo. The bed was done up in crisp white linens offset by navy blue throw pillows. A huge rug in shades of white, gray, and blue gave the illusion of standing on a sheet of ice.

Frank was drawn to a wall where several of his framed photographs showed off the inn and the lake on a clear, crisp winter day. Others depicted the aftermath of the previous winter's blizzard when snowdrifts had measured over six feet. He couldn't stop a little feeling of pride that his photos fit so well in the room and, in his opinion, provided just the right touch to the décor.

"It's pretty amazing," Frank said as he turned his attention back to Cassie. "I don't think it was quite done when I saw it last fall."

"I think you're right. We didn't get all the finishing touches in place until the last minute. It was crazy for a few weeks before the grand opening trying to get the inn ready and finish all the preparations for the wedding."

He felt a pang of guilt at the fact he hadn't been around to help. He knew the rest of his family had rallied around Susan and Cassie and had helped with everything from cleaning to folding towels to screwing in light bulbs. Before he could respond, Cassie was coaxing him to the bathroom to check out the huge Jacuzzi tub.

"The Igloo has the biggest bathroom of all the guestrooms. Since Riley was starting with a clean slate up here, Susan let her imagination run wild and ended up with a room straight out of a spa. I love how it turned out."

Like the bedroom, the bathroom was done mostly in white with gray and navy blue accents. The tub took up half of the room. Candles were placed around the edge and fluffy towels were piled in the corner. The separate shower was constructed out of clear glass blocks and its rounded design again reminded Frank of an igloo. He ducked his head inside and nodded his appreciation at the giant waterfall showerhead and massage jets.

"I could get comfortable in here," Frank commented as he headed out of the bathroom.

"If you want this room we can switch, I can stay here anytime, it's no problem—"

"Cassie, don't worry about it. The room next door is fine." Frank frowned at Cassie. Her nervousness was back, and he found himself wishing again he knew what to say, what to do, to help her get over it.

"The Hideaway is a very nice room, they all are. It's just not quite as posh as this one. But I love the wood stove in there. Too bad it's so late. I don't suppose you'll have much use for it. There's an incredible shower in there too, though. The same waterfall and massage jets as you saw in here. If you find you need anything, please let me know."

"I'm sure I'll have everything I need." Except you, he added silently to himself. Cassie appeared to be trembling and the thought that he was responsible was almost more than he could bear. He walked past her and out the door but not before adding, "If *you* find *you* need anything, let *me* know."

Frank tossed and turned and found sleep elusive. He couldn't stop his mind from imagining scenarios where Cassie knocked on his door, told him she'd made a horrible mistake, and threw herself into his arms. He had come up with at least a dozen before he finally dozed off.

Until the screaming jolted him awake.

He looked around wildly, first trying to figure out where he was, and then trying to figure out where the screaming was coming from.

"Cassie!" He jumped from his bed and hurtled for the door. His adrenaline pumping, he fumbled with the lock for a moment before throwing the door open and sprinting across the hall to Cassie's door. He tried the handle, found the door locked, and began to pound.

"Cassie! Open the door! Are you hurt?"

The screaming continued, and even through the closed door, Frank could make out the sounds of Cassie thrashing on the bed. Fear gripped him as he banged on the door and tried to force it open. He was ready to try to kick the door down when logic took over and he instead flew down the stairs and wound through the house to Riley and Susan's private quarters. And then began to bang again.

"Riley! Open the damn door! Hurry!" He

pounded and hollered until a squinting and sleep-tousled Riley opened the door a crack and peered out. Frank forced the door all the way open and succeeded in knocking Riley on the forehead.

"Ouch! What the hell was that for?" Riley grumbled.

"A key for Cassie's room—that white room—now!"

Rubbing his forehead, Riley looked confused. "Why are you standing here in your boxer shorts yelling at me?"

Susan appeared, pulling on a robe, pushing the hair out of her eyes, and looking from one brother to the other. "What's wrong?"

Hoping Susan would be more coherent, Frank grabbed her arm and pleaded. "A key, Cassie's room, that white one, she's screaming. Hurry."

His words didn't make much sense, but the desperation in his voice came through loud and clear. Susan ran to the reception area and, as quickly as her fingers would move, punched the code to unlock the key box and grabbed a spare for The Igloo. Frank was already on his way up the stairs. Susan and Riley followed.

Curious guests were poking their heads out of their rooms and Susan tried to reassure as she darted past. Everyone could hear Cassie's screams now.

Rationally, Frank knew it couldn't have been more than a few minutes, but it felt like an eternity since he'd first heard Cassie scream. All of his senses seemed to be on high alert. His heart pounded, he could feel sweat trickling down his neck, and he unconsciously clenched his jaw and his fists as he watched Susan's shaky hands fumble with the key.

As soon as the lock clicked open, he pushed past Susan, flung the door wide, and charged into the room. Cassie was on the bed, twisted up in the blankets and screaming, her arms flailing from one side of the bed to the other. Frank let his eyes scan the room before rushing to her side.

"Cassie, wake up," he pleaded.

She continued to writhe and scream. Susan joined him and tried to get through to Cassie. "Come on, Cassie, everything is okay. You're fine." Susan stroked Cassie's head while Frank took her hands and attempted to calm her.

Slowly, Cassie quieted, and after a moment her eyes flew open. She struggled to sit up, her eyes wide and haunted. Her breath came in short gasps. Her head jerked from side to side as she clutched the sheet to her chest and her eyes tried to take in the whole room at once.

"Cassie, what happened?" Susan asked. "Are you okay?"

"What?" Cassie rasped.

"Are you okay? You were screaming."

Cassie shifted her gaze from Susan to Frank and finally to Riley who was standing in the doorway looking exceedingly uncomfortable.

"Oh, God." Cassie fell back on the bed and threw an arm over her face.

"Cassie?" Frank began on a shaky voice. "There wasn't anyone in here, was there?" He still wasn't convinced it had just been a bad dream.

"What?" She let her arm fall enough to see him sitting on the edge of the bed, fear written all over his face.

"No, I'm sorry, nothing like that. Just a stupid dream. I'm so sorry I woke you." She replaced her arm and squeezed her eyes shut tight.

"A dream? Are you sure that's all it was? You were screaming, Cass." He couldn't get the sound out of his head. It had sounded as though she'd been fighting for her life.

Cassie attempted a laugh that got caught somewhere in her throat and turned into a coughing fit. She sat up again, trying to get herself under control. Frank darted away and returned with a glass of water he pushed into her hand. She took a sip, followed by a deep breath.

"I'm so sorry, I don't know what happened. I guess I was overtired or something. But I'm fine. Really."

Riley took a few tentative steps toward the bed. "Um, Red, there's a woman out in the hall demanding to know what's going on. She won't believe me when I tell her there's no ax murderer, or ghost, or anything else waiting to attack her."

"Mrs. Chamberlain," Susan guessed as she rolled her eyes. "Are you sure you're okay, Cassie?"

"Yes, fine. Please just go take care of Mrs. Chamberlain or the next thing you know, everyone will be up and asking questions."

Susan looked questioningly at Frank. Frank nodded so Susan reluctantly followed Riley into the hall to try to prevent a full-scale inquisition by their guests.

When the door closed, the room was thrown into darkness and Frank could feel Cassie's shiver. "Should I turn on a light?"

"Yes, please. That would be good."

Frank reached over and flipped on the bedside

lamp. With more light, he was able to see how pale she was, and despite trying to convince everyone otherwise, how terrified she looked.

He took her hand. "Will you tell me what happened?"

"I told you, just a stupid dream. Nightmare, I guess you'd call it."

"Seems like it has you pretty shaken. Want to talk about it? It might help."

She seemed to fight some sort of internal war. For a moment, Frank thought she was going to give in. She opened her mouth, but no words came. He wished he knew how to take the pain away. If she'd just talk to him…

"It's a nightmare I used to have a long time ago. I haven't had it in years, I hadn't given it a thought in years. It used to frighten me when I was a child. It's silly and it's nothing to worry about."

There was maybe a grain of truth to what she said, but no more. She couldn't lie to him, at least not well, and it gave Frank a glimmer of hope. She had to still have some kind of feelings for him if it proved so difficult to try to mislead him.

"I used to have a recurring nightmare when I was a kid. Whenever I was sick with a fever, it would strike. At some point I guess I outgrew it, but at the time, it was terrifying and it always took my mom at least an hour to calm me down. Pretty embarrassing now. I'm sure my brothers would love to tell you how I used to cry and scream until Mom laid down next to me and I finally felt safe."

"Tell me about your dream. What was it that could scare Frank McCabe?"

Some spark had returned to her voice and Frank breathed a bit easier. He'd gladly make a fool out of himself if it would help her.

"It's going to sound weird and not at all scary but, trust me, it was. I've never been able to explain it to anyone else, but it had to do with being trapped inside a huge factory full of whirling, grinding machines and me being expected to do something with the alphabet. I'm not sure if I was supposed to recite it and I couldn't or if I needed to find the letters and put them in order…it's all kind of fuzzy. And there were army men. Those plastic army men. Everywhere. Even as a kid, when I'd wake up it hardly made sense, but that didn't make it any less creepy."

Cassie put her hand to her face to try to hide her grin. "The alphabet? Were you secretly terrified of spelling tests or something?"

Frank chuckled. "I don't think so. I was actually a decent speller, almost always beat Riley. Like I said, it doesn't make any sense. I guess that's what made it so scary."

"Well, letters can be darn scary." She barely got it out before she started laughing.

"Wow, I tell you about my biggest fear and you laugh at me. Thanks a lot." He'd tell her anything if it would ease her mind.

"Sorry. I'm sure it was a horrible experience, I shouldn't make light of it." She seemed to try for sincerity, but failed. She was giggling again.

"It was, but it was just a dream. I did some research on recurring dreams when I got older. It was interesting. Apparently it's not at all uncommon to have the same recurring dream when you're sick, especially running a fever. It's almost like a hallucination. Are you feeling okay? Do you think that could be what's going on?"

"No, it's nothing like that." The levity of a moment ago was gone.

"I also read that sometimes it's possible to get rid of recurring dreams by digging into the subject. For example, if you're dreaming about being left alone at an amusement park, try to figure out if maybe something similar happened to you. Or maybe you heard an upsetting story about something similar. Many people have reported looking into their frightening dreams and, once they realized why they were dreaming what they were dreaming, they stopped. Just like that."

Cassie nodded tightly. "That's a good idea. I'll think about it."

"Cassie, I didn't mean to upset you, I'm just trying to help."

"I know that, and thank you. It's very kind of you."

"Are you sure you don't want to talk about it? Just talking it out can help too, according to what I read."

"Not tonight, I'm tired."

As much as he wanted to push, he knew he needed to let it go. "Okay, but if you ever feel like talking, I'm happy to listen." He looked around the room. "Are you going to be all right in here?"

Cassie hesitated. "Do you think you could stay for just a little while?"

"Of course, I can stay. As long as you want."

"Thank you, Frank. Can I ask one more favor of you?" When he nodded she continued. "Do you think you could run downstairs and make sure everyone is settled and Susan doesn't have a house full of crazed guests on her hands?"

"Sure, I'll check it out. After I put on some pants," he added with a grin.

8

"I can't believe they wanted to come in my room and see for themselves." Cassie snickered. "I'm sorry, I shouldn't laugh, you're the one who had to deal with it and I'm sure it wasn't very funny at two o'clock in the morning."

It was early afternoon, the inn was empty, and Cassie and Susan were cleaning and readying for their next arrivals. Susan knew Cassie was exhausted and still shaken by the nightmare, but she was doing her best to act as if the entire event was behind her.

"I'm just glad to see you laughing. You had me worried last night." Although Susan didn't really expect anything, she held on to a little hope that Cassie might open up and talk to her about what had her screaming in the middle of the night.

Cassie, instead, focused on their guests. "Did Mrs. Chamberlain really want to call the police? Frank told me you and Riley were doing everything you could to talk her out of it."

"Oh, she had her cell phone out and said if I didn't call she was going to. It took nearly thirty minutes to get her to put the phone away. The other guests were even trying to help settle her down. It was quite a scene. I told her, Riley told her, and then Frank told her that there was no one in your room, so then she started ranting about the place being haunted. I think it's safe to say the Chamberlains won't be back."

"Not a big loss. How did you finally convince her there was nothing to worry about?"

"It was the brandy that did the convincing. Riley was so fed up he went and grabbed a bottle and started pouring. At first she wrinkled up her nose and acted as if it was the last thing in the world she'd ever touch. But when her husband shoved a glass in her hand, she downed it like a sailor. And then another and another until she eventually staggered to her room."

Laughter bubbled from Cassie. "And the rest of the guests?"

"They were fine. Most woke up during all the commotion, but after that, it was Mrs. Chamberlain that was keeping them awake. Once she went to her room, everyone else followed suit. Things quieted down quickly."

"Good. You must be tired though."

"I've had more restful nights, that's true, but one night isn't going to kill me. How about you?"

Cassie was an expert with make-up, but Susan could still make out traces of dark circles beneath Cassie's eyes. And it was always a dead giveaway Cassie was tired or not feeling well when she started the day with her hair pulled back in a ponytail. Susan had never known anyone who looked as glamorous on a day-to-day basis as Cassie.

"A little tired, but I'm fine. And I really am sorry for everything that happened last night." Then before Susan could answer, Cassie changed the subject. "Did Frank talk Riley into taking a look at the plumbing?"

"He did. They left here at the same time this morning planning to stop by Frank's so Riley could check things out. Hopefully it's not a big deal."

"I hope not, and I hope the water can be turned back on today."

"We have a couple of open rooms tonight if you need one."

"Let's hope it doesn't come to that. I'm going to go take care of The Igloo and The Hideaway," Cassie called over her shoulder as she headed up the stairs.

Susan watched her walk away and realized that, once again, Cassie had avoided talking about anything even remotely personal.

Cassie gathered up used towels and emptied the trash before scrubbing down the bathroom in The Igloo. She'd had a wonderful soak in the Jacuzzi and had felt so relaxed when she'd gone to bed, the last thing she'd expected was to be blindsided by a nightmare. She'd been honest when she'd told Frank she hadn't had that dream in years. A couple years anyway. Making it seem as though it was a dream from her childhood, though, had been a little less than honest.

When she went to pull the sheets off the bed, she paused. Frank had spent the rest of the night in a chair next to her bed. She knew he hadn't gotten much sleep—neither had she—but he had been dozing when she'd woken in the morning. Cassie sat down on the edge of the bed and looked at the empty chair. Even in his sleep, she'd been able to sense his tension. He hadn't really settled down all night, jumping at her slightest movement. But in those few moments when she'd been able to watch him without his knowing, she'd seen past the worried forehead and clenched jaw and had seen the easy-going, quick-to-laugh man she'd fallen in love with.

She thought back to their two weeks together and couldn't help but smile. They'd been perfect for one another with similar tastes in music, movies, food, and books. They'd talked for hours and hours and had found only a handful of things on which they didn't see eye-to-eye. Cassie remembered how they'd joked that they'd need something to argue about when they were sitting on the porch in their rocking chairs surrounded by their grandchildren.

That's how certain they'd both been that they were meant to be together. Never before had Cassie felt anything close to what she'd felt for Frank. Or since.

If she'd gone straight to work that day, if Frank had stayed just a day longer, if... She shook her head. She couldn't think in what ifs. Just as hours earlier Frank had jerked awake and the illusion had been broken, Cassie now jumped to her feet and started yanking at the sheets. She couldn't afford what ifs.

Frank and Riley met up again later at Frank's, Riley armed with tools and supplies to tackle the repair job.

"You're sure there's nothing more than just this hose? No damage anywhere else?"

"As I've told you all three times you've asked,

everything else looks fine. The hose split, but you caught it early. There's no sign of water leaking to the basement and no indication of problems anywhere else," Riley answered less than patiently.

"Okay, fine, don't bite my head off," Frank snarled.

"What is with you? You've been in a mood since you got home. If you didn't want to come back to Misty Lake, then why the hell did you?" Riley barked right back.

Had he really been that hard to be around? Was the tension between Cassie and himself apparent to everyone?

"Sorry. There's nothing *with me*. Things have just been crazy since I've been back, trying to tie up the loose ends on the magazine project and, at the same time, trying to get my business here up and running again. And last night didn't help. Can't say as though I got much sleep."

Riley easily acknowledged Frank's apology with a quick nod then switched gears to genuine concern for Cassie. "What happened, exactly? Was it just a dream?"

"Well, there wasn't anyone in her room, if that's what you're getting at. I don't know…she says it was just a bad dream, a recurring nightmare she used to have often but that hasn't bothered her for years. She didn't go into detail. She never goes into detail," he added under his breath.

"Hand me that wrench," Riley instructed as he reached a hand out from behind the refrigerator. "Are you ready to tell me what really happened between the two of you?"

Frank was glad Riley was stuck behind the refrigerator where he couldn't see Frank's face. His twin would read him like a book. "There's nothing to tell. We met when I was in Chicago on that job with Keith. We spent some time together, then I came back to Misty Lake and it was over."

"If you don't want to talk about it, why don't you just say so? Do you seriously believe I don't know when you're handing me a bunch of BS? We shared a room for eighteen years and shared just about everything else along the way. You don't owe me an explanation, but the way I see it, you owe me the truth."

Frank sighed heavily and looked to the ceiling. "You're right. About all of it. It was a little more than just a casual thing with Cassie, but I can't talk about it. I don't know that I really understand it. Cassie doesn't want to talk about it, would rather it stays in the past, so that's where it will stay."

"Fair enough. No more questions…at least not from me. Look out if Mom gets wind of any of it."

And that had Frank grabbing a beer for the both of them.

9

As promised, Frank showed up with cameras, reflectors, tripods, and his intern who he introduced as Andrew. Susan frowned at the pile of equipment and turned to whisper to Cassie.

"I thought this was going to be a casual thing. He's got enough equipment here to work for hours. I don't want him to think he has to do this. Should I say something?"

"Don't worry about it, that's how it works. There's a lot that goes into a shoot. If he's trying to give his intern some experience, he's going to want to show him everything. My guess is he's using this as a pressure-free introduction. Sure, he wants the pictures to turn out well, but he can let Andrew try different things without worrying about making mistakes. It's actually a great idea."

Susan seemed unconvinced, but stood back, watched, and kept her mouth shut. Cassie could tell Susan was uncomfortable, probably worrying she was taking advantage of Frank. Cassie was uncomfortable for entirely different reasons. The last time she'd seen so much photography equipment was on her last shoot. It had been exciting. In spite of the tediousness of the job, Cassie had never tired of the thrill and excitement that came with the process. Setting the scene, adjusting the lighting, choosing the wardrobe…back then she had often thought about one day moving behind the camera. She never would have guessed the shoot where she'd met Frank would be her last. As she watched the process, still so familiar, she couldn't stop the chill that made its way up her back.

Cassie turned away and busied herself with work on the computer. They were planning special deals for early fall, and even though it was months away, it was time to prepare promotions for the inn's website.

Cassie fiddled and tweaked, adding and discarding pictures of the property ablaze with fall colors. She studied a photo she had taken herself the previous fall on a clear, calm day. She remembered being awed by the colors, grabbing her camera, and playing for nearly an hour. Most of her shots were nothing more than ordinary, but she had done something right with the one she studied.

Part of the inn's porch, overflowing with pots of gold and orange mums, filled the corner of the picture. The rest showcased the lake. Slightly blurred in the background, the water was a brilliant blue and without so much as a ripple on the surface. The maple and birch trees were at their peaks. The color exploded through the tree line and again where it was reflected on the surface of the lake.

Cassie jumped at a voice behind her.

"That's a great photo. Is it one of Frank's? He told me he's worked here before." Andrew looked over her shoulder at the computer screen.

Cassie tried to quiet her racing heart as she chided herself for letting the afternoon get to her. She looked back at the lanky intern, his dark blonde hair pulled back in a ponytail and a pale, wispy beard struggling to gain ground on his chin.

"No, I took this one."

"You did? It's incredible. You didn't try to balance everything, it works perfectly for the shot. And with all the color here," he indicated the potted plants on the porch, "it's good that the background is slightly blurred or you'd have too much going on. Are you a photographer too?"

Cassie chuckled. "No, just an innkeeper. I got lucky with this shot. Trust me, it doesn't happen often."

"Do you know Frank? He's awesome. If you want to learn how to improve your photography, you should talk to him."

"Um, maybe I'll do that."

"Andrew, do you have that reflector?" Frank called from the other side of the room.

"Coming," Andrew answered. "Gotta run…but really great shot."

Cassie watched for a while as Frank patiently worked with his intern. Frank had Andrew taking shots from different angles, using only the natural light from the windows, and then studying the outcome and explaining why some worked better than others.

When Andrew turned, looked at Cassie, and then turned back to Frank and mumbled something she couldn't make out, she figured he was telling Frank about the lucky shot she'd managed to capture. They talked for a bit before Frank straightened and his voice carried across the room. "I don't know about that, I guess you could ask her." Cassie was instantly wary.

Andrew loped across the room wearing a grin and looking as if he'd just struck oil.

"Hey, Ms. Papadakis, I didn't recognize you."

"Recognize me? Why would you recognize me?" She tried to keep the terror out of her voice, telling herself it was irrational to fear the pimply faced, innocent-looking man who had been nothing more than a child back then.

"Oh, I looked through some of Frank's portfolios a while back. There were pictures of you from a shoot for outdoor furniture. Frank said they were some of his earliest. Your hair's a little shorter." He cocked his head and studied her through inquisitive eyes.

"That was a long time ago."

Cassie realized she had never seen the pictures from that shoot. She'd put that part of her life behind her so suddenly and with such finality she'd never had any desire to see them.

"I'm wondering if you'd do me a favor. I'd love to try shooting with a person instead of just an empty room. Would you sit for me?"

"No." It came out sharper than she'd intended, but it was not a subject up for debate.

"Come on, it won't take long."

"I don't model any more, Andrew."

"You wouldn't really be modeling, I just need someone there. I won't even shoot you from the front so you don't have to worry about make-up or anything like that. Your blue sweater is perfect, just the right amount of color but no busy patterns."

He was bursting with enthusiasm and Cassie felt guilty telling him no, but she couldn't face it.

"I'm sorry, Andrew, but I can't."

His face fell. "Oh. I was really hoping to get something good for my portfolio."

He hung his head and turned away dejectedly. He looked like a little boy who'd just been told it was time for homework, not another game of baseball. Cassie couldn't stand it.

"Okay, just a few." She sighed and tried to convince herself she could get through it.

Frank moved back and Andrew took over. He moved furniture, pulled shades, and fussed with Cassie's hair. He positioned her facing the fireplace with a book in her hand and set up his camera behind her.

Cassie was surprised at how natural it all seemed. It had been seven years, but seemed like yesterday. She let Andrew move her into position and did her best to comply with his wishes. Once or twice, when she knew the shot wasn't going to come out as he hoped, she gently offered suggestions. But she soon realized Andrew had a great deal of talent. For someone just starting out, he made some very wise decisions. Slowly, Cassie relaxed, shut off her brain, and let instinct take over.

Not wanting his presence to affect Cassie, Frank stayed out of the way. But he was curious. He'd only had a few days to work with her in Chicago, but she'd been nothing short of genius. She'd known what he wanted without him having to say anything. He hadn't had much experience at the time, but since then he'd had plenty, and he'd come to learn that he'd worked with one of the best. Had she stuck with it, he was certain she would be doing something much different than running a bed and breakfast in Northern Minnesota.

Frank quickly realized Cassie hadn't lost a step. She angled her body just right so the light would catch her hair and touch the pages of the book. Andrew was in heaven. He bounced around the room moving lamps and other décor ever so slightly until he had just the look he wanted.

Susan walked into the parlor to find Cassie posing for Andrew, and Frank off to the side taking it all in. Intrigued, she observed with no one realizing she was there. Cassie, for as much as she said modeling was a thing of the past, seemed in her element. She looked graceful and completely at ease seated in the antique chair with her arm draped casually over the side and her gaze directed out the window. Just the slightest hint of her profile was visible, but even Susan's untrained eye could tell that Cassie's features were fixed in the appropriate lazy afternoon expression.

Andrew clicked away for a few more minutes before stopping and looking over at Frank. Susan knew what was coming before Andrew spoke, and she had to bite her lip to keep from cheering.

"Frank, would you be willing to help out? I think two people in this shot would work better. I'd like to angle the two chairs toward the fireplace, maybe set a bottle of wine on the side table, and shoot it from behind."

Cassie was on her feet in a flash. "Frank's not a model, Andrew, it might be more trouble than it's worth. I can move to a different location if you think it would work better. Maybe you could shoot me sitting on the window seat or on the hearth. There are lots of good possibilities."

"No, I'd really like a couple in the shot…if you're willing, Frank." Andrew looked hopefully to Frank while Susan crossed her fingers behind her back.

"I can try," Frank replied, "but I can't promise I'll be any good at it."

"Excellent. All you have to do is sit. I know exactly what I want."

When Andrew turned to look around the room, Susan scrambled and tried to make it appear as if she had just gotten there.

"How's it going? Are you getting some good pictures?"

"It's going very well, but I'm wondering if you might have a bottle of wine we could use for a prop. And maybe a couple of glasses? I have an idea for a shot I think will be amazing. I just need those couple things."

"No problem, I'll be right back," Susan said. This was going better than if she'd planned it herself, she thought as she skipped to the kitchen for glasses and a bottle of wine.

Inwardly, Cassie was a mess. She should never have agreed to help Andrew, that was clear. Outwardly, she tried to keep her cool. She drew on everything she had learned in her years of modeling and fought to keep her expression neutral. A glance at Frank out of the corner of her eye had her fighting the urge to run. Or scream. He was loving every minute of it.

Andrew arranged the wine bottle and glasses on a

side table, out of the shadows of the heavy drapes. He angled two high-backed chairs in front of the fireplace and positioned Cassie in one and Frank in the other. After stepping back and viewing the scene through his lens, he switched Cassie and Frank to the opposite chairs. Satisfied, he backed up and snapped a couple of quick shots to get a better idea for how it was coming together.

Andrew studied the results and asked Cassie to lean a little more toward Frank. Andrew arranged her long curls to flow down her arm. He clicked the camera again and scowled, indicating something wasn't quite right. He looked at his picture, back to Cassie and Frank, and back to his picture. Then grinned.

"Hey, I need you guys to hold hands. Not tight like you're holding on for dear life, just casual-like…as if you're comfortable with each other and confident in your relationship."

Cassie stole a quick glance at Frank. Things were getting worse by the minute. She told herself one more shot and that would be it. She did have work to do after all. She reached her hand across to Frank who took it in his own. Without being told, they linked fingers and let their hands hang loosely between the chairs.

"Perfect!" Andrew cheered. "That's exactly right. Now don't move."

They sat while Andrew moved around the room, clicking furiously.

"Look at each other," Andrew instructed as he set up directly behind them. "And don't worry, you're in the shadows, make-up isn't an issue," he added, addressing Cassie's argument before she could voice it.

Cassie didn't want to, she wanted to be done with

the whole thing, but she angled her face in Frank's direction and met his gaze. She tried to stay professional and to block out any emotion, but her efforts proved useless. Holding his hand and looking into his eyes was too much. She stopped resisting and just relaxed. She knew the moment Frank spotted the change in her because his expression softened and they were back in Chicago, looking at each other over a candlelit dinner, thinking about everything the future would hold for them.

Neither noticed Andrew stop in his tracks. For as feverishly as he had been working, now he clicked once and admired the shot captured on the camera's display screen.

"That's it," he whispered to himself. Frank and Cassie had fallen into an easy pose, casual at first glance, but the chemistry between the two was impossible to miss, even in the dim light. Love and longing infused their expressions.

Andrew found his voice and spoke so Cassie and Frank could hear him. "Thanks, guys, that was just phenomenal. I can't think of anything we could do to top it, so unless you have something else you want to try, Frank, I'd say we're done."

Cassie jerked at Andrew's words and pulled away from Frank. She gave Andrew a weak smile. "I hope you got something you like. I need to get to work."

And with that, she dashed from the room leaving Frank to frown after her.

10

They may be living in the same house, but Cassie had avoiding Frank down to a science. It had been four days since the photo shoot and other than one quick 'good morning' on her way out the door, she hadn't seen him in those four days. That was going to change in a few hours.

She'd gone into work early in the mornings, she'd stayed late into the evenings, she'd even spent another night at the inn, insisting Susan and Riley have a date night.

She'd suspected collusion when events lined up such that she'd had no choice but to agree to a meeting with Frank. She'd found a note from Frank on the kitchen table asking her if she'd be available that evening to go over the photos taken at the inn. He'd gone on to say that since she'd been reluctant to be photographed, he wanted to make sure she was okay with the images Andrew had captured. She had planned on using work as an excuse to bow out, but when she'd arrived at the inn, Susan had announced that after giving her a long night off, it was Cassie's turn to have one.

Fine. She'd meet with Frank. No big deal, she told herself. They were friends and they had business to discuss. She cursed the clock when she glanced at it and found it moving faster than it had any right to.

Determined to keep her mind on her work, she was delighted when her phone rang. Twenty minutes later when she ended the call, she was downright ecstatic and went to find Susan.

"Remember when I told you I had an idea for a sort of party favor for the guys at Angela's shower?"

"Sure. Did you figure something out?" Susan asked as she finished typing an email. She narrowed her eyes at Cassie. "You did more than just figure something out, didn't you?"

"Ooh, I think you're going to like it," Cassie teased.

"Tell me!"

"Well, years ago when I was in the Catskills, we had a bigwig from New York City wanting to rent out a big chunk of the resort for a week of meetings and parties. He turned out to be part of the Yankees organization. He had dozens of other baseball heavyweights with him. They were a fun group—rowdy, at times a little demanding—but mostly good-natured. I handled just about everything for them, got to know them, and they all left with promises to help me out if I ever needed anything from them."

Cassie grinned and bounced on her toes, barely

able to contain her excitement.

"And…"

"And, I called the guy I met from the Minnesota Twins. We chatted, reminisced about his week at the resort, and then I asked him if he could arrange for a group of guys to get the royal treatment at a game this spring."

"And he agreed?" Susan was on her feet now too.

"He agreed. The guys will get a tour of the ballpark and get to take batting practice before the team does, but from the way it sounds, the players get a kick out of joining, so the guys will likely have company. They'll have a private suite to watch the game, they can lead the crowd in *Take Me Out to the Ballgame*—assuming they want to and at least some of them can carry a tune—and one of them will get to throw out the first pitch. After the game, they can sit in on the press conference and have a chance to meet some of the coaches and players."

"Oh, wow," Susan finally managed. "They're going to flip. That's incredible, Cassie."

"It is pretty cool, isn't it?"

"Wow," Susan said again, shaking her head. "You know, I have a husband who's going to be downright jealous. His brothers, too, I'd guess. I wonder if Angela's fiancé is looking for a few more best friends?"

Cassie laughed. "I'd kind of like to go myself. It sounds like so much fun."

Concern clouded Susan's eyes. "I know there's no set limit on the cost, but this wasn't something on the radar. Do you think Angela's mother will balk? How much is it going to cost?"

"Hah! That's the best part. It's a favor, free of

charge."

"Are you serious?"

"I'm serious. I did hint at donations to the Twins' charities, but aside from that, it's absolutely free."

"Just what did you do for that group of baseball guys up there in the Catskills?" Susan asked as she raised her eyebrows.

Cassie threw her head back and laughed.

Cassie called the mother of the bride to run the idea past her, got her resounding approval, and then spent the rest of her shortened afternoon tweaking plans for the outing at the ballpark. She ordered baseball caps to give to the guys when they came for the party and found out about their surprise. Cassie buried herself in details until Susan finally kicked her out the door telling her to enjoy her time off.

Frank wasn't home yet when Cassie arrived so she did some cleaning, played in the yard with Trixie, and eventually poured herself a glass of wine, figuring if she had the time off, she may as well relax and try to enjoy it.

She wandered through the house admiring, not for the first time, the photographs Frank had on display. The family photos never failed to warm her heart. For the most part, Frank had stayed away from posed, formal portraits, choosing instead a collage of candid shots that captured the spirit and personality of those in the pictures. She lingered over a shot of Sean and Anna sitting on their patio and looking out over the yard where their children and their spouses were chatting, playing horseshoes, and enjoying one another's company. Sean and Anna were leaning toward one another with their heads angled in the direction of Joe and Karen who were somewhat off to the side, Karen with Dylan in her arms and Joe leaning over and tenderly running a hand over Dylan's head. Cassie figured the picture must have been taken when Frank had been home for Sam and Jake's wedding. It was a simple photo in some respects, but profound in the way it spoke to the generations of family.

She sipped at her wine and wandered to her favorite photograph. She'd hardly been able to tear her eyes from it the first time she'd been in the house and she'd returned to it time and again.

Nestled among pictures of Misty Lake and the surrounding areas during all four seasons was a photo of the aftermath of an ice storm. The sun had come out to reveal a city made of glass. Tree branches, thick with ice and bent low, brushed the sidewalk. Icicles hung at odd angles from mailboxes and street signs. Cars parked along the road appeared to be frozen in time, patiently waiting for the sun to free them from their ice prison. Everything sparkled and twinkled as if touched by magic. Frank had taken what had likely been a dangerous, perhaps deadly, storm and had captured its almost indescribable beauty. Cassie reached a hand out to the photo, tracing a finger along the frozen street certain she would feel the icy cold.

Lost in her thoughts, she didn't hear Frank come in until Trixie's excitement caught her attention. She turned to find Frank studying her.

"If I haven't already told you, I love this picture."

"Thanks, it's one of my favorites."

"When was the storm?"

Frank scratched his head as he remembered. "Years ago. I was still in high school, and the only thing I knew about photography was that I enjoyed taking pictures. I got lucky with that one. If I tried it now, I'd probably overthink things and the outcome would be very different." Turning his attention back to Cassie, he added, "Sometimes things just work out."

Not just in photographs, Cassie knew.

"How did Andrew's pictures turn out?"

Frank gave a quick nod, by now used to Cassie's skill at changing the subject. "They're very good. He's spent a lot of time editing and I think you'll be pleased. He has a good eye and will do well as a photographer. You thrilled him when you agreed to sit for him."

Cassie smiled, touched. "He's a sweet kid, so full of enthusiasm. It was hard to say no."

"Andrew wanted me to ask you about something. He's working on putting together a portfolio, so in addition to the photos for the inn's website, he's wondering if he can use some of them in his portfolio."

Cassie wasn't sure how she felt about her picture being used again after so many years. It had been a part of her life for a long time, but now the idea brought up mixed feelings.

"Show me."

Frank opened his laptop and pulled up the photos. He flipped through the shots they'd taken of empty rooms, pausing only to show her some he thought might be useful to showcase on the website.

"Here, these are the shots with you…and then with me, too."

Cassie examined each photograph and admired the way Andrew had used the low light and shadows to create a soft, cozy, romantic scene. In most, she was visible only from the back. The light bounced and played on her hair. Occasionally the slightest hint of her profile was visible. Cassie could envision several of them on the website as they highlighted the appeal of the parlor.

When she got to the shots of her with Frank, she drew in her breath and froze. There was no missing the pull of the photos. Cassie had worked with countless professional models during her years in the business, yet a photographer hadn't ever achieved such a natural and easy— yet subtly sexy—result.

She scrolled through the photos, drawn in to the story they told. When she got to the last photo, the one where Andrew had asked them to face one another, she felt a jolt of electricity surge through her. Seeing herself with Frank in such an intimate, private pose was shocking. She didn't have any pictures of the two of them from their time together in Chicago so she had never seen how they looked together.

Frank had to have seen it too. The connection between them was unmistakable. Cassie tried to study and dissect the photo as an impartial critic, but knew that anyone looking at it would pick up on the connection.

She thought back to the moment Andrew had asked them to face one another and had taken the picture. She remembered letting go for just a moment and allowing her real emotions through, something she hadn't done for a very long time. She was still in love with Frank. As much as she might try to deny it, to herself as well as to everyone else, she knew it was true.

Frank finally broke the silence. "What do you think?"

Cassie turned to look at him. Keep it professional,

she told herself.

"I think he did a remarkable job. You're right, he has a great deal of talent. As far as pictures for the website, I don't want to use any that show my face so someone might be able to tell it's me. I wouldn't want a guest coming to the inn and recognizing me from the advertising photos they'd seen online."

"Agreed. Andrew and I have already selected a few we think are the best and that we'll give to you and Susan to choose from. They're all either of the empty room or show you only from the back."

"Thanks."

"What about giving Andrew the okay to use some in his portfolio?"

Cassie hesitated. The fear was still there. Rationally, she knew the pictures would be seen by very few people, but she couldn't shake the uneasiness.

"I suppose he wants to use this one?" Cassie asked, indicating the photo of the two of them facing one another.

"He's pretty thrilled with it…yes, he'd like to use it."

"Hmmm…"

"What are you afraid of, Cassie?"

"I'm not afraid of anything," she lied, "it's just that I quit modeling a long time ago and I'm not sure I want my picture out there again." It sounded weak, even to her.

"The photo won't exactly be splashed on billboards, but if you'd rather he didn't use it, I'll tell him that."

It could be easy. She could let Frank tell Andrew

no, and it would be over. But then she thought back to Andrew's enthusiasm, his excitement at doing something he loved, and she knew she couldn't disappoint him.

"It's fine, he can use it if he wants to."

"You're sure? I'm not trying to pressure you."

"I'm sure. Like you said, it's not going to be on display for the world to see, is it?"

"Cassie, will you tell me what happened? Why you quit modeling, why you left Chicago, why you turned your back on us? Please?"

Cassie closed her eyes for a long moment. What could she say? No one knew what happened. No one. She wanted to keep it that way.

"I told you, it was a personal matter, something I needed to deal with…that's all."

"It must have been serious if it made you change your whole life. Won't you talk to me about it? I worried about you for so long. Now that you're here, I'm worrying again. Something's not right, Cassie, I can tell. Can't you let me try to help?"

"Help? What makes you think I need help?"

"Talking things out usually helps. I don't think it can hurt. I know it would help me if I understood what happened."

"Oh, Frank…" Cassie stood, needing to move.

"I don't know how things were for you before I got back to Misty Lake, but I do know that since I've been here, you've been unhappy. Unsettled. Tense. Not the Cassie I remember."

She hadn't seen that Cassie in years. Sure, she had fun at times, enjoyed her life for what it was, but Frank was right, she wasn't the same person. She didn't know how to go back, was fairly certain she couldn't.

"People change. Life changes. It's full of work, bills, responsibilities, lots of things that don't always add up to one carefree day after the other."

"But what made it that way, Cass? Why did everything change so suddenly?"

Cassie stopped in front of the window and stared out at the darkness. That day, the first part of it anyway, came back to her so clearly, as it always did when she let herself remember. What could she tell him? After a long moment, she started speaking, her voice not much more than a whisper.

"I was devastated that day you left, but also incredibly happy. Those two weeks were the best of my life, I hope you know that. I was sure we'd see each other again soon. I was ready to dig into school, to finish up the last couple of months, to graduate, and then see where life took me. Took us."

Frank waited, hardly moving a muscle, hardly breathing.

"I stopped at the grocery store on the way back to my apartment. I knew there wouldn't be anything in the refrigerator. I remember lugging my things up the stairs and down the hallway to my door. I was laughing to myself thinking about how we'd locked ourselves out of your hotel room."

Cassie dared a glance at Frank and saw a grin spread across his face for just a moment before it quickly vanished and he focused on her.

"I remember opening the door, sensing something wasn't right, and then things get kind of fuzzy." Cassie continued, but her voice lowered and became monotone.

"I remember fighting him off, screaming, kicking, scratching, doing anything I could to get him off of me."

"No. Oh, Cassie." Frank was on his feet and at her side in an instant. He tried to take her in his arms, to offer support, but she backed away.

Cassie knew if she let Frank hold her, she'd fall apart. Talking about it was harder than she'd imagined, but she'd started, so she'd continue. She owed Frank that much.

"I don't know how long it went on. I struggled, he fought back. I was pretty banged up when it was over, but I guess I managed to hurt him badly enough and, I think, scream loudly enough, that he finally ran."

This time when Frank reached for her, Cassie gave him her hand. Frank led her to the sofa and she sat. Aside from providing details for the police, she had never told a soul what she had just told Frank. She found she couldn't look him in the eye. She knew her hand was in his, but she barely felt the contact. It was as if she were numb from head to toe.

"Did he…I mean, were you…"

"No." She shook her head from side to side. "No, he didn't rape me."

Slowly, she started again. "I was in the hospital for several days. The police searched my apartment, checked my phone records, did what they could…"

"Why didn't you call me? I would have headed back to Chicago in an instant."

She knew that. She'd always known that. How to tell him the rest? How to tell him she'd let herself doubt him? How to explain that she'd been so insecure, so badly damaged, that she'd no longer believed in anything, including him?

"It took a couple of days until I was even with it enough to make a call. I had a pretty bad concussion, my face was badly bruised…it was difficult to talk. Later, I decided I needed to get away. I went back to my apartment only to pack up my things—there was no way I could stay there—then found a cheap motel and lived there while I finished up my classes and graduated. I left right after graduation. I knew a girl who had taken a job in the Catskills, she helped me get hired." Cassie shrugged as she tried to meet his eyes.

"Did the police catch the person who did it?"

At that, Cassie pulled her hand away and stood, starting to pace again. The tears were burning at her eyes, wanting to spill over. She wouldn't let them.

"Yes…yes, I guess." She took a deep breath and then the words came fast as if she had to get them out, had to get rid of them. "The police arrested someone, he had pictures of me, they told me it was all over, they said I didn't have to worry, said he couldn't hurt me anymore, they wanted me to identify him but I couldn't remember, couldn't remember much of anything, I don't think I ever really saw him, he had some sort of mask over his face, I, I, I tried—" Her throat closed and the tears she'd tried so hard to hold back started to flow.

This time Frank didn't wait to gauge her reaction, he just grabbed her and held on. They stayed that way for a long time, Frank rhythmically stroking Cassie's back as she sobbed.

The overwhelming relief that engulfed her came as a surprise. Fear, humiliation, regret, of course, she'd expected those feelings, but the relief was a surprise.

She thought back to when she'd been in the hospital and a social worker had come to talk to her. She had questioned Cassie mercilessly about family and friends, someone she'd have to lean on once she was released from the hospital. Cassie had lied, told her she had relatives she'd get in touch with, simply because it was easier and because it made the social worker feel better. There had been no one. For so many years, there'd been no one.

When Cassie was finally cried out, she pulled away from Frank and wiped at her eyes with the tissues he handed her. They moved back to the sofa and she nearly collapsed onto it. She couldn't remember the last time she'd cried. It didn't solve anything, she'd always reasoned, so why bother? Letting down her defenses enough to cry, even in private, had seemed not only fruitless but ridiculously silly. Now though, she had to admit she felt a little better. Drained, but a little better.

"I'm sorry I put you through that, but thank you, I guess I needed it," Cassie said, her voice husky in the aftermath of her tears. She focused her attention on a dark spot on Frank's shoulder where her tears had soaked his shirt. She studied it, reluctant to meet his eyes.

Frank tried to process everything he'd heard. It wasn't what he'd expected. Of all the possibilities he'd considered, that wasn't one of them. Her story left him feeling sick. Physically sick. He had to fight the insane urge to demand the name of the man that had been arrested and go hunt him down. Instead, still struggling with the fact that she hadn't turned to him when she'd needed someone the most, he ordered himself to calm down, took a deep breath, and prayed he'd say the right thing.

"I'm here for you, Cassie, and I'll do whatever I can, whatever you need. I hope you know that. And I can handle the crying," he added with a quick, one-shoulder shrug. "Shauna grew up in a house full of boys. I ended up being her go-to when she needed a shoulder to cry on."

"Really?" Cassie sounded intrigued and, Frank thought, for the moment anyway, focusing on something else.

"It started when she was about twelve. One day she came home from school with red eyes. She'd obviously been crying. My brothers and I were watching TV. They started teasing her, I may have joined in at first. But she flew into a rage, screamed at all of us, and stormed up the stairs to her room, tears running down her face.

"Mom wasn't home, I knew someone needed to talk to her, so I followed her. At first she yelled at me to get out of her room, but I managed to calm her down. Then she started talking, and I thought she'd never stop. I don't remember all the details, but I know it had something to do with Tommy Nelson and her best friend, Julianna. I do remember thinking it was silly girl stuff and I considered trying for a getaway, but she seemed so heartbroken, I stuck it out. She cried, I tried to help. And volunteered to beat up Tommy Nelson."

Frank puffed up his chest in an effort to get Cassie to relax. He was rewarded with the hint of a smile, though it didn't quite reach her eyes. "Ever since, I've been the one she usually goes to when she needs to vent…or cry."

"That's so sweet. I would imagine there were times when she felt like she was on the outside looking in with all of you boys. I'm glad she had a confidant. Has a confidant."

Frank looked deep into Cassie's eyes…eyes that were red and swollen and still guarded. Eyes that, he guessed, still held many secrets.

"I can be the same for you if you want. I know you told me your parents died years ago and that you don't have any siblings, but that's about all you told me regarding your family. Is there anyone else? Did you have someone to turn to after what happened?"

She gave an almost imperceptible shake of her head. "There's really no one. I don't have any family."

Frank couldn't imagine being so alone. Sure, there'd been times when he'd been younger and he'd foolishly longed to be an only child. Normal, he supposed. A kid didn't grow up in a house with three brothers, a sister, one bathroom between them, and not wish, at times, for solitude. But never having anyone to share his adventures, to join forces with him and plot strategies, to sneak downstairs with him early on Christmas morning? That he couldn't imagine.

"What did you do, Cassie? What did you do…afterwards? Did you talk to anyone? A therapist or someone trained to help?" Just thinking of her leaving the hospital, packing up her apartment, and moving into a lonely motel tore at his heart. No one should have to face something like that alone.

"A little, in the hospital. But I was fine. After a few days, I was fine."

"No one could be fine after something like that. Why didn't you call me?" he asked again. His voice came out rougher than he'd intended, but he couldn't help himself, the frustration was bubbling over and he needed to know, to understand.

When Cassie tried to get up again, Frank held her arm and kept her next to him on the sofa. A trace of anger began to smolder in her. Not warranted, she knew, but probably some sort of self-preservation mechanism. She'd never get through what she had to tell him without something fueling her.

"Fine. Do you want to know why I didn't call you? Because I was ashamed, that's why." She held up a hand to silence him when he opened his mouth to argue. "Not ashamed over what happened in my apartment, I know I had nothing to do with that, wasn't to blame, but ashamed of what happened afterward."

Now she did jerk free and resume her pacing. She couldn't sit.

"An investigation started almost immediately, I think. I don't know, I was in the hospital, didn't know what was happening for a while. But I know the detectives checked my home phone records and found repeated calls from the Regal—the hotel where you were staying…where we were staying. They had come at all hours and had all, obviously, gone unanswered. They also found a pen on the floor of my apartment, a pen from the Regal. I was almost certain I didn't have one on me, I couldn't recall ever using one, much less taking one. But when I told them I had been there, they began to question me about what I was doing at the hotel, about who I was with."

She glanced at Frank and saw his eyes flare. She had to turn away. It was obvious he knew what was coming.

"I tried to keep my comments vague but, in the

end, they suspected you and I started to believe them."

Frank spoke to her back, his voice a mixture of hurt and incredulity. "How could you think I would do such a thing?"

She didn't face him, choosing instead to focus on a tiny chip in the window frame as she tried to explain.

"I don't know. I've wondered the same for years. All I can tell you is I wasn't myself. The attack changed me, made me doubt everything, and I didn't know what to believe. The police made a good case. They tried to convince me it was possible you were jealous, that you thought I'd forget about you once you were gone, that you'd even been jealous while we were together, calling my apartment whenever I was gone to class or to work, trying to check up on me, and then once we parted, you snapped. They wanted to question you, were just about ready to, but then there was another attack…another woman, close to my apartment. They caught that guy and when they searched his apartment they found pictures of me along with other things from the Regal. He was a photographer. I guess I'd worked with him a few years back…I didn't recognize his name."

Cassie sighed, exhausted. Letting those memories back in hurt, and she was paying the price. Her head ached. She wanted to climb in her bed, curl up in a ball, and pull the covers over her head. But she continued.

"The detective wanted to charge him with the assault on me, but there wasn't a lot of evidence. Strong evidence, anyway. The guy claimed he'd just kept a few of his favorite pictures from the work he did with me and he denied ever being anywhere near my apartment. I guess he had some sort of alibi." Cassie shrugged. "I don't know.

The detective was convinced this guy was responsible, but the police focused their attention on the case they felt certain they could pin on him. I stayed as far away from all of it as I could. I didn't follow his trial, but I know he went to prison. It was enough."

Drained, Cassie pressed her hands against her eyes and rubbed. When she finally turned, Frank was staring at her. She could read the questions, the hurt, the anger, on his face. It's what she'd wanted to avoid. She'd learned there was no going back, nothing was going to change the past. Now he would have to learn to accept it too.

"I'm so sorry, Cassie. I don't know how to tell you how much I wish I could make it all go away, how much I wish I could go back and change my plans, stay a little longer…do something so it never would have happened."

Cassie sighed and ran her hands through her hair. With one swift twist, she had the binder off her wrist and around her hair, securing it in a loose ponytail.

"I know that. It was a long time ago, though. It's far in my past. I've come to terms with it and have moved on. I didn't want to tell you because I knew you'd feel just like you do…helpless, and probably guilty. You shouldn't. You can't. It won't change anything and it will only eat away at you. You have to try to put it behind you. Trust me, I know."

"Have you really, though? Have you really been able to put it behind you? I can't help but think the nightmare at the inn had something to do with what happened, and not something from your childhood."

It had been seeing him again, being at the inn with him, so many memories hitting her from all sides. The nightmare shouldn't have come as a surprise at all, she realized. But she couldn't tell him any more, so was grateful when, after a minute of silence, Frank changed the subject.

"You know what? That's enough. I never meant to turn this into such a difficult evening. What do you say we go to The Brick for a pizza then maybe see if there's a decent movie on tonight?"

Cassie breathed a sigh of relief and felt the tension start to melt away.

"Pizza sounds wonderful. But do they deliver? I don't feel much like going anywhere."

"They deliver…I'll call right now. Why don't you check and see what's on?"

When Cassie nodded and turned for the remote, it was Frank's turn to rake a hand through his hair. He gave Cassie a long look before heading to the kitchen to call in the order.

11

"We'd both have to go through their training, submit to background checks, the whole shebang, since we'd both be working with the kids and would be alone with them at times," Susan explained as she paged through the information packet. "And we'd have to figure out how to work things with Jennica and Jordyn. If we have kids from camp here in the mornings, I'm not sure if it will work to have the girls here at the same time." Susan paused and wrinkled her forehead at the thought. "I guess that's something we'll have to ask about. But, after seeing what an awesome experience it's been for Sam, I'm eager to give it a try, so long as you agree."

"I think it sounds like an excellent idea. I've heard Sam talk about it many times and have never heard any negatives. Let's do it."

"Great. I'll fill out the paperwork and get in touch

with the camp director, Tom Lindahl. I met him briefly the first year Sam volunteered. He's a good guy. Rumor was he took the job for just a year, but I think when things didn't go so well under his watch the first year, he wanted to come back and prove himself. This will be his third summer."

Cassie picked up a brochure for Project Strong Start and read over the mission statement and goals of the camp. Situated on Misty Lake and operating for well over ten years, the camp provided options and opportunities to at-risk and disadvantaged kids from the Twin Cities. From listening to Sam's stories, Cassie knew many of the kids who attended the camp had troubled pasts, because of mistakes they had made or because of family situations out of their control. Project Strong Start looked for business owners in the community to volunteer to mentor one or more of the campers for a summer. The kids were able to choose a business that interested them from the list of volunteers. They then spent twelve hours every week learning a skill or trade. Everything from woodworking with Sam to hands on work in a restaurant, an auto repair shop, or a day care was a possibility for the kids. Hopefully this coming summer they would also have the opportunity to learn what it takes to run a successful bed and breakfast, Cassie thought as she set the brochure back down on the desk.

"How many kids do you think we should offer to take?"

"I think maybe two or three. Sam has had six kids each of the past two years, but she has them in her workshop where she can supervise them all in one spot. Since we're responsible for them the entire time they're with us, I don't think we can have that many. Things are too spread out here."

"I think you're right. Not that I'm expecting them to try to make a break for it, but in order to give them our full attention, I agree that no more than three sounds good."

Susan looked off into the distance, a wistful expression on her face. "I hope it works out. I'd really like to try to help. So many kids just need a little self-confidence and someone to believe in them. If we can do that, we'll have made a difference." Her expression settled into one of a sad sort of resignation.

"You're thinking something like this program could have helped Danny?" Even though it had been over three years, Cassie knew the loss of Susan's cousin to drugs was never far from her mind.

Susan sighed heavily and shook her head. "I don't know. Actually, I doubt it. Sam and I have spent countless hours talking about what might have helped Danny. The reality of it is, I don't know that there's anything that could have helped him. We tried so many different things, so many treatment programs. We always thought we could cure him, but we've come to learn—and, I guess, accept—that drug addiction isn't ever really cured, it's managed. Addiction is a chronic disease and it takes a lifetime of work to stay healthy. Some people just can't do it." She shrugged. "If we can help steer even one kid along the right path, then any work we do, any hours we put in, will be worth it."

Cassie nodded. "Agreed. Finish up the paperwork and get it submitted…and let me know what else you need from me. I'm looking forward to getting the call telling us we've been accepted."

The call came just a few weeks later with the interview date set for a week after that. The days seemed to fly by with the weekend of Angela's shower quickly approaching and planning for the busy summer season in full swing.

Cassie sat in the parlor waiting for Tom Lindahl to arrive. She looked up as Sam jumped to her feet yet again. Sam had been more worried about the interview than either Cassie or Susan. Now, Sam chewed at her nail and looked at the clock.

"You're going to wear a hole in that rug if you don't stop pacing," Susan said without looking up from her work. "It's an interview, what's the big deal? Cassie and I have both done plenty before this."

"I know, I know, I just want it to go well. The idea of you guys having kids here this summer…well, it just has to work out." She turned to Susan and frowned. "Suze, you know the last time you saw Tom you yelled at him. I'd like to think he's forgotten about it or written it off to emotions running high, but be extra nice today."

Now Susan did look up. "Oh, for crying out loud. What do you think I'm going to do? Scream and holler and stamp my feet and demand he lets me take in some of his kids? I'm not an idiot. And besides, when I yelled at him I had every right to do so."

"I guess you did, but still…"

Cassie watched the volley between the cousins. Since neither had a sister, Cassie figured Sam and Susan were as close as you could get to the real thing. She knew they'd spent a great deal of time together growing up and guessed the fact that they hadn't lived together may have helped form their bond. Some distance most likely meant some of the petty annoyances and frustrations had never come to be. Not that she'd know…

Sam started again. "Remember to tell him about your experience with the teen program at the Catskills resort, Cassie, he'll like that. I know it's not quite the same thing, but it's still experience. And Susan, you have the information from your time volunteering with Big Brothers Big Sisters? You'll want to highlight that when you talk with Tom. I think—"

"I think you need to relax," Susan interrupted. "It's all going to go just fine. He liked our application, we're not hiding terrible secrets in our pasts, and we've got something of value to teach the kids. We're a lock."

"I'm sure you are," Sam replied, but looked less than certain. Before she could offer any more last-minute advice, the door opened and a smiling, gray-haired man entered. Catching sight of Sam, he lifted his hand in greeting.

"Sam, so good to see you," Tom said as Sam greeted him with a hug. "You look positively radiant. Congratulations once again."

"Thank you, Tom. It's good to see you too. Welcome back to Misty Lake. How was your winter in Florida?"

"Warm. At least warmer than here. It's almost April and there's still snow on the ground. I shouldn't be surprised, I lived in Minnesota long enough to know what winter's like. I guess I was just hopeful."

"It will warm up soon. I'm sure of it."

"Good, because if winter sticks around too long, Marilyn is going to start hinting again at staying in Florida year-round." He shook his head hopelessly. "I don't think I could take the heat in the summer, but when she wants something, well…"

"Project Strong Start wouldn't be the same without you," Sam argued. "And speaking of Project Strong Start…" Sam took Susan's hand and pulled her closer. "You remember my cousin Susan?"

"Sure, nice to see you again, Susan. You have a beautiful place here." Tom looked around approvingly before returning his attention to Susan and then to Cassie who had joined them.

"Thank you, we're rather proud of it. Mr. Lindahl, this is Cassie Papadakis. This place wouldn't be half of what it is if it weren't for Cassie. She's nothing short of a miracle worker."

"Cassie, it's a pleasure to meet an honest-to-goodness miracle worker."

"Mr. Lindahl, nice to meet you. Susan gets carried away sometimes, shall we say? May we show you around?"

"And I'm going to get out of your way so you can get to know Cassie and Susan. They do a remarkable job with the inn and they have a wealth of knowledge and experience ready to share with some kids. I hope things work out."

"Take care, Sam, it was nice to see you. I'll be in touch soon to talk details for the summer."

"Perfect, because I have an idea I'd like to bounce off you." Sam grinned over her shoulder as she waved and glided out the door.

"She doesn't seem to have slowed down any," Tom observed.

"Slowed down? Hah! If anything, it's double-time

with her. She's busier than ever with her business, she's building a crib and other baby furniture for the nursery, she's volunteering with the youth group at church, and she turns up here all the time wanting to know what she can do to help. I have to push her into a chair and tell her what she can do is rest." Susan rolled her eyes and shrugged.

"Then I guess my worries about her handling a group of kids while she's pregnant were unwarranted?"

"I suppose things could change as she gets closer to her due date," Susan said thoughtfully, "but I wouldn't worry about her. She can hardly wait to start working with your campers again."

With that, Cassie and Susan began a tour of the inn, the barn, and the rest of the property to give Tom an idea of where the kids would be, what they'd be doing, and how Cassie and Susan would supervise them.

"We already have three events booked that fall during the kids' time at camp. Susan and I are excited about the possibility of teaching the kids a little about event planning and hosting along with the business of running the inn. Party planning has become a lucrative business and we, in effect, run two separate operations here. The kids will get a taste of each. If we're approved, that is," Cassie said.

"It sounds like they would definitely benefit from spending time here. Shall we get started with the personal interviews? I'd like to talk to you each alone, if I could."

Cassie stole a quick glance at Susan and saw the surprise register on her face. They hadn't discussed it, but Cassie guessed Susan expected, as had Cassie, that Tom would talk to the two of them together.

"Sure, whatever you prefer," Susan said. "If you

and Cassie want to use the parlor, I'll be upstairs. Just call when you're ready for me."

Cassie didn't know why she was suddenly nervous, but as she took a seat across from Tom, her pulse started to race.

"So, Cassie, this is really just a formality. I've been over your application and your resume. Everything looks in order. I'd just like to get to know you a little better."

Tom smiled as he tried to decipher the emotions he saw flitting across Cassie's eyes. Nerves he was used to. Over the years he'd learned that anyone on the receiving end of interview questions tended to be a bit nervous. But the fear he didn't quite understand.

"Sure."

"I see you've spent your entire career in the hotel business. Is it what you always wanted to do or did you just fall into it?" He'd start easy to get her talking.

Cassie chuckled. "I don't know that I can say it's what I always wanted to do. When I first started, I think I was too young to know what I wanted to do. I needed a job, a hotel nearby was hiring maids, I got the job, and the rest is history, as they say."

Tom nodded. "You moved your way up quickly." He glanced at his notes and continued. "It only took six months until you were working at the front desk. Impressive."

"I don't know how impressive it was. There was a high turnover rate. I think maybe I just stuck around longer than most."

"I doubt that, I find most managers and owners are good at spotting talent and knowing who works hard and who doesn't. You must have been doing something right."

Since he didn't want to embarrass her or make her even more uneasy, he smiled and continued. "You graduated from college in just three years and then moved to New York for a time. First off, congratulations. I barely managed to graduate in four years. Next, how did you like New York? I spent a summer in the Catskills and loved it. Of course, that was back when I thought I was going to be a writer and live in a secluded cabin somewhere in the mountains churning out the next great American novel." He held up his hands and let them drop. "Alas, that wasn't meant to be."

"I met a few people that match such a description when I lived there. It's a good place to get lost, if that's what you're looking for."

Tom saw her jerk involuntarily at the words, but he didn't comment, just waited for her to continue.

"Graduating in three years isn't as impressive as it sounds. I managed to earn some college credits in high school and I took classes every summer. I always liked school and liked to study so it wasn't too much of a struggle."

"You've held a number of different positions at the hotels and resorts where you've worked. What do you enjoy the most about the business?"

"Oh, the people," Cassie answered easily. "For me, it's always been about the people. A lot of folks assume anyone heading to a hotel is excited about it, that every guest is eager for his or her stay and is looking at it as a long-awaited getaway. Oftentimes, that's true. But there are nearly as many guests who are dreading their stay.

They're there for yet another business trip, one that's taken them away from their son's baseball tournament or their daughter's school play. Or they're traveling to see a sick relative, to attend a funeral, to try to straighten out a mess a child away at college has managed to make. You'd be surprised what you hear at a check-in desk. For these people, I want to make their stay as pleasant as possible, given the circumstances. I know I'm never going to make everything okay, but I try to make it just a little bit better."

Tom was quiet for a moment. "I guess I never thought about it that way. Your guests are lucky to have you."

"Thank you. Now here," she said brightening, "our guests usually are looking forward to a getaway. It's a much different group of people than I saw in Chicago."

"What do you hope to be able to offer the kids from the camp? And what do you hope to get out of the experience?"

"It's not about me," Cassie answered emphatically. "I'm not looking at the opportunity to see what I can get out of it. I know a lot about the hospitality business—I have a college degree—but frankly, it's not a requirement. If some of the kids you have at camp are struggling with school, or don't like school, or think there's no way they can afford college, then I think this is a good place for them to learn about something they can do that is rewarding and where there is always going to be a demand, but that doesn't necessarily require a degree. We may not operate exactly like a big hotel, but the philosophy and many of the day-to-day operations are the same. It can be a good career."

Tom leaned back in his chair, rested his chin on

his thumb while his finger extended up the side of his cheek, and studied Cassie. He liked her, he believed her sincerity, but he still had one question for her and he worried it was the reason he thought he had detected a trace of fear in her eyes earlier.

"Cassie, part of the application process is a background check." He noticed her tense and sit up straighter in her chair. "Since Project Strong Start works with kids who have had problems in their past and who may have criminal records, we delve a little deeper into prospective volunteers' pasts than most other organizations. I need to ask you about an incident that occurred several years ago back in Chicago."

Cassie's heart thumped in her chest and she gripped the armrests of the chair. Her mind started to spin, and she focused on her white knuckles while terms Shauna had thrown at her when describing the antique furniture crazily raced through her mind. Maybe she could tell Mr. Lindahl about the heavy look to the furniture, the tendency toward dark finishes on the wood, the intricate carvings of roses, leaves, grapes…

Tom cleared his throat and Cassie jerked to attention. "I was asking about the incident in Chicago. I don't know all the details, nor do I need to, but I do know you were the victim of a violent attack. Depending upon the circumstances and depending how a victim has coped with the trauma, it is sometimes cause for exclusion from a volunteer position with at-risk kids—"

"Oh, but Mr. Lindahl, it's been years and I'm fine, really, it's in my past."

Before she could continue, Tom spoke.

"Sometimes we find people hold onto resentment they're not even aware of. Or, there's the fear of another attack. In either case, it's not a good situation for the volunteer or for the kids."

"I can assure you that won't be a problem. I've worked with kids, I've dealt with every type of person you can imagine…really, everything that happened is in the past."

Cassie nodded earnestly, needing to convince him. She knew how badly Susan wanted to volunteer and she couldn't stand the thought of her past getting in the way of them being accepted.

Cassie watched as Tom set his notes aside, steepled his fingers, and rested his chin on top. He scrutinized her over the top of his glasses. She met his eyes and fought for calm. After a minute he dropped his hands, sighed, and shifted in his chair.

"Okay, Cassie, I think that's all I have. Do you have any questions for me?"

"No, I've heard a lot about your program from Sam. She has done nothing but rave about her experiences. I hope you'll consider us and that you'll believe me when I tell you that there's nothing in my past that will affect the way I work with the kids." Cassie managed to shake off her earlier feelings and spoke with what she thought was confidence and professionalism. She prayed she was convincing.

"Good. Thank you for your time," Tom said as he rose and extended his hand to Cassie.

"Just one thing, Mr. Lindahl. If possible, please don't mention my past to Susan. It's not something I've discussed with her because, as I've said, it really is in my past and it doesn't have any bearing on my performance at work. If it becomes a reason for us being turned down as volunteers then I will explain things to her, but if there's no reason to, I'd rather it wasn't brought up."

Tom gave Cassie a strange look, but quickly recovered. "Of course. It's a private matter and it will stay that way."

"Thank you, Mr. Lindahl. Let me go get Susan for you."

"Oh, Cassie?" he called after her. "Just one more thing. Please call me Tom."

Cassie returned his smile, then headed upstairs to find Susan, crossing her fingers the entire way.

12

He was at the computer again, finalizing his plans. He'd contacted an old acquaintance—someone he hadn't seen, talked to, or thought of in years—but he'd heard the man was gravely ill, didn't have much time, and the situation provided the perfect excuse. He'd explained he needed to go see him, that they'd been close and he wanted to see him one more time if only to say goodbye. He'd have to actually do it, and that made him angry. It would use up valuable time, but they'd probably check up on him. At least the man lived on the way. He'd stop by for a few minutes, rehash an old story or two, and be out the door as quickly as possible.

He imagined what it would be like to see her again. For so long he'd only had his pictures. He thought about the last time he'd seen her...where she'd been, what she'd been doing, what she'd been wearing.

As he thought, he clicked. He looked through

pictures—some he'd taken and some he hadn't—newspaper and magazine articles he'd saved, a collection of ads where she had modeled. Then he typed in the website he was most curious about, the one he'd been checking for nearly a year, but hadn't visited in a few days. He didn't really expect any surprises, but when he made a seemingly innocent click, his blood turned to ice.

He stared. He moved quickly from shock to rage. And then it happened. He felt the darkness creeping in and he closed his eyes tight against it. The feeling was familiar, but that didn't make it any more welcome. He hated feeling out of control, hated when things started and he couldn't stop them. He tried again to focus on that last time he'd seen her, hoping it would calm him, but thinking was hard when the headaches started. He shouldn't have let it come to this, promised himself he wouldn't again. Too long. It had just been too long since he'd seen her.

He considered going for the medicine the doctor had prescribed, but instead leaned his head back against the chair, closed his eyes, and pinched the bridge of his nose. He was stronger than this, he told himself as the darkness engulfed him.

When he opened his eyes again, it was nighttime. He wasn't sure how much time had passed, but it must have been hours. He blinked and rubbed his forehead. The pain had dulled, but that other feeling was there, the one that told him he'd done something but he couldn't remember what. That feeling was familiar too, and it was worse than the pain.

He thought back to the period when he hadn't been able to see her for so long…that's when the episodes had started. Then, he'd gladly accepted the medication. Sometimes he'd lost hours, sometimes days, but it hadn't mattered. Then, he'd just wanted time to pass. Now, it was different. He needed to be able to account for every day, every hour.

Tentatively he got up from the chair and made his way around the house. The front door wasn't shut tight. Had it been? He thought so, but couldn't be sure. Had he gone out? He racked his brain. Blurry images flashed through his memory but, try as he might, he couldn't determine if they were recent or years old.

He gulped a giant glass of water and practically inhaled the two stale doughnuts sitting on the counter. An episode always left him feeling as though he hadn't eaten or had a drop of water in days.

Feeling a little steadier, he inched back to his computer. The screensaver bounced a series of pictures of her across the screen and he took a moment to admire them. Prepared this time, he refreshed the screen and studied the new information.

He would leave in the morning.

13

Cassie had spent the past few days going over the interview with Tom in her head. Now, as she drove home, she replayed their conversation again. She alternated between thinking it had gone reasonably well to being certain she had come across as unstable and unfit to supervise his camp kids. She'd trusted Tom when he'd said he wouldn't mention her past to Susan, but still jumped every time Susan spoke to her, sure she was going to ask questions.

Cassie used one hand to massage her temple in hopes of keeping the headache she could feel forming at a bearable level. She groaned a little as she remembered her planned bowling date with Frank. Crashing bowling pins and a splitting headache…not exactly a match made in heaven. She tried to recall if she'd picked up aspirin on her last shopping trip.

"Bowling," she groaned. She hadn't been bowling

since her middle school gym class had taken a field trip. It had seemed so simple…roll the ball and knock down the pins. It had been nearly impossible. She smiled at the memory of her ball jumping the gutter and rolling down the neighboring lane. It had gotten roars of laughter from everyone except her teacher. And it had been the last ball Cassie had thrown. She sighed and hoped adult Cassie would prove more adept than middle school Cassie.

When Frank had suggested bowling, she'd tried to talk him out of it, but he'd been adamant. 'It'll be fun,' he'd insisted. She doubted it. The bowling, anyway. A night out with Frank, she was finding, was always fun.

It had happened gradually, but over the past few weeks they'd started dating. Well, kind of. They went places, did things, but nothing was official. No relationship talk. She wasn't ready for that.

Cassie had been hesitant at first, still was, really. She was so afraid of hurting Frank again that she'd almost refused his simple offer to take her to a movie. But he'd been so sweet, so sincere, when he'd said he just wanted her to relax and have fun for an evening, she hadn't been able to refuse. It had led to a string of outings, and since there weren't all that many activities to choose from in Misty Lake, had led to bowling.

Cassie climbed from her car and unloaded a thoroughly exhausted Trixie from the back seat. Not only had the dog played with Gusto most of the day, but Sam had brought her Golden Retriever, Rigi, with her on her visit so for a couple of hours all three dogs had romped and raced until they'd collapsed in a pile, Trixie definitely the worst for wear.

"You are such a silly thing," Cassie said as she

nuzzled Trixie. "One of these days you're going to have to admit you're not as big, as fast, or as strong as your friends. I promise no one will hold it against you. And for the record, Gusto and Rigi already know."

She laughed as she put the dog down and saw her stumble a bit before gaining her footing. "See? You're so tired you can hardly walk."

As Cassie went to fit her key in the lock, she drew in a quick breath when, out of the corner of her eye, she caught a glimpse of something moving at the side of the house. Rendered motionless with only her eyes darting furiously back and forth, she struggled to catch her breath. It wasn't until she saw Trixie head around the house and heard her bark that Cassie snapped out of her stupor.

"Trixie! Come!" Cassie shouted as she trudged through the snow after the curious dog and tried to tell herself there was nothing to be afraid of. Just an animal…or maybe a piece of paper caught in the breeze. But she couldn't make herself believe it.

By the time she rounded the corner, the barking had stopped and there was no sign of the dog. Panicked, Cassie called louder. She turned in all directions, but couldn't spot Trixie. Or anyone or anything out of place. She looked to the ground as if she'd be able to pick out footprints—either the dog's or those belonging to someone or something else—but the snow was hard and icy after days of thawing and nights of refreezing so there was no sign of fresh tracks. Besides, there were enough old footprints from Trixie, Frank, and herself that she'd never be able to pick out new ones.

Frustrated and scared, she made a circle around the house, hoping that Trixie was busy somewhere and simply ignoring her calls. When she didn't find the dog, fear gripped her and she felt goose bumps rise even as she began to sweat.

Dropping her purse, she chose a direction and started to run. The fact that Trixie was a dusty gray color meant she was barely noticeable on dirty, salt-covered streets. It was always a fear of Cassie's. A driver could easily miss the dog if she darted out in front of his car. And given Trixie's proclivity for chasing cars…Cassie sprinted faster, calling for the dog as she ran.

She was so focused on scanning the yards and the street in front of her, she didn't notice the car coming up behind her until it slowed and honked. She jumped, startled at the noise, and was ready to take off in the opposite direction before she realized it was Frank. Out of breath, she rested her hands on her thighs and bent forward.

"Looking for her, by chance?" Frank said lightheartedly, holding Trixie in his arms. His tone changed when Cassie turned her head. "Cass, what is it? Trixie's fine, she's right here." He held the dog out to Cassie who just continued to stare at him with huge eyes.

"Where did you find her? Who had her?" Cassie demanded as she resumed her scan of the neighborhood.

"Joey Rafferty had her. I saw him standing on the sidewalk holding her and stopped—"

"Why did Joey have her? Did he take her?"

"Cassie, what's going on? Joey didn't take her, he wouldn't do that. You know how much he likes her…likes all dogs."

"Right, right, it wasn't Joey." The boy had helped Cassie out on more than one occasion when she'd been working late by feeding and walking Trixie. He'd never want to hurt the dog...or worry Cassie.

Frank took Cassie's arm and led her to the car. "Why don't you get in? We'll go home."

"What?" Cassie found herself in the car, unsure of how she'd gotten there. She squeezed Trixie.

"Tell me what happened. Did Trixie run away?"

Cassie didn't answer, instead asked a question of her own. "How did Joey find her? What did he say?"

"He said he was walking home from his friend's house and saw Trixie on the sidewalk, said it looked like she was eating something. He—"

"Was there anyone else around? Anyone he didn't recognize? Did he say?"

"He didn't mention anything and I didn't have any reason to ask him. He just said he knew she shouldn't be there, figured she was lost, so was going to bring her home. And he said it looked like muddy popcorn she was eating off the sidewalk and he didn't want her to get sick."

"Popcorn?"

"I don't know...I suppose someone could have spilled some. More likely, it was just ice chunks from all the refreezing."

Cassie looked skeptical as she nodded and narrowed her eyes. "Okay, so he didn't see anyone else?"

Frank stopped the car in the driveway and turned to Cassie. "Did *you* see someone? Did Trixie chase after someone?"

Cassie paused. She was no longer sure what she'd seen. "I don't really know. We got home, I was opening the door, she ran around the house and was gone. I guess I overreacted." Then, as Cassie climbed from the car and again scanned the sidewalks, she mumbled. "Kind of like last time…just disappeared."

"What?" Frank asked as he circled the car and met her.

"Oh, nothing, just thinking out loud. Trixie got lost once before, back in Chicago. She disappeared from a dog park. It was strange. The area was fenced, I had my eye on her the entire time except for just a minute when a friend's daughter wanted to show me her wiggly tooth. I looked up and Trixie was gone. Everyone helped me search, but we couldn't find her. Two days later I got a call from a vet. Some guy found Trixie wandering through his yard and dropped her off at the closest vet office." Cassie shrugged. "I got her back, she seemed to be fine, and I never found out what happened to her. It was weird."

"We had a dog once who liked to run…chased him all over town. No matter what we did, what kind of rope we used to tie him in the yard, he found a way to get free. We finally changed his name to Houdini."

Frank led her to the door where he found her keys still hanging in the lock. "Jake would have something to say about that."

"Sorry. Don't tell him."

They were inside before Cassie realized she didn't have her purse. It took her a minute to remember dropping it as she'd started to run.

"I have to go grab my purse," she said as she pulled the door back open. "I think I dropped it in the yard."

Waving aside Frank's offer to get it for her, she walked to the corner of the house and retrieved her purse. She took a moment to study the ground again, but like before, was unable to make out any distinct footprints.

"Just your crazy imagination," she muttered to herself as she headed back to the house. But she couldn't help one more glance over her shoulder.

14

Susan rearranged the magazines on the coffee table for the tenth time and swiped at imaginary dust with her sleeve. She fussed with the champagne flutes set on the sideboard, moving a few ever so slightly. Cassie was a little calmer, confident they'd done everything they could to make Angela's weekend one she'd never forget. The inn was spotless, the barn decked out for the festivities, and they'd confirmed and reconfirmed all the details. They were ready.

The sound of tires crunching over the gravel drive had both women jumping before looking at each other and, at the same time, giving an excited thumbs up. Giggles and shrieks confirmed the women's arrival. Cassie popped the cork on the first bottle of champagne as the door burst open and the room came to life.

It didn't take long to determine which of the women was the guest of honor. Angela's friends had dressed her in an elegant Miss America-worthy sash reading 'Bride to Be' along with a sparkling tiara. These definitely weren't party store finds. As the group took in their surroundings, Cassie squinted for a better look and couldn't rule out the tiara being real. Huh. Maybe she should have been a little more nervous about the weekend.

Her worries were quickly allayed when the petite, tiara-wearing blonde rushed forward and grabbed Cassie's hands. Angela's soft blue eyes danced and her peaches and cream complexion glowed. She looked as if she'd just stepped out of a sorority house. Her bow-shaped lips opened to a warm smile before she spoke.

"Oh my, this is so fabulous! Your inn is simply beautiful. Thank you so much for having us. No one would tell me where we were headed so I had no idea what to expect. This is better than anything I could have hoped for. We'll have the place to ourselves, we can relax, have fun, talk girl talk…I'm just so happy to be here! Thank you!"

With that, she threw her arms around Cassie. Touched by her excitement and her sincerity, Cassie hugged her back.

"We're glad you're here too. We'll do everything we can to make it a perfect weekend for you."

Two equally blonde women approached and Cassie didn't need introductions to know they had to be Angela's mother and sister. The resemblance was impossible to miss. Cassie extended her hand to greet them.

"Mrs. Whittington, Emma, I'm Cassie Papadakis. Welcome. How was your drive?"

"It flew by. Angela was so excited she kept talking

and talking. And please, call me Helen."

"Helen, I'm glad to hear it. We'll get you all settled in a minute, but I see Susan has started pouring the champagne if you'd like a glass?"

"Ooh, look! They have all our names. Are they ours to keep?" Cassie heard one of the guests ask Susan.

"They are." Susan smiled in response. "How about if I try to learn your names? Madison?"

Letting Susan handle the champagne, Cassie fielded questions about the inn, its history, and what the plans were for the weekend. She answered what she could about the inn, but kept a tight lid on all the upcoming festivities.

Gradually, the group moved to their rooms to get unpacked and settled. Susan and Cassie had broken one of their rules for this group and had purchased roll-away beds to accommodate everyone. Some rooms might be a little cramped, but the women wouldn't be spending much time in them. While Susan stayed to answer questions and handle any problems that might arise, Cassie dashed to the barn to be sure the caterers had everything in place for hors d'oeuvres and drinks. It was going to be a busy forty-eight hours.

It was nearly two o'clock by the time Cassie and Susan collapsed onto Susan's bed. They both laid flat on their backs staring at the ceiling for a full five minutes before either could muster the energy to speak.

"I'd say it went well, don't you think?" Susan managed.

"Very well. They all had fun, they all thanked me countless times and told me how much they enjoyed the food, the drinks, and the painting. Me? I may never move again. It's a darn good thing Riley is spending the weekend with Frank. There's no way I'm getting off this bed."

"You know this was only the beginning…we have to do it all again tomorrow."

Cassie drew in a deep breath and blew it out slowly. "I'll be ready to go tomorrow. I think the day—the past few weeks—just caught up with me. All the planning, the preparation, the worry…I guess I didn't realize how tired I was."

Susan turned her head to look at Cassie. Susan was exhausted too, but Cassie looked drained. It was more than just the weekend, it had been building for some time.

"Has something been bothering you, Cass? I'm wiped out from everything to do with this shower too so I know how you feel, but it seems like maybe there's something more going on. Is everything okay with Frank?"

Cassie hadn't admitted anything and Susan hadn't wanted to push, but news, especially when perceived as gossip, traveled fast in Misty Lake. Susan figured she knew about every time Cassie and Frank had gone anywhere together.

"Frank? What do you mean? Things are fine with Frank."

"Oh, Cassie, come on. I know you guys have been dating. You don't honestly think you can keep it a secret in a town like this, do you? Maybe if we were still in Chicago, but here people know what you're doing almost before you know."

"We've gone out to dinner, to a movie…it's no big deal. We're friends. I wish people would just mind their own business."

"Sorry," Susan whispered and moved to get up from the bed.

Cassie grabbed her arm and pulled her back down. "Wait, Susan, I didn't mean you."

Trying not to feel hurt, Susan dropped back down next to Cassie.

"Really, I didn't mean you. I mean all the people in town that I don't even know but who start whispering every time Frank and I walk into a restaurant. A while back we went bowling. A group of women were bowling a few lanes down from us. I didn't even have my shoes on yet when I looked over and every single one of them had a phone out and was either talking or texting while staring at us. If there's one thing I miss about Chicago, that's it. The privacy. The freedom to go where I want, when I want, without everyone knowing and commenting."

"It took some getting used to for me too. It was the same with Riley and me. Anna seemed to have some sort of hotline and her friends just couldn't wait to report on every little thing we'd done."

"I didn't even think about Frank's mom," Cassie said, horrified, as she threw an arm over her face. "She hasn't said anything to me yet. Do you think she will?"

"I think you can count on it. I'm kind of surprised you haven't heard from her yet. I was a little intimidated by her at first, but it didn't take me long to learn she's really very sweet. Anna loves her family fiercely and just wants what's best for all of them. She may come across as nosy, but she's only trying to help. She was very kind to Sam and to me when we were new in town and when we started spending time with her sons. Sam, especially, needed someone to talk to when she was all alone, and Anna made her feel welcome. Just be prepared. She'll corner you one of these days."

"Thanks for the heads up."

Susan paused then asked, "Is there anything else? Anything else bothering you?"

Cassie looked at her, and Susan was sure she was going to finally open up. But after a moment Cassie gave Susan a wide grin.

"I'm just trying to figure out how to go buy some new underwear without setting the phone lines in town on fire."

Saturday was a whirlwind of activity. The partiers slept in, so Cassie and Susan took advantage of the extra time to not only down a few extra cups of coffee, but to get a jump on preparations for the perfume and bath products stations. They laid out the aprons, fancy jars, decanters, and ingredients the women would use to create their own concoctions. They also set up a cozy corner with fluffy bath towels, body brushes, sponges, bath pillows, and eye masks…all the extras the women would be able to choose from to take home with them.

Brunch was done, the group had moved to the barn for the shower, and Cassie was making one more call to Angela's fiancé to make certain everything was on schedule for the evening when the surprise in Susan's voice caught her attention.

"What are you two doing here?"

Cassie looked up to see Sam and Karen peeking in the front door.

"Is it okay to come in? We don't want to interrupt anything," Sam whispered as she glanced around the parlor.

"They're in the barn, come on in."

"How's it going?" Karen asked.

"Couldn't be better. They're having a wonderful time and think The Inn at Misty Lake is, and I quote, 'The best place in the world for a shower.'"

"Hi." Cassie smiled at Sam and Karen.

"Hi, and congratulations on running the best place in the world for a shower," Sam said.

Cassie laughed. "They're an enthusiastic bunch. What are you ladies up to?"

"We thought we'd see if we could help with anything. Joe was so pouty, sure Frank and Riley were having all kinds of fun without him, I finally decided to throw him out and told him to go play with his brothers," Karen said with an exaggerated eye roll. "And since my mom has Dylan today, I called Sam. Turns out the same thing was happening at her house."

"Yeah, Jake was really feeling sorry for himself. He spent most of last night looking at his watch and trying to guess what Frank and Riley were up to. It was pathetic. When he started again this morning, I packed a bag for him and pushed him out the door. I didn't have to push very hard."

Susan shook her head. "Boys will be boys."

The door opened again and Shauna walked in.

"Do you all have some sort of radar or something?" Cassie asked.

"Hey, Shauna. What's up? Your hair looks fabulous, by the way," Susan said as she got closer to study the new highlights in Shauna's light brown hair.

"Thanks, I just came from the salon. And that's

why I'm here. I walked out the door after my appointment and *all four* of my brothers were walking down Main Street singing and laughing like idiots. They saw me and started hollering for me to come join them playing pool. I ran the other way. What in the world is going on? I haven't seen them act so stupid in years."

There were sighs and head shakes all around.

"A little early to start drinking," Cassie commented.

"Oh, I doubt they were drinking. Joe falls asleep after two drinks and Jake never has more than one when he's out in public…can't let the citizens of Misty Lake see their sheriff tipsy. Riley and Frank can put away a few more, but they rarely do. No, I know my brothers, they were just acting like dumb boys."

"They have the whole day to bond. Sam and I threw our husbands out after they started pouting about missing out on all the fun Riley and Frank were having."

"Ah, that makes sense," Shauna said, nodding. "They don't all get together for an entire day very often. They're going to be plenty grateful when they get home." Shauna wiggled her eyebrows. "I thought I'd stop by and see if I could help out with anything. I figured you'd have your hands full this weekend."

"You don't need to help," Cassie argued. "Why don't you sit down and I'll get you something to drink? The girls can have some fun too. Well, Sam, you'll have to have fun with grape juice."

"I'm getting used to grape juice. But we'll get to that later. Let us know what we can do to help."

Cassie was ready to argue again, but Susan raised a hand to stop her.

"It's no use, Cass, they won't listen. I'll tell you what. The shower portion of the program should be wrapping up shortly so we'll head out to the barn in a few minutes and guide them to their next activity. If you all want to lend a hand, fine. The more hands, the better."

Satisfied, Sam, Karen, and Shauna all grinned at one another before delving back into conversation about what they thought the McCabe brothers would be up to next.

By the time the ladies were done making their perfumes and bath goodies, had moved back to the inn for a light lunch, and the mobile spa arrived and began setting up, Cassie wondered why she'd ever considered turning down the offers of help.

The five of them had been running almost non-stop. Not that the group was demanding, quite the contrary, but there was just so much to do. Spills happened and Shauna was on every one in a flash. They forgot to bring the bottled water to the barn and before Cassie could say a word, Karen was out the door running to fetch it. One of the tables the caterer provided had wobbly legs so Sam stepped in with a quick fix. Cassie knew she and Susan would have managed, but having the extra help made the afternoon run much smoother.

And even with five of them making countless trips back and forth to the barn, no one ever noticed the man watching intently from behind a massive, twisted oak tree.

Lunch was over and the group was relaxing in the parlor when Cassie and Susan, along with their helpers, came in loaded down with giant, purple gift bags.

"Okay, ladies, we think you're going to enjoy the

rest of the afternoon," Cassie said.

Some who had been looking a little droopy perked up and took notice as the bags were handed out.

"Go ahead and look inside," Susan said.

Oohs and ahhs filled the room as, one by one, they held up the plush robes, some rubbing them on their cheeks and some slipping them over their shoulders.

"These are heavenly," Angela cooed. "I could just snuggle right in and take a nap."

The women began kicking off their shoes and slipping their feet into the cozy slippers.

"Are we taking naps next?" the raven-haired Calley asked on a yawn.

"Not yet. You'll have some time to rest a little later…unless, of course, you want to skip the spa that's set up in the barn?" Cassie asked.

All signs of tiredness vanished. The women were on their feet, their excitement palpable.

"A spa? Really?" Angela's eyes were like saucers. "I keep thinking there's no way this weekend can get any better, and then you do something to top it. You guys are amazing."

Susan accepted the compliment with a nod and a bit of a blush. "I think you'll enjoy the spa. It's all set up with massage therapists, estheticians, nail techs…the works. They're just waiting for clients."

Angela's friends were nearly bouncing out of their slippers, all talking at the same time and all eager to make their way to the barn. Angela, however, turned to Susan and Cassie.

"Surely you'll join us? All of you," she said as she turned to include Sam, Shauna, and Karen. "I'd love to have you all there."

"Oh, thank you, but we'll get you set up and then let you enjoy the afternoon with your friends," Cassie answered for them all.

"But I want you there. You're all my friends now too. Please come. You deserve a little pampering after all you've done for us making this weekend just so unbelievably special. Please," she added again when her hosts continued to look skeptical.

"Well," Susan said turning to Cassie. "I don't know…"

Angela's mother came to stand alongside her daughter. "Please join us. Angela is right. You've done a marvelous job planning this weekend for us. I couldn't be happier. Relax with us for a while. You've more than earned it."

The five glanced at one another, all clearly wanting to say yes, but hoping someone else would say it first. Cassie spoke up.

"I guess I wouldn't say no to a massage…"

"Wonderful," Angela answered, giving a little clap and then wrapping Cassie in a hug. "It's going to be even more fun with all of you there." And she then proceeded to hug everyone else she could get her hands on.

Cassie was infinitely glad she hadn't said no to the massage. As she sat in the parlor with her feet up and sipping a glass of sparkling water, she admired her nails and ran a hand over her cheek. She hadn't felt so relaxed and hadn't been so pampered in…well, ever. She looked around her at Susan, Sam, Karen, and Shauna. They all looked equally relaxed as they sat chatting. Karen's eyes were closed and Cassie was fairly certain Karen had drifted off. Cassie wondered how long it had been since Karen had had a day like this to herself. Working and caring for a husband, a toddler, and a home couldn't be easy. They'd made the right decision joining the ladies at the spa, Cassie told herself again as she felt her eyes start to close.

Because she knew it would be easy to doze off, she forced herself to stand and peek out the window. The limos were due in thirty minutes, but Cassie couldn't help worry they'd show up early and ruin the surprise. It was time to wander upstairs and be sure the ladies were dressed in their jeans and ready to head back to the barn.

Wide eyes accompanied by more oohs and ahhs filled the barn when the group got a look at the evening's decorations. The room had been completely revamped by a slew of talented decorators while the ladies relaxed back in their rooms.

Thousands of tiny lights were strung in the ceiling beams, and more lighting came from countless mason jars filled with candles. Bushel baskets overflowing with purple and white flowers were placed around the room and more flowers were wrapped around the posts framing the dance floor. A stage had been erected for the band, and tables were set for dinner with thick, white dishes, shiny silver, and sturdy glassware that reflected the dozens of tiny candles on each table. A purple cowboy hat hung from each chair. Straw bales, rustic crates, and wine barrels were situated around the perimeter, doing double duty as they gave the room an unquestionable charm, but would also serve as tables and chairs once the dinner tables were cleared to make room for the dance floor. The effect was breathtaking.

Angela had tears in her eyes as she turned to Cassie and Susan. "My goodness, this is incredible. It's exactly what I would have chosen for this night. Thank you. You have all my favorites…it's just too much." She swiped at her eyes as she hugged her mother and sister. "Thank you," she repeated to them.

Once she'd gathered herself, she looked around, scrutinizing her surroundings. "It smells delicious in here. I'm starving and unless I'm mistaken, I smell barbequed chicken," she said with a grin. She looked closer and knit her brows together. "There are so many seats. Why are there so many seats?"

She barely had the words out when the doors opened again and a group of men, escorted by Shauna, made their way into the barn.

Angela gasped and her hand flew to her mouth. "Karl!" She darted across the room and launched herself at a tall, dark-haired man who was grinning from ear to ear and who had eyes for only one woman in the room.

Cassie watched as one by one, the women spotted their husbands and boyfriends and greeted them enthusiastically. A dignified-looking man with graying hair and intense dark eyes made his way across the room, walking somewhat stiffly in neatly pressed jeans, a denim shirt, and cowboy boots. But he carried himself well and seemed to take control of the room without uttering a word. The man was clearly better suited for a board room and a designer suit than for jeans and a country-themed dance in a barn.

"Helen." He smiled at his wife as he dropped a kiss on her cheek.

"Oh, Bradford, you look…" Helen stifled a giggle.

"I look foolish, that's how I look," he grumbled, but couldn't keep the corners of his mouth from curving up in a grin. "I still don't know why I agreed to wear this ridiculous getup."

"You agreed because you love your daughter," Helen answered as she reached around him and gave his behind a pinch.

"You're right about that." He looked at Angela who still had her arms wrapped around her fiancé and was beaming up at him.

"Bradford, meet Susan and Cassie. They are the ones responsible for making this weekend an absolute delight."

They shook hands as Angela rushed up, pulling her fiancé along with her.

"This is Karl. Karl, this is Cassie, and this is Susan. They are both amazing. They have given me the best weekend. If there was one thing missing from all the fun it was you, and now they've given me you too. Thank you both so much. This is just the best surprise. I can't wait to tell everyone I know about your inn." Turning to her fiancé, she said, "You know who would love it here? Mark and Tilly Westbrook. They are always looking for somewhere new to visit when they're not in Washington. We'll have to mention it to them. They both love being outside, fishing, hiking, all those things. It would be perfect for them."

Angela was talking a mile a minute while Karl just listened, nodded, and smiled at her. Cassie shifted her glance to Susan. Mark Westbrook? Angela couldn't mean *Senator* Mark Westbrook, could she? Susan must have had the same thought because her eyebrows nearly disappeared into her hairline as she gave Cassie an almost imperceptible shrug.

The rest of the night flew by. The food was delicious, the band was a hit, and everyone, even Angela's father, took a turn on the dance floor. As exhausted as Cassie was, she almost hated to see the night—and the weekend—come to an end.

15

"I've said it before and I'll say it again…hiring Jordyn and Jennica was the smartest thing we've ever done." Susan yawned as she leaned back in her chair and closed her eyes."

"Agreed."

Angela and her friends had just left after lengthy goodbyes and promises from many to return. The girls were already at work cleaning the guestrooms to prepare for the next arrivals. Susan and Cassie were sitting at a table in the corner of the kitchen, sipping yet another cup of coffee, and trying to muster the energy to get to work.

"Sometimes I wonder why I stick with the hotel business," Cassie mused. "The hours are impossible, the work can be frustrating, back-breaking, and, at times, downright disgusting, and nothing about it is exactly glamorous. But then we get guests like Angela's group and I realize there's really nothing I'd rather do. When people enjoy themselves, relax and have fun, and appreciate the fact that someone worked hard to make it all possible for them, well, then all the work is worth it."

"I know what you mean. What an awesome group. They were fun and friendly and, like you said, so appreciative. I wish all our guests could be just like them. It was a great weekend…even if I feel like I could sleep for a week."

"Ah, sleep. You shouldn't tempt me with something so far out of reach."

"I wonder how much sleep anyone got last night? The girls were all pretty wound up. I heard them upstairs chatting away for hours. And the guys? I'll never forget the looks on their faces when we told them about their day at the ballpark. They didn't have any trouble replacing their cowboy hats with baseball caps, did they? They were practicing *Take Me Out to the Ballgame* as they got into the limos." Susan laughed at the memory.

"I think everything went better than we could have hoped for. Here's to us." Cassie raised her coffee cup in a toast.

Jennica walked outside loaded down with garbage bags. She and her sister had just finished cleaning the guestrooms and since Jordyn won their game of rock, paper, scissors, she was replacing a burned out light bulb while Jennica hauled trash to the dumpster at the end of the drive.

From what she'd heard, there had been a full house, and then some, all weekend. She'd never have known from the state of the rooms. They were as neat as she'd seen them in all her months working at the inn. It had come as a bit of a shock when she'd first started and had seen the messes some people left behind. She'd cleaned up everything from spoiled food to tiny beads spilled all over the bed and floor to the disaster made by a cat a guest had smuggled into her room. It was nothing, though, compared to the stories she'd heard from her friend Ruthie who worked at the discount motel a few miles down the highway.

Jennica shuddered as she heaved the first bag up and over the edge of the dumpster. As she bent to pick up the second, she saw a pair of heavy black boots next to the bag.

Startled, she looked up and couldn't help but gasp when she found a man staring at her.

Taking a step back, Jennica looked toward the inn before she uttered a shaky, "Hi."

"Hello. I'm looking for Cassie Papadakis. Is she here?"

Jennica breathed a little easier. "No, she had to go into town, but she should be back soon. Do you want to talk to Susan McCabe? She owns the inn."

"No. I'm just here to see Cassie. I'm an old friend of hers and I'm surprising her, so don't tell her I was here, please." He smiled crookedly behind a hand that shielded most of his face.

"Um, okay. Are you going to come back later?" Jennica wasn't sure why, but she didn't trust the man.

He nodded. "Yes, I'll stop by again later so I can surprise her. Be sure not to tell her I was here." Just as suddenly as he had appeared, he disappeared into the trees.

Weird, Jennica thought. She couldn't figure out where he had come from and why he didn't have a car if he was visiting from out of town. When she heard an engine start, she figured he must have parked down the road, probably unsure of where he was going.

Still, it seemed odd. He seemed odd. She should probably tell Cassie about it, or Susan, but just as she started to head back inside, her phone buzzed and the cute picture she'd taken of her boyfriend at the Snow Daze carnival when he'd won her the stuffed penguin popped up on her screen. Grinning, she answered, and all thoughts of the strange man and of telling someone about him were forgotten.

His brothers had finally cleared out after what had been a good weekend. A really good weekend. Frank couldn't remember the last time they'd all hung out with nothing to do but whatever seemed like a good idea at the moment. In one afternoon and evening they'd played pool at Mick's, stuffed themselves with pizza at The Brick, held foosball and darts tournaments in Frank's basement, watched some playoff hockey, staged their own round of playoff knee hockey, and watched *Slap Shot* for what he guessed was at least the twentieth time.

Frank pulled open the refrigerator door and stared at the empty shelves. Except for some salad ingredients and other green things Cassie kept in the crisper drawer, he'd been cleaned out. Sometime in the early pre-dawn, Riley had eaten an entire jar of pickles after complaining there was nothing else worth eating.

Frank had made his brothers stick around and help clean up, but the grocery shopping would fall on his shoulders. He shrugged as he shut the door. A marathon shopping trip would be worth it, he figured.

As Frank sat down to scribble a few things on his grocery list, he rubbed at the bruise on his shin where Jake had whacked him with the mini hockey stick. The game had gotten rough, complete with checking and all-out cheap shots, but they had laughed themselves hoarse and everyone had been able to at least limp away from the game. He remembered the brawls that were, at one time, commonplace in his parents' basement when they'd all grab sticks and whack away at the ball and at each other. Shauna had even joined in the action more often than not, and as much as Frank and his brothers still hated to admit it, she'd always had a way of sneaking past them and finding the back of the net with the ball.

Since a couple of his brothers had been unable to go the entire night without checking in with their wives, Frank knew Shauna had been with all the rest of them at the inn helping out with the group there for the shower. He'd teased Joe and Jake mercilessly when they'd snuck off to make their phone calls, but then he'd hung on every word when they'd reported on the goings on at the inn, waiting for any mention of Cassie.

He checked the clock. Cassie would be back in a few hours. As busy as he'd been and as much fun as he'd had with his house full with his brothers, it had still seemed somehow empty without Cassie. Even more so now.

He did some quick calculating. He needed to put in a little time at his office before his meeting the next morning. Most of the work was done and ready to present to Jared Wright, owner of JW Office Furniture, but Frank wanted to go over some of the shots he planned to show Jared. As usual, ever since he'd done the editing on the photos he'd chosen to highlight the new JW campaign, he'd been going over them in his head, thinking about how he could tweak them just a little more to make them pop. JW was a new client and while Frank didn't find office furniture particularly exciting, he was determined to make it seem as though he thought it the most fascinating subject in the world and to wow Jared with his photos.

A couple of hours in the office and he'd still have time to stop by the grocery store to pick up steaks for dinner. He'd grab some bread, throw together a salad, and since it was finally warm enough to fire up the grill, dinner would be a snap. Cassie would most likely be exhausted by the time she got home, and as she tended to do, would probably want to grab a yogurt and call it dinner. Frank was determined to see that didn't happen.

Twenty minutes later he was unlocking the door of his office ready to fine-tune his presentation and already looking ahead to his evening with Cassie. He made a mental note to pick up a hunk of parmesan at the store since he knew Cassie loved it grated on her salad. As he pocketed his key and started across the room, the feeling that something wasn't quite right struck hard. He stopped and looked around, studying everything carefully and while he couldn't spot anything damaged, overturned, or glaringly out of place, the feeling remained.

Thinking back to Friday afternoon when he'd locked up, he tried to remember if he'd left anything on his desk. He strived to make it a habit to put everything in the desk drawers or in one of the file cabinets before leaving, but acknowledged the fact that he didn't always follow his own rules. Since the desk drawers and the file cabinets locked, it gave him a little sense of security, even though he knew those locks would be easily bypassed by anyone wishing to do so. He went to his desk and paged through the papers he found. Most were for his upcoming meeting and could have been left out on Friday afternoon. He had been in a rush knowing Riley was coming over.

At the bottom of the stack he found a picture of the inn and it stopped him cold. Had he taken it out? No, he was sure he hadn't. There was no reason for it to be mixed in with the papers for his meeting. He knew it was one of the exterior shots Andrew had taken, and he knew all of those photos had been filed away once they'd handed over some of them to Susan. Maybe Andrew had taken it out, he'd been working on his portfolio again. The print could have gotten mixed up with the other papers and prints they'd had out on Friday.

He crossed the room to the file cabinet and yanked on the drawer containing the file for the inn. It held firm, locked securely. Drumming his fingers on top of the cabinet, he scanned the room again. The chairs around the table he used for client meetings caught his eye. Normally the chairs were all pushed under the table. Today, one was pulled out, angled sideways to the table, as if someone had been sitting in it, maybe focusing on something he was holding rather than something lying on the table. Strange, but not proof of anything untoward. A cleaning crew came in on Friday evenings and while they normally left the room in perfect order, it was certainly possible they'd missed a chair.

Still, the feeling that something was wrong nagged at him as he got to work. He thought back to a break-in that had occurred at the New York offices of *Country Chic*. A disgruntled former employee had been arrested within twenty-four hours after the state-of-the-art surveillance equipment had captured clear video of him forcing his way into his old office and proceeding to smash a computer keyboard and empty the contents of the file cabinets on the floor. Frank's friends at the magazine had hardly believed him when he'd told them his office in Misty Lake not only didn't have any surveillance equipment, it didn't even have an alarm system. It had taken him the better part of an afternoon to explain life in Misty Lake and to convince the lifelong New Yorkers he was telling them the truth.

Less than two hours after he arrived, Frank was locking up his office, certain he'd done everything he could to put the final polish on his presentation. He hadn't found anything else out of place, but locked and double-checked all of the desk drawers and file cabinets. Then, smiling, he headed out, ready for the evening ahead.

He and Cassie were making progress, he assured himself. She hadn't talked any more about their past, but they talked about most everything else. She shared things from her time in the Catskills, and he entertained her with stories of some of the more colorful clients he'd had over the years. They were starting fresh and Frank felt ready to take on the world.

16

Cassie felt a little more at ease than she had the last time she'd headed to a gathering with the entire McCabe clan. Maybe it helped that this time they were at Sam and Jake's house instead of at Sean and Anna's. Sam was her friend, it was easier for Cassie to feel as though she belonged. Sam loved to entertain and had insisted on having a Mother's Day get-together so neither of the mothers in the family would have to lift a finger. Any and all arguing by Anna and Karen that Sam deserved a day off as well since she was going to be a mother soon had been promptly poo-pooed by Sam. She'd convinced them she'd take her turn the next year.

Since Cassie and Susan had hired Molly Olson as a very part-time, on-call employee, both were able to spend the afternoon away from the inn. Molly was nothing short of a godsend. They hadn't done more than toss around the idea of maybe looking for another employee when Molly had shown up and asked if they needed any help. She'd come with a resume in hand, one that had warmed Cassie's heart.

Molly had spent the majority of her time raising her family, but had taken a few part-time jobs over the years. On the experience section of her resume she'd listed, in addition to her stints waitressing and working the front desk at a motel, Household CEO and Organizer Extraordinaire. She'd also added a section titled Special Skills where'd she'd boasted an unending supply of love, patience, and sound advice. Cassie and Susan had hired her on the spot. So Molly was tending to the inn while Cassie and Susan spent a rare afternoon off together.

Cassie had just stopped her car at Sam and Jake's place when her phone rang. Fumbling in her purse, she grabbed it and looked at the display. Not a number she recognized, but an area code she did. Chicago. She almost didn't answer, but in the end, pushed the button.

"Hello?"

"Hello, is this Cassandra?"

Cassie clutched the phone a little tighter. "Yes. Who's calling?"

"Cassandra, it's Detective Zalinski. How have you been?"

Cassie struggled to find her voice. "Detective Zalinski. Fine, I'm fine." She didn't know what else to say. "Please, call me Cassie."

"Good, I'm happy to hear that, Cassie. I, um, I've been meaning to contact you but I had to track you down and, well, things have been so busy that I'm afraid it's taken longer than I intended."

He paused and Cassie tried to brace herself for

whatever was coming. "Yes?"

"I need to tell you that Martin Santos was released from prison. He's been free for...for over a year now. I know you said you didn't want to know anything about him, but I'd been checking on his status over the years and when—"

Cassie didn't hear any more after she dropped the phone. She watched it bounce off the car seat and onto the floor, unable, or unwilling to reach for it. She hadn't heard that name in years and had hoped she'd never have to hear it again. Unwanted memories bombarded her as she sat, frozen in place.

Seeming to move in slow motion, she reached for the phone and managed to get it back up to her ear.

"Cassie? Cassie, are you there?"

She struggled to catch her breath. "Yes, I'm here."

"I'm sorry to spring this on you but, well, I just thought you should know. I checked up on him, he's been sticking to the rules of his probation...there haven't been any problems, any...incidents of any kind."

Cassie didn't answer. What could she say when she didn't even know what to feel?

"I don't think you have anything to worry about, but I want you to be alert."

At that, Cassie almost laughed. Alert? Had she been anything but alert for nearly eight years? "Okay."

"I checked in with his parole officer a couple of months ago, seems like things are fine. So far, so good, I guess. Now, I know you're not in Chicago any longer and the conditions of Santos' parole are such that he's not allowed to leave the state, but that doesn't mean it would be impossible. He could break parole, he could plead for leniency in the case of a funeral or something like that…"

"I see."

"But you're not an easy woman to find. The phone number I had on file for you was disconnected several years ago, you don't appear to be active on social media, your former employers from back…back then didn't have any current information on you. Those are all good things if you don't want to be found."

Cassie started to bristle at the fact that he'd dug into her privacy the way he had, but then let it go. He was a cop, after all. It was his job. Instead, she focused on what he'd said. '…if you don't want to be found.'

She'd never had any desire to join any of the social media sites that she'd seen suck up so much of her friends' time. When they stuck their phones in her face to show her the latest picture of their cousin's neighbor's puppy, she smiled and made some sort of comment, but mostly she found the whole thing ridiculous. Who cared, really? And who wanted the entire world to know their every move? No, she hadn't cared about those things…but had she not cared because she'd been afraid? Because she wanted to stay hidden?

The detective's voice pulled her away from her thoughts. "So, what do you think?"

"Excuse me?"

"Do you want me to keep you updated on any change in his parole conditions, his whereabouts, that sort of thing? I'm happy to do so."

"No. No, thank you. I don't think that's necessary."

"How about if I leave you with my direct number? That way, if you have any questions, you can contact me."

"Sure, that would be good."

Cassie scribbled the number on the back of an old receipt, thanked the detective, and rushed to end the call. When she disconnected, she did so with trembling hands.

Why now? Why did he have to call now when things were finally moving—albeit slowly—in the right direction? She hadn't heard from Detective Zalinski since he'd called that final time to tell her Martin Santos was on his way to prison. Since then, she'd changed her cell number, severed ties with everyone from that period of her life, and moved several times. He was right. She didn't want to be found.

As much as the phone call had bothered her, and as much as she wished she hadn't answered, she knew Detective Zalinski had her best interest at heart. Always had. He'd been almost frighteningly driven to solve her case, but had never been anything but patient and kind when he'd questioned her. His mild manner, at least when he was sitting next to her hospital bed, had been so different from that of the others who had come with their questions and had seemed impatient, angry, or even bored. Detective Zalinski, though, with his chestnut hair, gold-flecked hazel eyes, and lean, athletic build, had made Cassie think more of a model, a co-worker, than of a police officer. That had made it easier to talk with him, even if the subject had been nearly impossible.

It wasn't until one of the other cops who had talked to her let it slip that Zalinski's wife had been raped and murdered and the assailant never caught, that his intense focus on her case started to make sense. She'd always wished she'd been able to recall more details in order to help the investigation, as much for Detective

Zalinski as for herself.

Now, though, she wished she could, once and for all, put it all behind her. She inhaled deeply and exhaled slowly, calling on her yoga experience to try to calm her racing heart. It didn't help much. Knowing she couldn't face the McCabes in her current state, she gave Trixie a pat on the head, started her car, backed out, and drove around the lake for fifteen minutes until she had herself convinced that Detective Zalinski's call wouldn't change anything…and that she definitely wouldn't tell Frank.

Cassie was barely inside, had barely greeted everyone—pleased to find she was able to do so calmly—when Frank got everyone's attention.

"Since everyone is together, I thought this would be a good time to show you all something." He reached into the bag he was holding and held up a copy of *Country Chic*. "It comes out next week, but I got a few advance copies. Check out the cover."

Cassie gasped.

Susan shrieked.

A stunning photo of The Inn at Misty Lake, taken in the fall with spectacular color all around, was splayed across the glossy cover.

Susan grabbed the magazine from Frank's hand. "Oh, Frank, it's gorgeous. Are there more pictures inside?"

"Take a look."

Frank took a few more copies from the bag and passed them around. Cassie went to look with Susan. The entire issue was dedicated to the restoration and preservation of farmhouses and barns. It was filled with breath-taking photos and, it appeared, short stories on the history of each subject.

When they got about halfway through the magazine, Cassie and Susan gasped simultaneously. There were four pages of photos of the inn and the barn complete with a lengthy article.

"This is incredible, Frank, I can hardly believe it. When I spoke with the writer at the magazine and answered his questions about the inn, I had no idea he had anything like this in mind. When did you find out?" Susan appeared close to shock.

"A while ago. I thought it would be more fun to wait until you could see it instead of just hearing about it."

"You're good at keeping secrets. I don't think I would have been able to hold something like this inside," Susan said.

"Are all the photos in the magazine yours, Frank? They're absolutely stunning," Cassie said, her heart bursting with excitement for Frank.

"They are. And thank you. I'm pleased with how it all turned out."

"You should be. Congratulations. You'll be getting calls from all over the country. Everyone will want to hire Frank McCabe."

"And everyone will want to visit The Inn at Misty Lake," Frank answered.

"Riley's name is in here! Riley, your name is in here. Look!" Susan was bouncing up and down, holding the magazine out for Riley to see.

As everyone else had a chance to page through the magazine and to congratulate both Frank and Riley, Cassie wandered across the room, grateful to be right where she was, with the people she was with. The call from Detective

Zalinski seemed like a distant memory.

It was a beautiful spring day, the leaves starting to open on the trees, the grass greening, and the birds that had left for warmer climates the previous fall, slowly returning. As Cassie gazed out the huge picture windows in Sam's living room, the lake glittered a bright blue and looked deceptively inviting even though Cassie knew it would be closer to the Fourth of July than to Mother's Day before she'd dare dip a toe in the frigid water.

She let her gaze wander around the room. Anna's aunts, Kate and Rose, were seated by the window, enjoying the sunshine, and chatting animatedly while paging through their copy of *Country Chic*. Cassie had met the sisters, but didn't know them well. Most of what she knew of them was through the stories that circulated throughout the family and throughout the town and that seemed to be the stuff of legends. The women were not afraid to state their opinions or to share their vast knowledge of most everything, and everyone, in Misty Lake.

As she studied the two, Cassie noted the similarities, and the differences. They both sat erect in their chairs, Kate's shoulders perhaps a bit more rounded than Rose's, but still proud. Both wore long-sleeved dresses with cardigans thrown over their shoulders, sturdy, square-heeled shoes, and heavy nylon stockings. The years had been kind to them in that both had relatively unlined faces and their eyes had remained wide and alert. The sisters both had their hair permed in tight curls, but Kate had let hers go gray while Rose continued to color hers a dark brown. Their personalities showed through in their choice of jewelry. While Kate opted for a gold chain and simple pearl earrings, Rose had plump red strawberries dangling from her ears, and instead of a necklace, a sparkly brooch featuring a motorcycle and the words, 'Born to be Wild' secured to the front of her dress.

Trixie chose that moment to wander over to them and snuggle her way near Rose's legs where the sun had warmed a spot on the floor.

"Oh!" Rose exclaimed, startled at the brush of fur against her legs.

Cassie was there in a flash, ready to grab Trixie out of the women's way. "I'm sorry she barged in like that. I think she was searching for the sunniest spot in the room."

"She's no trouble," Rose insisted. "I've been looking forward to meeting her. I've heard quite a lot about her."

"You have?"

"Let me have her," Rose said as she reached for the dog.

Somewhat uncertainly, Cassie handed over the dog. Rose settled her on her lap and ran a hand down the dog's head and back. Never one to pass on some pampering, Trixie melted under Rose's touch.

Delighted, Rose fussed over the dog. "Isn't she just the sweetest little thing? We can have cats in our apartment building, but not dogs. If I could, I'd have one just like her. Now, let's see if the stories I've heard are true."

Stories? Where had Rose heard stories about her dog? And what kind of stories? It took only a moment for Cassie to find out. Rose looked into the dog's eyes and started to belt out Elvis' *Blue Suede Shoes*. When Trixie started to sing right along with her, Rose threw her head back and laughed before continuing with the song.

The howling—and the singing—reached fever pitch.

"Oh, for crying out loud, Rose, what are you trying to do, attract every dog within ten miles?" Kate scowled and scolded her sister.

"Maybe I should take her," Cassie said. Conversation came to a halt as the McCabes all looked on curiously. Kate was still scowling, both Rigi and Gusto had started to whine and pace, and Rose showed no signs of slowing.

Frank came up behind Cassie and flung an arm around her shoulders. "Is this our pre-dinner entertainment?"

Cassie, wide-eyed and helpless, whispered, "I'm sorry, I didn't know she was going to do that. What should I do?"

"Probably just relax and enjoy the show. My guess is Rose isn't going to quit until the song's done."

"Are you sure? Is it bothering everyone? Do you think they're angry?"

Cassie looked around the room and found everyone still watching, some with brows creased in confusion, some with amused grins lighting their faces.

"Angry? No. Everyone knows Rose. This isn't unusual behavior. She likes to have fun."

Frank was smiling, seemingly relaxed, but Cassie wasn't convinced. She tapped her toe impatiently along with the song, willing Rose to hurry. When Rose finally belted out the final notes, Cassie rushed to grab her dog.

"Oh, I haven't had that much fun in a long time," Rose said, wiping her arm across her forehead. "That dog of yours is a gem."

"Well, yes, I guess so…"

"Kathryn, do you remember that foolish dog Mayor Gilman had for so long? That thing spent his days wandering around town begging for food, and if no one would oblige, stealing it. Once he stole blueberry pies right off Mavis Trumble's kitchen table."

"Hmpf," Kate snorted. "That dog was nothing but a menace and Dicky Gilman was worthless. He let that monster run wild all over town and never did a thing to control it. Every spring, as soon as I put in my petunias, that dog would come and dig up the garden and trample every last one of them."

"You don't know it was Dicky's dog, Kate," Rose scoffed. "Your petunias never did any better after the dog died. I don't know why you can't admit you just don't know how to grow petunias, never did."

"How dare you?" Kate yelled at her sister. "I won a ribbon at the fair for my flowers, and you darn well know it."

"Yes, you won a ribbon…once, for dahlias, and that was when Janelle was growing them for her 4-H project…" Rose let the thought hang.

Kate drew in a sharp breath before narrowing her eyes. "You take that back. I did not enter my daughter's dahlias in the fair. I grew those flowers, I babied them all summer, and they were perfect. You're still jealous because the jam you entered that year didn't win squat!"

Frank stepped between the two before Rose could respond. "How about I refill your drinks for you?"

Nearly in sync, both women studied the glasses in their hands and then twirled their ice cubes.

"Why, thank you, Frank, it looks like we could use refills." Kate smiled sweetly before turning to Rose. "Do you think it really was Dicky's dog that stole those pies from Mavis? Or, do you think that was just an excuse because she didn't want to admit she couldn't bake a blueberry pie? She was supposed to bring those pies to the church festival as I recall. She'd never offered to bring blueberry pies before. I still think they didn't turn out and she was trying to save face."

Cassie stared, dumbfounded. Just a moment before, the women had been shouting at one another, seemingly close to an all-out brawl. Now, they were rehashing memories from years ago as if nothing had happened. Cassie looked around to see if anyone else noticed, but everyone had gone back to their conversations and she appeared to be the only one listening to the sisters. When they continued to talk about pie and then moved seamlessly to simultaneous conversations about one neighbor with shingles and another who was 'building a wall for the Facebook,' Cassie's head started to spin. She scooped up her dog and headed for the door. Time for a break. For both of them.

She thought she'd snuck out unnoticed, but it wasn't thirty seconds before she heard the door open behind her. She turned to find Frank's mom following her into the yard.

"I love springtime," Anna said, lifting her face to the sun. "So full of promise."

Cassie nodded. "Is it your favorite time of year?"

Anna looked contemplative. "I don't know that I have a favorite time of the year…I think my favorite thing is the changing of the seasons. I don't know that I'd enjoy living somewhere that didn't have distinct seasons. You appreciate the warmth of summer, or the snow in the winter, when you don't see it all the time."

"True. I guess I've always loved fall because my mom was so thrilled when the leaves started to change—" Cassie caught herself and threw Anna a nervous glance.

Anna paused a beat and then asked, "You were close to your mother?"

Cassie considered deflecting, but it was a simple question. The answer, however, wasn't so simple. "Yes, we were close. We really only had each other."

"Your father…?"

"He died before I was born," Cassie answered flatly. She never knew what to feel when someone asked about her father. Mostly, she didn't feel much. She couldn't say she missed him, she'd never known him. She couldn't say she'd loved him because, again, she'd never known him. He was an enigma to her…an unknown, plain and simple. She assumed she would have loved him had she known him since her mother clearly had. She'd longed, at times, for a father, but didn't know if she'd longed for *her* father or just *a* father.

"I suppose you've heard it's easier because you never knew him. While it's heart-breaking to lose a parent—or anyone you love—I have to believe not knowing, wondering what things would have been like if he hadn't died, is just as heart-breaking."

Cassie turned away. Anna was right, exactly right, but Cassie usually didn't let herself think about the past, and Anna was getting a little too close. Cassie picked up a stick and tossed it to Trixie who promptly caught up with it then started to chew on it. The art of fetching was lost on her Lhasa Apso.

"I'm on my way to Sam's shop to take a look at a rocking horse she's making for us to give to Dylan. She wanted me to check out the progress, see if I like what she's done so far. Walk with me?"

"Sure."

Anna moved ahead of Cassie when they reached the shop, then fit the key into the lock. Anna pushed the door open and motioned Cassie inside.

The smell hit her first. Crazy how the sense of smell was so powerful…more so, she believed, than any other. It took only a hint of the fresh-cut wood to transport her right back to Hans' shop. And it never failed to make her feel warm, loved, and safe.

"What is it, Cassie?"

Cassie closed her eyes and allowed herself one last moment to remember before she answered. "Oh, it's just walking in here. It reminds me of being a kid."

"Sam's shop? Did you know someone who was a woodworker?"

"Our neighbor, Hans Kramer. He was retired and spent most of his time in his garage workshop. He let me hang around with him after school." Cassie didn't add that she'd had nowhere else to go. "I used to love to sit and watch him work. He used old-fashioned hand tools almost exclusively. I didn't know anything different at the time, but once I got older and thought back on those days, I realized how amazing his work and his methods really were. My favorite days were those when he'd get out the plane to thin and shape and he'd make delicate little curls as he slid the plane across the wood. I'd collect them, make a big pile, and play with them." Cassie smiled at the memory. She could still feel the fragile twists between her fingers. "I wonder if Sam has one of those," Cassie said, looking around her.

"Did he teach you how to work with wood? You should spend some time here with Sam."

"He showed me a few things, but I was young. He'd let me pound nails into a board, saw small pieces in half, maybe play with a screwdriver, but mostly I just liked to watch." And talk, Cassie thought, because in Hans she'd had someone who would always listen. "I was mesmerized by the way he took a simple piece of wood and turned it into something beautiful. Trust me, I'd never be able to keep up with Sam."

"She has a gift, that's for certain. Look at this rocking horse. It's magnificent, and a couple of weeks ago it was nothing but a stack of boards."

Grateful for the distraction, Cassie ran her hand along the smooth, wooden mane on the horse's neck, made out of a darker wood so it stood out against the lighter wood of the horse's body. She nudged the horse to set it rocking and delighted in the way it glided silently and effortlessly. Crouching down, she studied an adjustable footrest. Clever. For now, it could be raised to the highest level so Dylan's feet would reach. As he grew, it could be lowered to accommodate his longer legs.

"Isn't it something? I can just picture Dylan rocking furiously back and forth and whooping with laughter."

Cassie stood and nodded her agreement.

"It's coming up on a year already…are you feeling at home in Misty Lake?"

Another question Cassie had always struggled to

answer. She'd been asked if her apartment felt like home, if New York felt like home, and now if Misty Lake felt like home. But she didn't really know what home was supposed to feel like. In the place she'd called home for seventeen years she'd felt, at times, frightened, alone, and sad. Other times, she'd felt happy and loved. Now, though, she knew what Anna was looking for.

"I'm comfortable here. I'll admit that there are times I miss the anonymity of the city, but I'm growing accustomed to the idea of a tight-knit community."

"Hmmm, diplomatic," Anna chuckled. "I suppose it's hard to ignore the gossip. For that, I'm sorry. Misty Lake is really a very nice place to live, but there are some who think they're not doing their civic duty unless they're reporting on everyone's comings and goings. I hope you believe me when I say I'm not one of them. I can't deny many of them like to report to me on every move my children make so it's inevitable I hear the gossip, but I don't contribute to it."

Cassie figured she must have looked skeptical because Anna continued.

"It's hard, at times, to stay away from it, but I made a promise to myself years ago that I would try my best to do just that. There's a difference between gossiping and simply caring for your friends and neighbors, keeping in touch and knowing if there are health issues, family circumstances, anything that means they may need some help. In those cases, I will spread the word. What I won't do is spread rumors and half-truths. And I think you'll find that people who know me well feel free to talk to me because nothing they say that they don't want spread around town will ever leave my lips."

Cassie nodded, noting the sincerity in Anna's eyes. It was obvious the woman wanted to convince her.

"I don't doubt that, Mrs. McCabe. Other than poking fun at one another, I've never heard any of your children say a derogatory thing about someone else. That sort of character is learned at home. And I know you've been a big influence on Frank. He told me he's long been Shauna's confidant, and I'm guessing she's not the only one who has confided in him in the past. It's not hard to see where he learned to listen."

A blush touched Anna's cheeks. "Yes, Frank and Shauna have always had a special relationship. Let me tell you a little about Frank. Oh, don't worry." Anna laughed at the brief flash of panic on Cassie's face. "I'm not going to tell you anything you don't want to hear. I just want to help you understand him better."

Anna had, of course, heard that Cassie and Frank had been seen around town together on several occasions. She'd also heard rumblings about them having a prior relationship. That, she hadn't yet confirmed. She suspected her other children knew more than she did, but she'd long ago learned they were more than capable of circling the wagons. While it frustrated her at times, mostly she was pleased they were all as close as they were.

There was something different about Frank's relationship with Cassie. Normally, Anna might push just a little, ask questions and see if Frank would open up to her, but she sensed that in this instance, he needed space while he worked some things out for himself. He'd come to her when he was ready.

"Of all my boys, Frank has always been the most

soft-hearted. Oh, he tried to hide it with all the hockey and sports and tough-guy things he did, but he's really a gentle, caring soul.

The others liked to try to keep secrets from me, and while I usually found out in the end, it never took long with Frank. No matter what happened—he got in trouble at school, he did something he knew was against the rules or that I wouldn't like—he could never keep it to himself. I would tuck him in at night and within ten minutes he'd be creeping down the stairs saying he needed to talk to me. And he was always so sorry, I had a hard time punishing him."

Cassie smiled. "I can believe that."

"Another thing about Frank that I always found so endearing was the way he appreciated—truly, sincerely, appreciated—everything he was given. Now, I think I can safely say all the kids grew up with a sense of appreciation, we didn't spoil them and they were all grateful for what they had, but with Frank it was different.

"I will never forget when he and Riley were just little boys, not yet in school, and they and Shauna would come along with me to do the shopping. There was one aisle in the grocery store that had a section of toys, little things like coloring books, bubbles, toy cars…but there was a set of plastic handcuffs that, for some reason, caught Frank's attention. I suppose it had to do with his father being the sheriff and the fact that handcuffs seemed cool. Maybe he was hoping he could lock up his brothers and sister for a while. But, whatever the case, he would ask me every time if he could please, please, please have them. Well, they were hardly more than junk, just some flimsy plastic, and I always said no. With five children, I couldn't let them think that every time we went to the store they would get something.

"Then one day I was shopping alone. I can't remember how that happened, it was a rare occurrence, but I found myself in the toy aisle and I spotted those handcuffs. And do you know what I did? I bought the silly things. Frank had been behaving very well, he'd managed to stay out of trouble when the other three boys had found themselves in a heap of it earlier in the week, so I figured, what the heck? I'd surprise him. You should have seen his face."

Anna's eyes teared as she looked away, remembering the moment. Her voice was thick as she finished her story.

"He threw his arms around me and thanked me over and over. And it didn't stop there. For months, out of the blue, he would come up to me and say, 'Thank you for my handcuffs, Mommy,' with the sweetest expression on his face. It was the best three dollars I ever spent."

"You raised incredible kids, Mrs. McCabe, you should be proud."

"I am proud...of them, that is. It's easy to look back and think about the things I should have done differently when they were young, but you're right, they are a pretty incredible group."

Anna was quiet for a time, remembering, but also deciding how to proceed. When she spoke, it was with great care.

"There's still a lot of that little boy in Frank. He's grateful for what he has, he's kind and considerate always, and, even if he doesn't show it, he's easily hurt. Now, I don't know what the situation is between the two of you and it's none of my business, but I do know Frank has had a lot on his mind lately, and I can't help but think that much of it has to do with you."

Cassie opened her mouth—to protest, Anna figured—but Anna continued before Cassie could sneak a word in.

"It's in Frank's nature to try to help, to try to fix things. It's hard for him to see anyone hurting. If he pushes too hard, I can promise you it's only because he cares."

"I know that, but there's nothing to fix. Frank and I are friends. I know he cares, the same way he cares about all those he considers friends. Like you said, he's kind and generous. But as far as things between the two of us, there's nothing to worry about. We happen to have ended up living in the same house so that means we spend a lot of time together. I enjoy Frank's company, and I think he feels the same way about me. I hope you're not worrying there's any sort of problem between us because there isn't."

Anna considered giving another nudge, but decided against it. As much as she sensed Cassie needed a shoulder to lean on, Anna knew in her heart she couldn't push. Cassie would come to her when, and if, she chose to. She wouldn't be rushed, that was clear. For now, Anna needed to be certain they remained on good terms.

"I'm glad to hear that. I suppose we should head back inside before they send out a search party."

Cassie blew out her breath. "You're probably right." She called Trixie who was dozing in the corner of the shop and they headed to the yard.

Anna tilted her head and studied the dog as she

bounded across the grass. Turning to Cassie Anna said, "You do have to tell me one thing…how in the world did you ever teach her to sing?"

17

It had been two weeks and everyone was settling into a routine. Stu, Molly's husband and a volunteer driver for Project Strong Start, dropped off the kids by eight thirty every Monday through Thursday and they spent the next three hours learning the ropes at the bed and breakfast. Things had fallen into place with Jordyn and Jennica. The girls had asked for Tuesdays and Thursdays off during the summer so they could run a youth program at the park in town. That meant on Mondays and Wednesdays the inn was full with kids, but on Tuesdays and Thursdays it was just the camp kids and on Fridays just Jennica and Jordyn. It was working out well.

So far, there hadn't been any big mishaps. Sure, a tray of cinnamon apple French toast had ended up on the dining room floor…well, on the floor and on Mrs. James, but everything had been cleaned up and Mrs. James had been very understanding. And maybe a couple dozen reservations had been deleted from their spreadsheet, but they'd been able to go back to saved files and recreate them. Of course, the day Tyrell had volunteered to clean up Gusto after the dog had gotten into a tangle with a skunk—and had decided the industrial sink in the kitchen, with its large basin and handy spray nozzle would work much better than the hose on the back of the inn—they'd lost a good part of the day when they'd had to disinfect and scrub down every surface of the kitchen. But the kids had learned about food service sanitation regulations that day.

Now, Cassie cringed as Matt balanced at least a dozen plates with one hand and reached to open the cabinet with the other. The kitchen was already a few plates lighter than it had been before the camp kids had come on board. She'd told him before to take his time, that unloading the dishwasher wasn't a timed event, but he was so eager to please…and to him, that meant the faster the better. Miraculously, all the plates arrived safely in the cabinet before Matt slammed the door and rushed back to the dishwasher to gather another load.

"Hey, Matt, why don't I finish with the dishes and you wipe down the counters?"

"Oh, okay Ms. Papadakis, I can do that."

He dashed for the sink, reached underneath, snagged the bottle of disinfectant and a rag, and began spraying and wiping furiously. His longish, dark blonde hair swayed back and forth across his forehead and his narrow shoulders hunched and strained as he scrubbed. Cassie watched for a minute, wanted to remind him to slow down, but just sighed and got to work on the dishwasher.

She truly liked the boy and empathized with his situation. He'd grown up with an abusive father, his mother had died when Matt was very young. From his file and from their talks with Tom Lindahl, she knew that Matt lacked self-confidence, never having lived up to his father's expectations. Whenever the young boy had made a mistake, his father had taunted, and more often than not, had become physical with him. A couple of years back, the father had finally been arrested after a teacher reported signs of abuse and the police had been called in. Now, Matt was bouncing around in foster care. Cassie knew he desperately needed positive role models, people to let him know he was capable and smart, and, above all, patience. It hadn't been easy.

Once they had the kitchen clean and orderly, Cassie directed Matt to the parlor. Today was his day to spend time at the reception desk. He'd be checking email for reservations, answering phone calls—with Cassie's assistance—and getting a peek at the website and what was involved in maintaining it. Cassie put a hand over Matt's to slow him down when he immediately started banging on the computer keyboard.

"Okay, Matt, let's take it one thing at a time. First of all, if the phone rings while we're at the desk, I'd like you to try answering."

Cassie proceeded to instruct on the proper way to answer the phone, how to take a message, and how to put the call on hold if he wasn't able to answer a question or if he needed to find someone while the caller waited. As usual, Matt was eager to give it a try.

"We may not get a call, we'll just have to wait and see. A lot of people prefer to make reservations online and even to ask questions online, so let's take a look at the email."

"I know how to check email, I've done it before." He sounded hurt.

"I'm sure you do, but there are a few things about our email that might be a little different than what you're used to. For example, you have to use a password every time. A password we change frequently. And, we try to be careful about opening emails that seem like they might be spam. We have some filters, but things get through. We don't want to end up with some sort of virus."

"Have you ever had one?"

"No, but we're very careful."

They logged into the email account and sifted through the new emails. Since one was a request for information, Cassie showed Matt how to find the files for their brochures and their detailed pricing information, and how to send a reply with the files attached. While they worked, the phone rang. Matt lunged for it.

"Remember to use the greeting we went over," Cassie reminded him.

Matt gave a quick nod then grabbed the phone. "Good morning. Thank you for calling The Inn at Misty Lake. How may I help you?"

Cassie smiled and nodded her approval. She leaned over to listen as Matt held the phone away from his ear as she'd asked him to do. The caller questioned the check-in time for that evening; Matt confirmed. Cassie was congratulating Matt for the way he handled the call when she heard a crash upstairs. Their guests had all checked out, and she knew Tyrell was upstairs removing used towels and linens from the guestrooms.

"That didn't sound good. Stay put, Matt, I'll be right back," Cassie said as she dashed up the stairs.

It took no time at all to learn the reason for the crash. Tyrell was standing in the doorway to Pine Woods with an overturned housekeeping cart at his feet and toiletries rolling in every direction. While Cassie knew Matt would be distraught if he'd been in Tyrell's position, nothing much got to Tyrell. He merely nodded and surveyed the hallway.

"Man, Ms. P, that stuff sure does make some noise, don't it?"

"Yes, Tyrell, it sure does." Cassie sighed as she righted the cart and began collecting wayward shampoo and lotion bottles. "What happened?"

"Well, I'm not real sure," he said as he looked from the room to the hallway. "I went in to get the towels like I was supposed to, and when I came back out here to dump them in the laundry cart, I must have bumped this cart. Huh. That's a lot of shampoo."

"Why don't you give me a hand getting this cleaned up?" Cassie suggested when the boy continued to lean against the doorframe and watch her work.

"Oh, sure, Ms. P."

Cassie watched him as he pushed bottles and packages into a pile with his feet before lazily bending over, grabbing a few, and dumping them back on the cart. The boy was tall and thin, very tall and very thin, and his arms and legs seemed to extend forever. His dark eyes were heavy-lidded and helped further his aloof personality. He kept his hair in tight cornrows that ended at the back of his collar. Cassie had already determined the diamonds in his ears were real.

Tyrell, she'd learned, never worked harder than he figured was absolutely necessary. So far, he hadn't shown much interest in anything related to the inn. He had seemed bored when she'd tried to show him the inn's website, had wanted nothing to do with—and actually seemed a little frightened of—the kitchen, and Susan told her it hadn't been any different when he'd been in the barn helping to prep for an upcoming family reunion. The only time Cassie had seen the slightest flicker of interest from him had been when he'd eagerly volunteered to help with Gusto. While the result had been something of a disaster, he'd handled the dog well. Too bad Dr. Fischer, the town's vet, wasn't taking kids. It might be a better fit.

Tyrell's past was filled with arrests for shoplifting and vandalism, and stints in juvenile detention. He came from a very wealthy family, but his parents were apparently more interested in their country club lifestyle than in the well-being of their son. Much of the trouble he'd gotten into was nothing more than a way of demanding his parents' attention. According to his school records and test scores, the teen was very intelligent, but had no interest in school. He routinely argued with the teachers until more often than not, he wound up suspended. Probably considered that more of a reward than anything, Cassie figured.

Cassie tensed and looked to the stairs when she heard the phone give a half ring before being answered. Matt was manning the desk alone. She pictured him lunging at the ringing phone. She could only hope for the best as she made sure the hallway was cleaned up and that Tyrell got back to work on the guestrooms.

A long morning, she thought, as she headed back

down the stairs and pulled her hair into a ponytail. Matt was happily banging on the keyboard. Bracing herself, she joined him at the desk.

"What happened up there?"

"Just a little spill, it's all taken care of. What's going on down here?" It had only been ten minutes, but she found herself extraordinarily nervous.

"I answered an email about the October promotion." Matt sat up straighter and squared his shoulders with pride.

"You answered it? You mean you sent it already?"

"Yep."

"Can I see what you sent?" Cassie pasted a smile on her face, but on the inside, she was frantic.

"Sure." He clicked and opened the most recent entry in the 'sent' folder.

Cassie read it. It seemed okay, the wording was similar to the email they'd answered earlier together. Then she noticed the attachments. "Um, what did you attach?"

"It's the information about the fall promotion and the other file you showed me about the event center. I thought maybe she'd be interested in that, too."

"She didn't ask about the event center..."

"I know, but I noticed on her original email she copied four other people. I searched for her on Facebook, found out the others were her sisters and brothers, and saw that some of them had been posting about planning a family reunion for the fall. I figured they could use the space."

Cassie was dumbfounded. "You did all that? *You looked at their Facebook pages?*"

Matt shrunk in front of her. "I'm sorry, is that

bad? The pages weren't private, all the information was right there, I was just curious, I didn't tell her I'd looked at it…"

The boy seemed terrified and Cassie felt awful. "No, Matt, you didn't do anything wrong. In fact, you did a good job. I never would have thought to do all of that searching. I think you're right, they might be very interested in the event center."

He didn't seem convinced. His eyes were wary, and he inched away from the desk.

Cassie's mind raced. Had he crossed a line? Probably. Was it going to be an issue? Probably not. She needed to reassure.

"Matt, it's okay. Your email is perfectly worded and attaching the information about the event center shows a lot of initiative. I'm proud of you." He seemed to relax some. "Now, we wouldn't ever want to look at personal information or ask questions that aren't any of our business, but I agree with you that what she has posted on her Facebook page isn't really all that private. It's good you didn't say anything about seeing the mention of the reunion on Facebook, though. That might seem a little pushy and intrusive. I guess what I'm saying is we have to be careful. We want to promote the inn and all it has to offer, but we have to be sure to do it the right way."

Matt didn't answer, and he still looked upset. Cassie tried changing the subject. She hoped the result of her next inquiry would be better.

"I thought I heard the phone ring while I was upstairs. Did you answer a call?" She tried to make her voice light and carefree. Matt seemed to perk up.

"Yeah, there was one call. It was a guy who

wanted to talk to you."

Cassie smiled and glanced at the desk hoping to see a message. There wasn't one.

"Was his name Frank? He's a friend and I'm expecting a call from him today."

"I don't know, he didn't tell me his name."

"Oh, then it must not have been Frank. What did he want?"

"He didn't say, he just asked to talk to Cassie Papadakis…but he said your name weird. I told him you were busy, I asked if I could take a message just like you told me to do, but he didn't want to leave a message. He was kind of hard to understand."

"Hard to understand? What do you mean?"

"He talked with some kind of accent."

Cassie's heart started to pound. "Are you sure he didn't say anything else? Anything at all?"

"That's all he said. After he said he didn't want to leave a message, he just hung up. It was probably someone trying to sell you something, they never leave messages," Matt said knowingly.

"Sure, you're probably right," Cassie mumbled. She wanted to ask more questions even though she was afraid of the answers, but before she could, Susan walked into the parlor followed by Kendra, their third camper.

"We got the last of the cleanup done in the barn," Susan announced. "It's ready for the caterers. I think it's going to be a fun weekend for the Miller family."

"Good, thanks for handling all of it," Cassie said. "What do you think, Kendra, did we forget anything?"

Cassie and Susan had quickly learned that Kendra was nothing short of a perfectionist. She asked question after question, demanded detailed answers, and offered countless suggestions…most of which were very well thought out and some of which they had already adopted. She'd made it clear from the start that she hated the time she had to spend at Project Strong Start and would much rather spend her time working at the inn where she felt she fit in much better.

"No, everything is in place. I asked Mrs. McCabe, and she said you got a final confirmation from the caterer?"

There was doubt in Kendra's voice and Cassie had to look down at the desk and pretend to scribble a note so Kendra didn't see the grin. In so many ways, Kendra reminded Cassie of herself at that age. If you want to be sure something is done, and done right, do it yourself.

"I did. I called this morning and went over all the details one more time. Everything is in order."

"Okay. Then as long as the guestroom assignments are done, we should be ready for the Millers."

Cassie got a kick out of how Kendra, after only two weeks, so easily included herself in the collective 'we.' Cassie wished Kendra could share some of her self-confidence with Matt.

"The guestroom assignments are all noted on the reservation page. I used your suggestions, taking into account which families have kids, who is older and won't want to climb to the attic, and who is younger, without kids, and would likely appreciate one of the more romantic rooms. You did a good job."

"Thank you." Kendra looked pleased with the compliment even though Cassie suspected it hadn't come as a surprise to the girl. "You know, I could ask again if I could help out this weekend with the Miller family reunion. If you explain to Mr. Lindahl that you really need help, maybe he'd let me come."

"Kendra, you know he's not going to change his mind on that. He's responsible for everyone at camp. He can't have people going in all different directions on the weekends," Cassie said.

Kendra huffed out a frustrated breath, but didn't argue.

"What's next on the schedule?" Susan asked effectively changing the subject.

"Why don't you and Kendra sit down and take a break? I'm going to run upstairs and check on Tyrell."

It had been suspiciously quiet and Cassie was curious. As she passed by Susan on the way to the stairs, she whispered, "Keep an eye on Matt if the phone rings."

It was still quiet as Cassie reached the guestrooms. She found Tyrell in the second room she checked.

Sound asleep on the unmade bed.

She closed her eyes and counted to ten before she rapped her knuckles against the wall.

"Hey, Tyrell, what's going on?"

If he was startled—or embarrassed—to be caught sleeping, he didn't show it. "Oh, hey Ms. P. What's up?" He lazily ran a hand over his face, but made no move to get up from the bed.

"Just wondering what you're doing. Weren't you supposed to be collecting all the used linens?"

He brightened. "Oh, I did that. They're in the bin in the hallway."

"Okay, but then why didn't you take them down to the laundry area?"

The boy appeared positively puzzled. "No one told me to do that."

This time Cassie only made it to five. "We've gone over what you're supposed to do when you straighten the guestrooms…collect the used linens and gather them with the rest of the laundry."

"Huh. Okay." He slowly sat up, hung his feet over the edge of the bed, and stretched.

"Tyrell, what do you do when you're at home? Or at school? Or at Project Strong Start? You must be able to figure out when it's time to go to school, when it's lunch time, when you need to do your homework—any number of things—without someone telling you. You need to do the same here."

He pondered for a long time and then shook his head. "No…I usually just wait for someone to tell me what to do. That seems to work out pretty well."

Cassie simply couldn't stop her sigh. "Okay. I need you to gather all the linens then take them downstairs and put them with the rest of the laundry. When you're done with that, come back up here and make sure all of the toiletries are stocked in each room, and when they are, return that cart to the supply room. When you're done with that, please come find me in the parlor."

"Sure. I can do that."

He shoved to his feet, stretched once more, and made his way out of the room. As he passed Cassie, she gave him a genuine smile and a pat on the shoulder. As frustrating as he could be, he really was a sweet kid. Part of her wished she could be as easy-going as Tyrell. Life would be a whole lot easier.

"Thanks, Tyrell."

18

Cassie eased her car into a parking space and stared at the cozy and compact building in front of her. Originally a home, it gave visitors a much more welcoming feel than a more traditional medical facility ever could. This was her fifth visit, but it wasn't much easier than her first. Dr. Willard was kind, intelligent, and seemed to want to help, but Cassie still wasn't entirely comfortable with the idea of sharing her personal life with him.

Was it helping? She'd asked herself that question repeatedly in the past month. Probably. At least a little. But she still hadn't let Frank get any closer and she still didn't have a good reason as to why. Maybe today, she told herself as she gathered her purse, and her nerve, and made her way from the car to the office door.

When she sat down in the comfortable brown leather chair in Dr. Willard's office and looked across the desk at him, she felt the familiar nervous flutter in her stomach.

Dr. Willard had a kind face. His light brown eyes were intelligent and inquisitive but, Cassie had learned, never bored into her as though looking past what she was saying to try to find what she was really thinking. His pink, full cheeks, snow white hair, and rounded belly had Cassie thinking he'd be the perfect grandfather in an advertising campaign if he weren't busy trying to solve seemingly unsolvable problems such as hers.

"How are you today, Cassie?" The doctor smiled over his half glasses as he opened the file in front of him.

Cassie couldn't help but wonder what he'd written in there about her. What kind of notes did a psychotherapist make about his patients? 'She's one clothespin short of the loony bin?' Cassie liked to think not. It was unsettling, though, to watch him nod and scribble notes as she talked.

"Cassie?"

"I'm sorry, Dr. Willard. I'm fine."

"And how was your week?"

"Normal, I guess. The kids we're working with keep us hopping, but that's a good thing. We've been nearly full with guests, the reservations keep coming in for the summer…"

She was rambling and she ordered herself to stop. Dr. Willard never changed his expression, just eyed her with calm and understanding.

"Good. How about what you wanted to work on this past week? How did things go with Frank?"

Even after four visits, Cassie still bristled a bit when the doctor used Frank's name. She had been reluctant to even give him Frank's name at first, thinking it was too personal for her and some sort of invasion of privacy for Frank. Part of the reason she'd found a doctor thirty miles out of town. Once she had realized she'd be telling the doctor details far more personal than someone's name, she'd relented. But she still wasn't completely comfortable.

She didn't answer right away. She'd known he'd ask, that was why she was there after all, and even though she thought she'd been prepared, she didn't know how to answer.

"Things went well, I guess. The same as always."

"You were going to try for something other than the same as always."

"I know. We spent time together, watched a couple of movies, went out to dinner last weekend, but…" She faltered.

"But nothing more?"

"No. Nothing more."

"Okay. That's fine. Things stayed the same. That's better than you thinking things got, in some way, worse. Do you agree?"

"I guess so."

"You're not sure?"

Cassie lifted her hands just to let them drop again. "I don't know, Dr. Willard. I guess I just feel like I'm not making any progress, not getting any better. Shouldn't I be better by now?"

"I explained from the outset that no matter how much I would like to give you a time frame, that's just not possible. Everybody is different. If you ask me, though, I think you've come a long way."

"Really? How do you mean?"

"Think back to your first visit. You were barely able to tell me why you wanted to see me. As I told you then, that's perfectly normal, but you also didn't want to tell me much else—didn't want to talk about your childhood, your family, the incident in Chicago, any of it. Last week you talked at length about the attack, about how you felt immediately afterwards, and how you feel about it now. I call that excellent progress. And that progress made you feel like you were ready to try to move things along with Frank. You shouldn't view the fact that you feel you didn't as some sort of failure. Just acknowledging that you want to, that you feel like you're ready, is a big step."

"It all makes sense when I'm here, but when I get home, it all seems so impossible again." Cassie was embarrassed, but she looked over the doctor's shoulder and continued. It was easier if she didn't have to meet his eyes. "When we were watching a movie, Frank put his arm around me and pulled me close on the sofa. It was fine, it was nice, I was comfortable. Later, he leaned over and I could tell he wanted to kiss me. I jumped up and claimed I needed to let the dog outside. I felt like such an idiot, but I panicked. I just panicked."

"Do you know why? Were you thinking of the attack at the time?"

"No, that's just it. I wasn't thinking about it, I didn't feel like it had anything to do with what was happening between us, but something wasn't right. It's just so frustrating. I thought we had it figured out. I thought that dealing with those feelings would make things better, but it doesn't seem to have worked." She was near tears, but didn't give in to them. In a weak voice she said, "What's wrong with me?"

"Cassie, listen to me. There is nothing wrong with you."

He was quiet for a while, studying her, and she braced herself for the 'but' she was afraid was coming.

"But, I think there's more to it. I think there's something else that's standing in your way, something—"

"I told you everything. Really. There haven't been any other men, no unhealthy relationships, nobody that I had unreciprocated feelings for, nothing. Nobody."

"I believe you. What I'm thinking is there might be something you're not even aware of, something you don't remember."

She stared at him for a full minute. She felt sick. When she finally spoke her voice was trembling.

"You think I have some sort of repressed memories? Something happened to me that I don't remember?"

"I'm saying it's a possibility. It's something we could investigate. Maybe we don't find anything, but maybe we do. And it's nothing to be ashamed of, it's not at all uncommon."

Cassie stood and walked to the window. She needed to think without his eyes on hers. Was there something? What would happen to her if there was? Would she end up even worse off?

"What would you do? Hypnotize me or something?" The thought terrified her.

"No, nothing like that. There are a few different techniques I've used over the years, but trust me, you'll be fully aware of what's happening the entire time."

She just didn't know. She didn't want to think that there could be something, but she also didn't want to go on the way she was…unable to fully trust anyone, unable to confide in anyone, unable to really love anyone. She wanted to be able to love Frank, she had once before, and she hated what she was doing to him. He'd been so patient with her, but she couldn't expect him to keep trying, to wait for her forever.

"Think about it, Cassie, and let me know at our next session. No pressure. If you don't want to try it, that's fine. Just give it some thought."

19

The next week passed in a haze for Cassie. She couldn't get her mind off her upcoming session with Dr. Willard and worrying about what she might learn. Or, maybe worse, that she wouldn't learn anything. She still hadn't told anyone she'd been seeing him, scheduling appointments on her afternoons off and claiming she was taking a yoga class out of town. She'd even gone to the yoga class once, just so she could have some legitimate details in case someone asked. Of course, Susan did.

"I'm still jealous you're sneaking away for yoga, you know." Susan stretched her arms over her head and moved them from side to side. "How's the instructor? Anything like Petunia?" Susan giggled.

"Well, I haven't heard 'Flower your buttocks,' or 'Fold over and just let your brains spill out of your head' even once." Cassie laughed along with Susan. "She was a good instructor, if you could tune out some of what she said."

"I wish your class wasn't so far away...we could ask Molly to come in for a couple of hours and we could go together. But with the long drive, it would just be too much time away. And I don't feel like going by myself."

"That's the hard part about this, isn't it? You're tied down. Is it starting to bother you?"

"No, not really. I love what I'm doing here. But I think it's starting to get to Riley. He hasn't said much, but I think he's getting tired of always having strangers around. We've talked more about putting on an addition and I think we're going to go ahead with it so we'll have a separate living area for ourselves, but I worry it won't be enough."

"What then?"

"I guess I don't know. It's something I haven't let myself think too much about. And I'm making it sound worse than it is. Riley hasn't complained about it or anything, I just sense a disturbance in the force once in a while."

Cassie started thinking. When she'd first come to Misty Lake, that had been exactly what she'd expected. Riley would tire of living at the inn, Susan and Riley would move to town, or somewhere else nearby, and Cassie would move into the inn. Now, she tried to picture herself living there...and moving out of Frank's house. She couldn't. That led her to thinking again about her upcoming appointment, what she might learn, and that made her stomach lurch. She was relieved to be able to turn her attention to the kids walking through the door.

Kendra immediately got down to business. "Did the shipment come yesterday?" she asked, referring to the order she'd help place for some tablecloths and napkins in fall colors.

Cassie pointed to the corner behind the desk. "It's all here. I left it for you to open."

Kendra's eyes twinkled. "Really?"

"Sure, you were the one who chose the patterns and entered the order online. You may as well be the one to unpack all of it."

Kendra bounced to the boxes. She carefully removed the packing list, reached for a pen, and began sorting and checking.

During their talks with Tom Lindahl, Cassie and Susan had learned Kendra was one of the most hesitant campers he had this time around. She wanted nothing to do with Project Strong Start and had tried everything she could to get out of being there. She had a history of some drug use, primarily at home, and her social worker was convinced some time away from that environment would be the best thing for her.

The only child of two addicts, Kendra had been around drugs her entire life. Then, when she was in her early teens, her parents had offered her marijuana and she wound up in and out of trouble with drugs for several years. According to her records, a high school teacher had taken notice of Kendra and had made an impact on her. Kendra had been drug-free for over nine months and seemed committed to staying clean.

For as confident as she seemed, however, there were times when she struggled with self-doubt. Too much of that doubt had, in the past, led her back to drugs. Cassie and Susan were determined to do whatever they could to help Kendra realize her value and potential, and Kendra was making their job easy.

"When you're done there, will you please put the linens in the storeroom and then help Mrs. McCabe in the kitchen? I'm going to take Matt and Tyrell out to the barn to do some cleanup."

"Sure, Ms. Papadakis."

Cassie almost told Kendra the news she had just learned earlier that morning, but held her tongue knowing it should come from Tom and guessing he may want to wait until the camp group returned from their annual trip to the Boundary Waters over the Fourth of July week. But Cassie just couldn't resist a wide grin and wink as she passed Kendra on the way to the barn.

Frank was just starting to think about heading out to get lunch when he heard his office door open. Looking up, he smiled at Shauna. She was dressed in a white silk blouse, a short, bright blue skirt that Frank guessed pushed the limits of what bank president Bob Bell considered appropriate business attire, and oversized sunglasses that she pushed up on her head as she walked in.

"You need to brighten this place up. It's boring. You should let me decorate for you."

Used to her complaints about his boring office, Frank ignored them. "What's up, Shauna? Want to get some lunch?"

"I guess. Maybe. Were you heading out? I'm not really hungry. Maybe just coffee."

She was rambling. Frank knew it meant she was working up to something. He waited her out.

"How's business?"

"Business is good. I've been busy since I got

home. A few new clients, some return clients. It's good."

Shauna nodded and looked around the office. "That's new." She pointed to a framed photo on the opposite wall.

"Yep. One of the shots from a campaign I did for an office furniture company. Maybe not the most interesting subject matter, but I liked the way that one turned out and since I didn't have anything like it displayed, decided to hang it up."

"Good, that's good."

The fact that she didn't comment on the ultra-modern furniture in the photo and refrained from launching into a lecture on the countless reasons antiques and art enhance a work environment, made Frank even more certain she had something on her mind.

"What's new with you?"

She sat down across from Frank and rested her elbows on the desk. "What do you think about yoga?"

"Um, I guess I don't?"

"No, I don't suppose you would. Well, what do you think about me teaching yoga?"

"You teach yoga? Since when?"

"I don't. Not yet, anyway. But I'm certified and thinking about starting. Maybe."

"You'd quit your job at the bank?"

"Oh, no, I couldn't afford to do that. I'd just teach some classes in the evenings."

"How did you manage to get certified? When did you do it?"

"A few years ago. Remember I started with yoga as soon as I started college?" Frank nodded and she continued. "I took some teacher classes while I was there and ended up getting my certification. I never taught except for filling in for my instructor a few times. Guess I got too busy with school."

"Understandable with a double major."

Shauna shrugged. "For the past few months I've been driving to a yoga studio out of town and I've been working with an instructor there, kind of a refresher course. And I went on a weekend retreat for instructors a couple of months ago."

"You did all that? Seems like I would have known."

"You don't always know everything about me." Shauna rolled her eyes.

"Okay, not everything. Just most things." Frank was curious. "You know, Cassie's been going to yoga classes somewhere out of town. Have you seen her where you've been taking classes?"

"No, but I didn't even know she was going. There aren't that many places that aren't super far away so it's probably the same place. I guess we haven't been there at the same time."

"I guess."

"Well, anyway, what do you think?"

"I think if you want to do it, if you think you have time to do it, then you should give it a try. If it doesn't work out, you can always quit."

"True."

"Where would you have classes? At the school?"

"That's what I'm planning. We had an instructor here for a while—remember Melinda Summers?—but she got married and moved away. She held her classes at the elementary school. I went for a while. Not the greatest environment, but it worked."

"So what's holding you back?"

"I don't know. I'd be running my own business, more or less. I guess I'm worried I won't be able to handle it. All of it."

"I've never known you to back down because you're afraid you can't handle something. Is there more to it?" He knew there had to be.

Shauna didn't answer right away. After a sigh, she said, "It's just that I always thought I'd leave Misty Lake. And I always thought I'd open my own business, but I thought it would have something to do with art or antiques and, therefore, probably wouldn't be here. If I start teaching yoga, it seems like just one more tie to Misty Lake. One more thing that makes it seem like I'll never leave."

Frank understood. He'd been in the same place a few years ago. He chose his words carefully.

"You know, Shauna, life can change in the blink of an eye. Just because you're making some decisions, some choices, now, doesn't mean you're making them forever. The yoga idea sprung up because the yoga instructor in town left and you saw an opportunity. You could stumble upon another opportunity like that at any time. What I don't think you should do, though, is look at this opportunity as something you're just settling for. It will be whatever you make of it. Who knows where it may lead?"

"You're happy here? In Misty Lake? You really don't want to chase after a high profile career? You always talked about that, you know."

"I know. And I always thought it was what I

wanted. Now, I know it's not. My months away taught me that. That's not to say it's not for you, though. Time will tell."

Shauna nodded and grinned. "Thanks, Frank. You always know what to say."

Frank couldn't help but think of Cassie. He wished he was as confident as Shauna that he always knew what to say. Instead, he felt like he was making mistake after mistake where Cassie was concerned, and he didn't know how to make it better. They seemed to make progress one day, then the next, seemed to move even further backwards. He doodled on a notepad on his desk while his mind wandered.

"Hey, earth to Frank. I asked if you think you'll give my yoga class a try."

"Me? Yoga? I don't know about that." The thought of a yoga class was horrifying. "You should talk to Cassie. I bet she'd take you up on it. It would save her a lot of time driving to wherever she's been going."

"I'll do that, but you have to come too. Surely you'd support your only sister."

Shauna flashed him a helpless look and all he could do was laugh. She was about the furthest thing from helpless he'd ever encountered. Then her expression changed and she was studying him through narrowed eyes. Frank knew there was more coming.

"What's the deal with you and Cassie? I still don't get what went on between the two of you. And what about now? Are you guys together?"

"That's a lot of questions."

"Answer them one at a time. It won't seem like so many."

"Cute. There's nothing to tell. We knew each other a long time ago and now…well, now we're friends. We go out, I know there's talk, but friends go out. It's no big deal."

"I don't believe a word of that, but I can tell by your tone you're not going to tell me any more, at least not right now, so I'll drop it. But remember, you don't have a monopoly on being a good listener."

"Thanks, Shauna, I know."

20

The temperature was near scorching, the humidity tropical, and the sky heavy with clouds. That didn't stop the buzz of activity at the McCabe house. Cassie had, of course, heard about the McCabe family's annual Fourth of July picnic, but this would be her first time attending the bash. She had argued with Susan that Susan should go to the party. Susan was a McCabe, after all. Susan had argued right back that Cassie was now a Misty Lake resident, and it was only right she experience the party of the year. In the end they'd agreed that Cassie would head over early, Susan would join her later in the day while Molly took a late afternoon shift at the inn, and then Cassie would relieve Molly.

Cassie had arrived with Frank a few minutes earlier, but Frank had already disappeared, having been nabbed by Riley and put to work carrying chairs. Cassie felt a little helpless and a lot out of place as she watched the flurry of activity in the yard.

"Hey, Cassie."

Cassie turned to see Shauna, her hands full of paper plates and napkins, trying to open the screen door with her foot. Cassie pulled the door open and then reached out to grab a stack of teetering plates.

"Thanks. They go over here."

Shauna led Cassie to a long buffet table next to the house. Dozens of other tables and countless chairs were scattered around the yard. While Cassie and Shauna arranged plates and napkins at the end of the buffet table, Jake and Joe hauled even more chairs into the back yard.

"Your family can't possibly own all of this?" Cassie asked, waving her arm to encompass the overflowing yard.

"No, not even close. The party has sort of taken on a life of its own. Every year, a few days before the Fourth, people start dropping off tables and chairs. We always wind up with plenty by the day of the party."

"Nice," Cassie said, and meant it. A true family—and community—event. And something she had never experienced. Not by a long shot.

As she found herself doing more and more lately, she wondered how different her life might have been if she had grown up with a big family or with extended family nearby. Or even with friends…the kind of friends you have because your parents are friends. They'd be kids you've grown up with, and even if they're not always your closest friends, they're still the ones you're always happy to see and who you share a lifetime of stories with…

"Cassie?"

Shauna was looking at her, head cocked and

confusion on her face.

"Sorry?"

"What do you think? Would you come to my class?"

How much had she missed? Cassie wondered, feeling guilty. "Your class?"

Shauna threw up her hands. "My yoga class. I'm going to go ahead with it, I already talked to people at the elementary school about using space. Did Frank talk to you about my plans?"

"He didn't. You're going to teach yoga?"

"Yes, I'm really going to." Shauna bounced on her toes. "It's exciting and terrifying at the same time. I mean, what if no one comes? Or worse, what if people come but they hate me? But you'll come, right?"

"Well, I used to do yoga back in Chicago, Susan and I took classes together for a while, but it's been a long time. I'd probably have to start in your beginner class."

When Shauna looked more confused than ever, Cassie realized her mistake. She felt her face heat.

"I thought you've been taking classes somewhere out of town? That's what Frank told me. He thought maybe we'd been going to the same—"

"Oh, um, yes, but just a few times. I don't think I've been there often enough for it to really count. It's taking me a while to get back into the swing of things…" Cassie ran out of things to say and hoped Shauna wouldn't press.

"You should definitely take one of my classes. And you have to convince Frank too. I told him he needs to come and he tried to talk his way out of it." A sly grin spread across Shauna's face. "I'm going to make all of my brothers take a class. They at least have to give it a try. That's fair, don't you think? I've put up with them for all these years, they owe me."

Cassie relaxed and smiled at both Shauna's enthusiasm and at the mental picture of all the McCabe men in a yoga class. "Definitely. And I'll come to that class for sure."

As the two headed back inside to see what else needed doing, Cassie looked up at the sky. "Do you think the rain will hold off?"

Shauna took a turn looking upward. "I hope so. About five, maybe six years ago, we got rained out. The day started out a lot like this, super hot and humid. About two o'clock the rain started and people began to leave. By three o'clock it was storming and everyone was gone except for some close friends and family. Mom and Dad herded everyone into the basement and the party continued down there. You know, it ended up being one of the more memorable parties. We taught Mom and Dad how to play beer pong."

"Beer pong?"

"I thought you went to college?"

"I did, I guess I just didn't go out much."

With that, Cassie hurried to the kitchen hoping to put an end to the discussion of her college days.

The party was a roaring success. People flooded the yard and even though Cassie thought the number of chairs had been overkill, as she looked around, every one was filled. She stood a little off to the side, enjoying herself but somewhat overwhelmed. Sam joined her.

"Quite something, isn't it?"

"That's an understatement. Is the whole town here?"

"Just about, I think. You know, I was in your position a couple of years ago. When Jake brought me here, I hadn't met many people in town…not even in his family. Everyone was so nice, so welcoming, but…I don't know, I guess I wasn't quite prepared."

"For the crowd?"

"For any of it. It was a difficult time. I wasn't ready to let anyone inside the wall I'd built around myself and I didn't know how to handle all the well-meaning questions. Part of me wanted to sneak away." Sam paused before adding, "It looks like you may be feeling the same way."

Cassie found herself slowly nodding. She had just been peeking at her watch, calculating how much longer until she could claim work as an excuse.

"I've never been to anything quite like this. I didn't grow up with a big family, my mother was not at all out-going, so get-togethers like this just weren't part of my life. I can honestly tell you I've never been around so many people at the same time before."

"I know what you mean. With the McCabes, it seems the more the merrier. It's growing on me."

Cassie stayed quiet while her eyes scanned the yard. From young children to those using walkers or wheel chairs, everyone seemed to be having a good time. A group of girls stood on one side of the yard giggling and eyeing the group of boys on the other side of the yard. The teams currently on the volleyball court were working up a sweat and looking like they were second-guessing the decision to play. Hoots of laughter erupted from all corners of the yard. Maybe it was growing on her too, she thought. Slowly.

"How are you handling all this heat?" Cassie asked Sam.

Sam's hand made its way to her belly and she began rubbing slow circles as she sighed. "I'd like to tell you I'm doing great, the heat's not a problem, and I'm full of energy. But that would be a lie. I'm hot and tired and am considering lobbying to have a national holiday instituted in honor of the inventor of air conditioning."

As if on cue, Jake appeared at Sam's side. "Hey, beautiful," he said as he kissed her on top of the head. "How about we go inside for a while and cool off. I don't know about you, but this pregnancy thing is wiping me out. If I don't sit down, I'm going to fall down."

Sam shook her head and laughed at her husband. "Well, we can't have that. Want to join us, Cassie?"

"No, go ahead. I have to head to the inn soon so I think I'll say a few goodbyes."

As Jake and Sam made their way into the house, Cassie went in search of Frank. She found him in the middle of a group of senior citizens, most of whom were staring glassy-eyed at his great aunts. Kate and Rose seemed to be holding court but, at the moment, in the midst of an argument.

"You are full of beans!" A blush crept up Kate's cheeks as she rolled her eyes at her sister. "That never happened."

"Hah!" Rose shot back. "Don't you try to deny it. You were drunk as a skunk and you know it…singing at the top of your lungs and waving your unmentionables over your head. And at Anna's wedding! It's a wonder she ever spoke to you after that." Rose threw her head back and howled.

Frank gave an apologetic shrug as Cassie snuck in beside him.

"What's going on?"

"I didn't hear the whole thing, but from what I gathered, Kate was picking at Rose about an incident during their weekly card game and Rose took offense. She started dredging up stories from the past and landed on one of her favorites. My parents' wedding. I heard them from across the yard and thought I should check on them."

"Is it true? About the wedding?"

"I think it's rooted in the truth, but as stories have a way of doing, it's grown over the years. This is the first I've heard of underwear flying."

Cassie did her best to muffle her giggle, but Rose must have heard because she turned and spotted Cassie. Rose seemed to forget all about teasing her sister.

"Cassie, dear. So nice to see you. Now where is that darling dog of yours? I was just telling my friends here about her. Let me show her off."

"I'm sorry, she stayed at home today. She doesn't always do well in a crowd."

"Oh, that's too bad. Everyone was looking forward to hearing us perform."

From the looks on the others' faces, Cassie guessed that was likely far from the truth, but she offered her apologies again.

"Next time you be sure to bring her with you. We could use something new to talk about." With that, she threw a nasty look at her sister. "Speaking of new, did you hear we're getting a new man in the building?"

Now Rose had Kate's interest. "Is that so? In Lola's apartment?"

"Of course, in Lola's apartment. It's the only one vacant."

One of the other women in the group piped up. "I heard that too. His name is Harold and he's been a widower for three years. Story is he used to live in town, but moved away years ago after getting married." She seemed tickled to have information the rest of them didn't.

Kate's forehead creased. "Interesting." Turning to her sister, she asked, "Rose, do you remember Harold Benson?"

"Scary Harry? Sure, I remember him. You don't think it's him, do you?"

"It could be. I don't remember too many Harolds getting married and moving away. And he wasn't really that scary once he stopped hiding behind trees and growling at the girls on their way to school."

"Kathryn, could it be you're still sweet on Scary Harry after all these years?"

"Oh hush, Rose, and mind your own business." With that, Kate turned and stomped away.

"I think it's safe, at least for the time being." Frank put a hand on Cassie's back and led her away from the group.

"I just came to say goodbye. I need to head back to the inn so Molly can join the party before it starts to rain."

Frank studied the sky. "We've got a few hours."

"Oh, now you're a weatherman, are you?"

"Trust me. At least three hours."

Cassie laughed as they walked across the yard, stopping to greet people as they meandered.

"I wish you'd stay a little longer. We've hardly had any time together."

"Don't worry about it, you've been busy, I understand. And I've had plenty of people to talk to."

"Did you have a good time? Was it too much? Did everyone ask you a hundred questions?"

"Just you." Cassie smiled at the worried look on Frank's face.

"Sorry. It's just that I know how people can be. They're always curious about the new person in town."

"I'm not really that new any longer."

"Until you've been to a McCabe Fourth of July party and everyone has had a chance to interrogate you, you're new."

"I wouldn't call it interrogating, exactly. Most people were very nice and welcoming."

Cassie realized they'd wandered to the front of the house and she hadn't said goodbye to, or thanked, Sean and Anna. She didn't feel like going back.

"Do you think you could tell your parents goodbye and thank them for me? I really did have a good time, but I need to get going, and I've learned goodbyes can take a long time around here."

"I'll tell them. You know, I was hoping to watch the fireworks with you tonight. I wish you didn't have to work."

Cassie found she wished the same thing. "I told Susan I'd cover tonight. She needs a night away from the inn."

Frank nodded, looking dejected until a glint

appeared in his eyes and he started to smile.

"How about I head out to the inn after things wrap up here. I'll bring a bottle of wine, some sparklers, and we can sit in that fancy gazebo Riley built and watch the fireworks over the lake. There are always people who shoot them off right around the lake and we should be able to see some of the show from town too."

"Oh, Frank, you don't need to do that. I've heard about the party on the garage roof. Sam told me you've all been climbing up there for years to watch the fireworks together."

"They won't miss me, and besides, I'd rather be with you." He reached for her and toyed with the ends of her hair.

Cassie's heart melted. "Okay, I'd like that."

"Yeah? Fantastic! I'll be there as soon as I can."

"What about your prediction of rain in three hours? The fireworks might be rained out."

Frank looked up at the sky again and studied the clouds.

"Nope. Fireworks are too important. The rain will come, but it will only last a couple of hours. It will be over by dark. Mark my words."

Six hours later Cassie sat in the gazebo with Frank, sipping a cool glass of Chardonnay, twirling a sparkler through the air, and marveling that Frank had nailed the forecast. The rain had come, along with the thunder and lightning, but had moved out in plenty of time for the night's fireworks that were just now beginning at several spots around the lake.

"Ooh, look at that one," Cassie said when a

particularly bright green light shot high into the night sky before opening into a cascade of twinkling sparks.

Booms echoed and the colors were reflected in the smooth, black surface of the lake. Frank fiddled with his camera.

"Do you want to brave the mosquitos and get closer to the water? We'll see more if we get away from the trees."

"Sure. And I'm guessing you want to take pictures?"

"It's what I do."

They watched the show, turning to try to see everything at once. It seemed as though every house on the lake had something to set fire to. A huge bonfire on the shore directly across from them lit up the night and laughter rolled across the water from the party.

"Is all this legal? The fireworks I saw in the store here in town were nowhere near this big."

"No, only little stuff is legal in Minnesota, but some neighboring states sell the big stuff. It makes its way here."

"And people don't get into trouble?"

"Not usually, unless they're pretty stupid. Jake likes to tell a story from a few years ago. Some guy took his pontoon out into the middle of the lake and started putting on a show big enough to rival the one in town. Someone with a little more sense than that guy called the police. Jake found the guy with gas cans right next to the fireworks. A wayward spark and he could have blown himself up. Anyway, Jake fined him, confiscated his fireworks, and tried to explain how dangerous his idea was. I guess the guy said he'd never thought about the fact that the gas could explode."

Cassie just shook her head.

"Look that way." Frank pointed and Cassie followed with her eyes. "The show in town is starting."

They watched as one explosion after another filled the sky. From the twisting, turning rockets that seemed to fly miles into the sky before whirling into a frenzy, to the slower, gentler flashes of light that shattered into millions of showering sparks, the show was breathtaking.

Cassie was so caught up in the display, she wasn't aware that she had found Frank's hand and had intertwined her fingers with his. It wasn't until she went to swat at a mosquito and her hand met with resistance that she realized she'd likely been holding his hand for several minutes. She was pleased when she realized it felt right.

"I thought you were going to take some pictures?"

"I decided it's more fun just watching. Besides, I have enough pictures of fireworks." He reached his arm around Cassie's shoulders and pulled her close.

They watched until the grand finale set the sky on fire with burst after burst of color and more booms and pops than Cassie could count. Some of the revelers on the lake were still shooting off their bottle rockets and Roman candles, but the activity was dying down.

"That was quite a show. Is it better from your garage roof?"

Frank was so slow to answer that Cassie turned to look at him.

"This was better, by far."

His voice was low and soft. Cassie could barely make out his eyes in the darkness, but she sensed them studying her. Slowly, Frank bent his head toward her. He hesitated as if expecting her to pull away, but Cassie surprised them both by closing the small distance between them.

When Frank's lips touched hers, Cassie's world lit up again, far brighter than any fireworks display could ever manage. Her head started to spin and then the memories bombarded her. She remembered how it had always felt so right to be in Frank's arms, how they'd fit together like two adjoining puzzle pieces, how he'd made her feel like she was the most special and beautiful woman in the world, how much she'd loved him…and how much she still did.

Cassie felt Frank's hand make its way up her back to find her hair at the same time she reached her hands behind his neck and pulled him even closer.

It wasn't until a firecracker exploded, sounding like it was right next to them, that Cassie pulled away. She was grateful for the darkness that, she hoped, kept Frank from seeing the confusion and turmoil she was certain was evident on her face.

As if sensing her emotions, Frank paused only a moment for a deep breath and a long, slow exhale before announcing, "Let's have some fun. Stay put, I'll be right back." With that, he dashed to the gazebo.

Cassie used that minute to try to make sense out of what she was feeling. She kissed Frank! For all the weeks and months she'd spent worrying, analyzing, and speculating, she had just gone ahead and done it with hardly a thought. And that was how it was supposed to work, she told herself. For normal people, anyway. Maybe she was finally getting to normal?

Before she could dissect things any further, Frank was back with his arms full.

"Here."

He passed Cassie a huge handful of sparklers and a lighter. He then got to work setting up a tripod and attaching his camera to face toward the lake. He adjusted dials and knobs on the camera, but before Cassie could ask any questions, he took her by the hand and led her right to the shore.

"Stand here."

Frank then took all but one of the sparklers out of her hands and set them on a large, flat rock.

"Okay. You're going to light the sparkler and then I want you to wave it in the air. Hang on just a minute."

He bounded back to his camera, adjusted a little more, looked through the viewfinder, and then told Cassie, "Light it now."

Cassie wasn't sure where it was all going, but she followed Frank's instructions. She held the flame from the lighter to the tip of the sparkler and heard it sizzle before it burst to life. Then she began waving it.

"What do you want me to do with it?"

"Just what you're doing…wave it around for a minute."

So Cassie did just that. She made circles as high as she could reach. She traced a crazy zigzag up and down in front of her. She made a series of tiny circles like a coil. She continued until the sparkler burned out.

"Now what?" she asked.

"Now come here and look."

She joined Frank at the camera and he pointed at the small display screen. She was mesmerized.

"How did you do that?"

"It's simple, really…tweak the aperture, the

shutter speed, the balance, and you get this."

"I'm not sure what all that means, but it sure makes for cool pictures."

Cassie crouched lower for a better look. The lines she had drawn with the sparkler glowed against the inky backdrop of the lake. Whatever magic Frank had worked preserved the path of the sparkler's glow. One photo showed the overlapping giant circles. On another, the screen was split in the middle with a long, tight spiral. Still another was filled with what looked like a jagged, repeating W.

"Could I try to draw a picture?"

"Sure. I wanted to show you how it worked. Now that you know, try whatever you want."

Cassie felt like a kid as she skipped the few steps back to the edge of the water and grabbed another sparkler.

"Ready?"

"Whenever you are."

Cassie dove in. She drew stars and hearts, ran along the beach twirling a sparkler in each hand, and wrote her name. It took a few tries to figure out how to write it backwards so it looked correct in the photo.

When Frank didn't use the flash, only the sparkler trail was visible. When he did use the flash, Cassie and some of the background was visible as well. She spun in circles creating a tornado effect around her. She drew a picture frame around her face and posed. She even tied a sparkler on the end of a rope and spun it crazily overhead. And she had more fun than she could remember having in a very long time.

Cassie finally convinced Frank to join her. He

used the camera's remote and the two of them joined forces to create more elaborate designs. They played for nearly thirty minutes until the pile of sparklers dwindled and then disappeared.

Out of breath from running up and down the beach, Cassie panted. "I guess it's time to call it a night. Thank you, Frank. That was a lot of fun."

"I like to see you smile."

Cassie cupped his cheek with her hand and repeated, "Thank you. I'm going to grab the things from the gazebo and head inside. Can I carry anything for you?"

"No, I've got it. I'll be right behind you."

Frank watched as Cassie headed for the inn. Once she was out of sight, he pulled a hidden sparkler from his pocket, clicked the remote, and created one last picture.

21

He paced around his living room as he relived his time in Misty Lake. The memories of his days there were never far from his mind, but it wasn't often that he allowed himself to set aside time to do nothing but relive every detail of the trip. This time he ticked off items on his fingers as he mumbled to himself.

"Dog. Good. Lucky thing I remembered about the popcorn. That yapping mutt probably would have bitten me if I hadn't stuffed its mouth full. Maybe I should have kept it. Hmmm, no. That would have made her too sad. Just need her to feel unsettled, uncomfortable, not sad. Don't want that. I don't think so, anyway. Do I?"

He paced more. "His office. Good? Don't know, didn't really learn much."

Begrudgingly, he admitted to himself that the guy took good pictures. But that still didn't give him the right to photograph her. That was only for him to do.

"Girl. Don't know about that girl. That could have been a mistake. Shouldn't have talked to her."

He slapped himself in the head repeatedly as he mumbled, "Stupid, stupid," over and over.

After a minute, he twisted his fingers together to keep his hands in place and forced himself to think of something positive.

"But I know no one saw me that night. They were too busy running back and forth to the barn. And I was so close." He was near giddy at the thought of how close he'd been to her.

"I could have gotten her into the car, could have her back here right now."

Suddenly he stopped moving, his face contorted, and he shouted, "Then why didn't you?"

He cowered. "I don't know, I don't know, it didn't seem like the right time."

The shouting resumed. "Act like a man and do what a man would do! If you want her, take her."

"I should have taken her then? That night?"

"I don't know, should you have taken her that night?" He shouted in a mocking voice. "How long are you going to wait? Too long, probably."

His voice was barely more than a whisper now. "No, no, I won't wait too long. I won't." He fell on the sofa and grabbing a pillow, buried his face in it.

It was forty minutes later when he stood to resume his pacing, but he wasn't aware any time had passed. He picked up right where he'd left off. In his mind, he could see her jogging between the inn and the barn holding a clipboard and glancing at it as she hurried. His hands began to tremble as he remembered how close she'd passed to the tree he'd been hiding behind. He'd been able to smell her perfume, the same scent she'd worn before. It had nearly driven him mad. Soon, he promised himself. Soon she'd be his.

It took some time, but he finally convinced himself he'd handled the evening visit to the inn as well as he could have. He'd seen her, he'd gotten a feel for how she was interacting with those around her, and he'd gotten a look at where she was working.

As much as he didn't want to, he forced himself to consider the man she was living with. Of course he knew it was the same man as before, the one at the hotel in Chicago, but he tried to remain clear-headed as he added up everything he had learned. There was no ring on her finger, he had checked. A good sign. She had spent the weekend at the inn and not with him. Another good sign. There had been no framed photo of her on his office desk. Also good. What kind of man wouldn't want to show her off if he had the right? He told himself again there was no indication that they were together.

But she had seemed relaxed, more so than she ever had in Chicago. That may signal a problem. But then again, maybe not. Maybe time had just dulled her memories, maybe she was just relaxing. Forgetting. A change of scenery, a change of attitude. He wondered if he'd left her with enough to think about when he'd paid his visit. He wondered if she'd found the gift he'd left for her.

He was certain nabbing the dog had been the right thing to do. She'd remember the time the dog disappeared in Chicago. That was good. He'd been able to watch her much more closely that time and she'd been distraught.

She had gone back to the dog park a half dozen times looking for the mutt.

He could still picture her face as she traipsed through the trees surrounding the park. So sad, so incredibly sad. But frightened too. Always looking over her shoulder. He'd kept the dog just the right amount of time then, he told himself. It had been much briefer in Misty Lake, less than an hour, but he felt confident it had accomplished what he'd wanted. Those feelings of helplessness would resurface.

Absently, he rubbed his head where he'd slapped at it earlier and his pacing slowed. But what about that girl? Had she told Cassie he'd been there asking for her? Even if she had, what of it? The girl wouldn't be able to give a good description. A good description might not make much difference, anyway. It had been a long time.

Then he couldn't resist any longer and he moved to his computer. He pulled up the file with the photos he'd taken while he'd been there. He hadn't looked at them in weeks because the last time he'd pored over them, the headache had come. He hadn't been able to control it and when he'd woken, hours had passed. He still hadn't been able to account for those hours.

So now he gritted his teeth and clutched the edge of the desk. He wouldn't let it happen again. He couldn't let it happen again.

There weren't many, he'd been so afraid of being seen, but those he had were magnificent. He'd gone so long without new pictures of her that these were truly a gift. He studied every one…and cherished every one. But sooner than he wanted, he forced himself to shut down the computer. No point in taking chances. Proud of himself, he moved to his old, worn recliner, sat down, and reached for the journal he kept on the side table next to his chair.

It still grated at him that he was forced to keep a journal. That ridiculous doctor told him it wasn't optional. He was supposed to write down what he did every day, how he felt, and most importantly, make notes of any times he felt like he forgot a period of time. What utter nonsense. Like he'd tell the doctor.

He scribbled a few notes about going to work, doing a load of laundry, and ordering some food. That would be enough to satisfy the doctor. Then he opened the drawer in the side table and took out the real journal.

He'd been keeping it for a few years. It was exactly the same as the journal the doctor forced him to keep, but in it he wrote what really mattered. He wrote when he saw her, when he learned new information about her, about his plans for their future. And in this journal, he did try to account for all of his time. It scared him when he lost minutes, hours, or even days, and he'd found that writing things down helped. Maybe the fool doctor was on to something.

As he paged through, there were things that made him smile, but there were also things that made him angry. Very angry. Today, though, he was going to focus on the good. He was proud that he'd rehashed his trip to Misty Lake and that he'd looked at the photos he'd taken without losing control, so he made meticulous notes about how he'd done it.

Pleased with his accomplishments, he tucked the journal back in the drawer before leaning his head back, closing his eyes, and drifting off to sleep.

22

"Are you ready?" Susan asked Cassie as she glanced at the clock.

"I'm ready. You know, I kind of missed the chaos of having them around. Even with having the inn full of guests all week, it's seemed quiet."

"That's about to change."

"I wonder what they'll have to say about their week?"

"I'm guessing Matt loved it, Tyrell tolerated it, and Kendra hated it."

"I'm guessing you're right. And judging from the way Kendra is almost running up the sidewalk, I'm guessing Tom talked to her," Cassie said as she watched through the window.

The kids filed in, Kendra in the lead.

"Is it true? Mr. Lindahl talked to me this morning and told me I could work here for you, I mean more than just in the mornings, but is it true? Is it okay with you guys? I was afraid he hadn't discussed everything with you yet. If it's okay, I promise I'll work hard. I already know a lot about what needs to be done, but I'm willing to learn more. And I'll do whatever you need done, even if it's gross. I really want to work for you, I—"

"Kendra, slow down. It's true." Cassie smiled as the girl exhaled and relaxed somewhat, but still eyed Cassie warily. "If you want, you can work here. Mrs. McCabe and I talked with Mr. Lindahl and we have some of the details worked out. We can talk more about it this morning and figure out how many hours you think you'd like to be here, what works with your schedule…all the details."

Kendra lowered her voice and glanced back as if worried Tyrell and Matt would overhear. They weren't paying any attention. Tyrell had reunited with Gusto and was already back outside racing through the yard with the dog. Matt was watching the action from the safety of the doorway.

"I want to be here as much as you'll let me. I don't like it much at camp. People are nice and everything, but it's boring. I don't want to play basketball or go swimming or do most of the other things we're supposed to do there."

Cassie had to remind herself that the girl was at camp for a reason. She needed help, no matter how sure and confident she may seem at the moment. Cassie needed to tread carefully so as not to undermine the work Project Strong Start was trying to do. Before she could continue the conversation, however, the boys came back inside with Susan.

"We'll talk later this morning. I promise," Cassie

added when Kendra gave her a doubtful scowl.

"So, how was the camping trip?" Cassie asked the group.

"It was pretty cool," Matt answered. "Did you know the Boundary Waters is over a million acres?"

"Really?" Cassie asked. She looked to Susan with raised eyebrows.

Susan shrugged. "I don't know. A million?"

"It's true." Much to Cassie's surprise, Tyrell was the one to answer. "We had to learn about it on the bus ride there. It's a protected area of over one million acres with over twelve hundred miles of canoe routes and something like two thousand campsites. It's rugged and remote and you hardly ever see anyone. Everywhere you look, it's trees and water. Nothing like I've ever seen before, that's for sure."

Cassie glanced at Susan again and found Susan staring at Tyrell with wide eyes. The kid was full of surprises.

"So you enjoyed the trip?" Susan asked Tyrell.

Tyrell leaned his hip against the sofa table and scratched his head. "It was all right. I mean, we had to walk a lot, that kinda sucked, and we had to cook our own food which was a pain in the ass, but, you know, it was all cool."

There, Cassie thought, that was more like the Tyrell she knew.

"Oh yeah, it was great if you like bugs," Kendra grumbled. "More mosquitos than I thought possible." She scratched at a welt on her arm.

"How about you, Matt, what did you think?" Susan asked.

"I had fun. It was kinda scary at night, there are wolves and bears there and just about every night we heard the wolves howling. We had to put our food in bear-proof containers and hang the containers between trees, but the bears still came around. One night we heard them right outside our tents. Our guides told us if the bears come, we should try to make noise and that would scare them away so people were getting out of the tents and banging pots together and screaming. Crazy," he said, shaking his head. "I stayed in the tent."

"I think I would have done the same thing," Susan said with a shudder.

"But during the day we went swimming and hiking and canoeing…it was so fun. We saw lots of deer and loons and eagles and stuff, and one kid said he saw a moose, but no one really believed him."

"It sounds like an incredible trip. I'm glad you guys were able to go. But I'm glad you're back. We missed you. And we have a busy week ahead."

With that, Cassie directed Kendra and Matt to the kitchen to get ready for the late breakfast crowd and sent Tyrell to the dining room to make sure everything was ready in there. Using only subtle gestures, Cassie and Susan agreed Susan would follow Tyrell to the dining room and Cassie would handle the kitchen.

Later, after breakfast was done, the kitchen and dining room cleaned up, and the boys outside doing work on the beach under Susan's watchful eye, Cassie had a chance to talk more with Kendra.

"We're looking forward to having you here, Kendra, but we need to balance it out with the obligations you have at camp. You know you're required to attend counseling sessions and you're responsible for the chores you've been assigned. Those things take priority over any extra time you spend here at the inn."

"I know, Mr. Lindahl told me the same thing, but I can make it work. I always get my camp chores done on time and the individual and group sessions we have to go to are mostly at night. That leaves plenty time to be here."

Cassie studied the girl. Kendra was focused, determined, and above all, persistent. Admirable qualities, for sure, and coupled with her stunning looks, made for a young woman with a world of potential. Cassie wondered if Kendra realized it.

The sun had done its work on the teen's long, blonde hair, drawing even more attention to the natural highlights that catapulted her tresses from ordinary to extraordinary. Her oval-shaped face with its smooth, even complexion held full lips, high, chiseled cheek bones, and wide, laser-beam blue eyes. Not for the first time, Cassie imagined Kendra in front of a camera. Her tall, athletic build would be well-suited to print ads. She debated bringing up the subject of modeling with Kendra, but decided against it. Cassie's job was to help Kendra navigate her life as it was, not make it more complicated. Instead, she tried to calm the anxiety she saw in those vivid blue eyes.

"It does leave you time to be here. We thought it might work for you to stay a couple of hours longer every afternoon. Either Mrs. McCabe or I will give you a ride back to camp instead of you going with the boys in the van."

"Just a couple of hours four days a week? I know

I could handle more. And what about weekends? Weekends at camp are usually just laid back with games and speakers and things like that. I wouldn't be missing anything, and I know I'd learn more here than I would there."

Cassie had expected Kendra to push, but she hadn't expected the desperation in the girl's voice and in her body language.

"What is it, Kendra? Is there some reason you don't want to be at Project Strong Start?"

"I told you, it's boring," Kendra answered quickly, her eyes avoiding Cassie's.

Cassie was on high alert, her imagination running wild. She did her best to stay calm.

"It seems like there's more to it. Are you afraid there? Did something happen?"

"Oh, no, nothing like that. It's just, well, I…"

Spotting the tears welling in Kendra's eyes, Cassie reached her hand across the table and covered Kendra's.

"You can talk to me. I promise I'll try to help if there's something you need, and I promise that if it's possible, I won't discuss what you tell me with anyone else."

Cassie worried she might be crossing a line, might be delving into territory where she had no business being, but she decided that at the moment, she didn't care. Kendra needed someone, and right now Cassie was that someone.

Kendra's lip trembled before she bit it and took a deep breath. She met Cassie's eyes.

"I need to learn how to do something. I need to get a job and I don't want it to be just fast food or something like that."

"Okay. That sounds like a good idea. Are you thinking about a job for after you graduate from high school?" Cassie believed the girl, but there was more. She was certain there was more.

"I'd like to start working right away, before I graduate, but I'm not sure I can. I don't have a car right now so I'd have to find some place I could get to on the bus. But I need to make some money. As soon as possible. So I figured if I knew more about how things work in a business, maybe I'd be able to earn a little more than if I didn't have any experience."

"It sounds like you've thought things through. Good for you. Are you trying to earn money for college?"

At this, Kendra looked away. "No, I don't think I could afford to go to college." She took a deep breath. "I'll be eighteen soon and when I am, I want to move out."

"Before you finish high school?"

"Yes."

Cassie knew Kendra had problems at home, but was suddenly very afraid there was more she didn't know.

"Can I ask why you want to move out?"

Kendra was quiet for what seemed like a long time. She pulled her hands to her lap and twisted her fingers. She crossed, then uncrossed, her legs. She stood, walked to the sink and filled a glass with water, then returned to the table. Cassie waited. When Kendra spoke, the confident young woman of a few minutes ago was gone, and in her place was a sad, desperate girl.

"I hate it there. I've always hated it there. I have to get away, Ms. Papadakis, I just have to."

Cassie's stomach twisted, and in the back of her

mind, something nagged at her though she couldn't put a finger on it.

"My parents don't care about me, don't care what I do. They're wasted most of the time. The only time they pay any attention to me is when they try to convince me to get wasted with them. I don't want to do that anymore. I don't want to end up like them. And I'll make it work this time, I will. I had a job once before, even had a car, but one day I came home from school and the car was gone. My dad sold it, said he needed money. That night they bought some really serious stuff, said they were splurging. I left for a few days, went and stayed with a friend, I don't think they ever noticed."

She was crying now and Cassie went to her. Cassie held on as Kendra's shoulders shook. After a few minutes, Kendra pulled away, swiped at her eyes, and looked embarrassed.

"I'm sorry, I shouldn't have done that."

"Don't apologize, you didn't do anything wrong. I told you that you could talk to me and I meant it."

"I don't usually cry. It doesn't solve anything."

So much like herself, Cassie realized again. In so many ways.

"You know, I used to think the same thing, but not long ago someone helped me realize that, sometimes, crying can help."

The hint of a smirk flitted across the girl's face. "Mr. McCabe's twin brother?"

Cassie drew back and raised her eyebrows. "Excuse me?"

Now Kendra giggled through her tears. "I've seen the way you look at him. He looks at you the same way, you know."

"Really? Do you think so?"

"I know so. And he's gorgeous, you have to know that."

"He is, isn't he?" Cassie answered before she caught herself. She stood and threw her hands up in the air. "How did we get to talking about Frank and me?"

Kendra sobered. "I'm sorry. I didn't mean to be inappropriate."

"Oh, you weren't. I guess I'm just embarrassed, that's all. I'm not so good at talking about personal things either."

Kendra nodded.

"Why don't I talk to Mr. Lindahl and see about you spending some time here on Saturdays too? We're busy and could use the help."

"Do you mean it?"

"Of course, I mean it. If you're willing to give up part of your weekend, we'd love to have you."

"I won't be giving up anything. I'll enjoy it here way more than I would at camp. Do you think I can start this weekend?"

"If I can work it out then yes, you can."

"Thank you, Ms. Papadakis. You won't regret it, you'll see. I'll work hard."

"I know you will. And, you know we'll pay you for the extra hours you spend here."

Kendra's eyes grew wide, and quick, jerky movements had her head shaking no.

"No, no way, I don't need to be paid. I didn't mean to make it seem like I expected you to pay me…I just wanted you to understand how much I wanted to be here, to be able to spend more time here, to learn more…I wasn't trying to make it seem like you needed to pay me or you should feel guilty about it or something—"

"Kendra, it's okay. Mrs. McCabe and I have already discussed it. We don't expect you to work here for nothing, we never did." Cassie held up a hand to stop further arguments from Kendra. "We'll pay you the same thing we pay Jordyn and Jennica. It's already decided," she said with finality.

"Well…I, I guess if that's what you want." Now a grin moved up Kendra's face, starting with the corners of her mouth and making its way to her eyes…eyes that seemed to shoot vivid blue sparks.

"It's what we want. I know you'll work hard and give us your best, so it's only right you're compensated for that."

"Thank you. Can I run outside and thank Mrs. McCabe?"

"Sure." Cassie glanced at the clock. "Actually, she and the boys should be wrapping up, it's almost time for Stu to be here with the van. Give her a little reminder."

"Will do."

Kendra bounded from the kitchen. Cassie watched out the window as the girl skipped across the lawn, gave a little hop, then stretched her arms up over her head before breaking into a run and executing some sort of gymnastic move that had her flipping head over heels.

Cassie noted the long, athletic frame and the way Kendra moved gracefully no matter what she was doing. Cassie pondered. She chewed at her nail and then reached for her phone.

23

Cassie wasn't sure what to expect as she headed into Misty Lake Elementary on a warm, sunny Friday evening. Shauna had convinced all four of her brothers, their wives, and Cassie to attend a yoga class. Well, not exactly a class as Shauna had been sure to point out. More of a trial run. She wanted to practice in the space she planned to use in the school gymnasium to see how things flowed. Having her brothers and Karen there meant she could focus on beginners. Having Susan and Cassie there meant she could try a few things for more advanced students. And with Sam, she could test some of what she was hoping to offer in the class catering to pregnant women.

So with her yoga mat tucked under her arm, a towel around her neck, and a water bottle in hand, Cassie gave Frank a shove toward the door. "Come on, Frank, no backing out now."

"I seriously can't believe I let her talk me into this.

Yoga? I mean, really. I have no idea how to do yoga. I'm going to make a fool out of myself."

"Well first, you won't. There's no judging in yoga. Second, don't worry, your brothers are all in the same boat. Finally, you're athletic. A little yoga shouldn't be a problem."

Cassie bit her lip to keep from laughing as Frank squared his shoulders and stood taller. But, she noted, there was still doubt in his expression.

"I guess even if it's horrible, I get to look at you in those yoga clothes for an hour. It's worth it."

Cassie wanted to tell him that after a few minutes he most likely would forget all about what she was wearing, but decided against it. He'd find out for himself soon enough.

They were the last to arrive. Jake, Riley, and Joe were standing about as far away from Shauna as they could get, huddled together and, Cassie guessed, trying to figure out how to make a break for it. Shauna was bustling around, laying out mats, and glancing at her brothers. The other women were grouped together near the front of the room. Cassie joined them.

"You're here! We almost started taking bets on whether Frank would be the one to back out," Karen said as she reached an arm around Cassie and gave her a hug. "Glad you both made it."

"Are the rest of them complaining as much as Frank? He's been griping about this for days. I actually thought he might back out, but I don't think he could do that to Shauna."

"Jake has been complaining, that's for sure. He claims he runs and lifts weights, he doesn't need to do yoga too." Sam lowered her voice. "You know, I think he's just afraid he won't be able to do it. I caught him watching a yoga video online the other day. He slammed his laptop shut when I walked in the room. He looked like a kid caught with his hand in the cookie jar." Sam giggled as she snuck a peek at Jake. "I didn't say anything, just acted like I hadn't noticed."

"Riley claimed he didn't feel well this morning." Susan rolled her eyes. "He's scared to death of yoga, scared he's going to make a fool out of himself, and most of all, scared his brothers are all going to be better at it than he is. I think the whole thing is hilarious."

"I tried to tell Frank on the way in that yoga isn't a competition or about being the best."

"With them, everything is a competition," Karen said as she draped her arm around Cassie's shoulders and the group headed for their mats.

"Okay, first, thank you for showing up today. I really appreciate all of you taking time out of your days to give this a try and to help me figure out what's going to work and what's not going to work."

Shauna stood in front of the class smiling but, Cassie thought, looking just a little nervous. She wasn't the only one. Her brothers seemed to be hardly listening. Instead, they were shifting from one foot to the other and throwing nervous glances at each other.

"Next, a few things I want you to know before we start. Since many of you are new to yoga, I want you in the right mindset before we begin. Yoga is not a competition. We're not here to see who's the best, that will never be our goal. Yoga is for you. Over time, your practice should improve, but the goal in any given session is for you to feel relaxed, free of stress, and full of energy to face the rest of your day."

"So it's not really a workout." Joe seemed confused but pleased at the same time.

"I didn't say it wasn't a workout," Shauna answered. "You'll be using muscles you didn't know you had. You'll be moving in ways you've likely never moved before. And I'll be asking you to try things that will be out of your comfort zone. And that's okay, pushing yourself a little. I like to remind people that a little uncomfortable is good, pain is not. If at any time you feel pain, stop, take a break, and above all, don't worry about what the person next to you is doing. Your practice is just that. Yours. It has nothing to do with the person next to you just as their practice has nothing to do with you."

"Why do you keep saying practice?" Riley sounded genuinely curious.

"Because that's what yoga is. For as long as you continue to practice yoga, your practice will evolve. You should find, after a time, that certain poses become less uncomfortable or you're able to get into poses you weren't able to get into before, but a yogi never reaches a point where he or she feels like everything has been mastered, that there's nothing left to learn. There's always something to learn. And I'm not just talking about yoga poses. Yoga is about so much more. The word yoga can be defined as union. A union of mind, body, and spirit. You're working to understand yourself better."

Cassie was impressed. She had come to think of Shauna as fun, full of big ideas, and more often than not, flitting from one of those ideas to the next. She'd always seemed somewhat unsettled to Cassie. Now, in the gym of the town's elementary school, she was witnessing an entirely different side of Shauna. One that was focused, calm, and in control.

Cassie peeked around the room. From the looks on the faces of Shauna's brothers, they were seeing a new side of Shauna, as well. They seemed a little in awe of their youngest sibling.

"Okay. Let's get started. The first thing I want to stress to you is breathing. Your breath is going to be the single most important component of your practice today. Every move you make should be connected to your breath. Concentrate as we move through our positions. Inhale and exhale through your nose. Don't hold your breath…that's very important. We have a tendency when we're working hard to hold our breath, so I need you to make a conscious effort not to do so. Let's get started. Cassie?"

Cassie picked up her mat from its place next to Frank's. She gave him a little shrug before she moved to the front of the room.

"I asked Cassie if she'd help me out today. You can watch her if you're unsure about a position. I'll explain what I want you to do and do the poses facing you, but I'll walk around to help you out, as well. Cassie will be your guide. Watch her. With her back to you, you'll see the way she moves and you can follow along. Let's start with Mountain Pose. Remember to pay attention to your breath."

As Shauna began explaining the proper way to align the body from the toes up, Cassie turned her back to the class, inhaled deeply, and hoped she hadn't forgotten too much.

It didn't take long until Cassie heard thuds and muffled oaths behind her. The jabs she'd heard the guys throwing at one another at the beginning of the class had ceased, and she figured they'd realized that their concentration was a very necessary part of their practice.

Shauna had the group move through some basic poses, occasionally modifying the movements for Sam in order to accommodate her growing belly.

"Inhale, feel your belly rise, exhale, feel your belly fall," Shauna intoned. She stood in front of the group. "Exhale, back to Mountain Pose. Now we'll try something called Tree Pose. Shift your weight to your left leg. Inhale, slowly turn your right knee to the wall on your right and move your foot up your inner thigh as far as is comfortable, and only to a point where you're able to maintain your balance. Exhale. Inhale, move your hands to Prayer Position. Hold this position and breathe. If you're feeling steady, you can try lifting your hands up over your head."

As Cassie demonstrated slowly stretching her arms up, she heard what could only be described as a crash. Distracted, she whipped her head around.

Jake had apparently lost his balance as he was on the floor, more on Frank's mat than his own. Cassie watched, mesmerized, as Frank's eyes grew wide, he tilted his head slightly in Jake's direction, but seemed to forget he had the ability to put his arms and foot down. Instead, he struggled to maintain his balance while his brother twisted below him. Then, as if in slow motion, Jake got to his hands and knees in an attempt to get back up, but managed to clip Frank's out-turned knee and then Frank began to fall. His arms windmilled wildly. He tried to put his right leg down, but now Jake was on his hands and knees directly below him and Frank's leg never found the ground. Instead, it landed on Jake's back. Jake collapsed, Frank on top of him, and they managed to both roll into Joe.

"Ouch!" Joe ended up on the floor, his shoulder taking the brunt of his fall.

Riley howled with laughter. Sam's hand flew to her mouth as she gasped. Karen stared as if unsure what she was witnessing. Susan started to giggle, but quickly swallowed her laugh after catching sight of Shauna's devastated expression.

"Are you all okay?" Shauna asked as she rushed to the tangle of arms and legs.

"Dammit, Frank, get your foot out of my face!" Joe pushed at Frank's foot as he tried to extricate himself from the pile.

"I can't move my foot until Jake gets his fat ass off my leg!" Frank shot back.

"Come on, get up you guys," Shauna pleaded.

Riley kept laughing until Susan elbowed him in the ribs. Susan looked at her husband and then directed her eyes to Shauna. Riley took the hint. He stomped over to his brothers and began plucking them from the floor. Once everyone was back on their feet, Shauna tried to regain order.

"No problem, things happen. Let's move on. Can we try to finish out the class?" Her soothing voice was back in place, but uncertainty was written all over her face.

Joe looked out of the corner of his narrowed eye at Jake and Frank in turn. Karen guided him back to his mat and ran a hand up and down his arm while muttering something to him. He sighed and stood on his mat, looking resolutely forward. The rest followed suit.

Cassie was impressed with the way Shauna kept her cool and got everyone back on track. They moved through a few more poses, and though Cassie didn't turn to look, she was fairly certain there were a few more bobbles and stumbles as they worked on Extended Side Angle Pose and Triangle Pose.

Shauna guided everyone down onto their mats and eased them into gentle spinal twists. "Bring your right knee into your chest. Now, take that bended knee across your body and move it toward the floor. Make sure you're breathing. Stretch your arms wide, trying to pin them to the floor. Turn your head to the right, the opposite direction of your knee. You should feel a wonderful twist in your lower back. Hold this position and breathe. Twist as far as is comfortable without putting strain on your back. Breathe."

There was a hiss and loud whispering from the back of the room. "I can't put my knee down on one side and my head and arm on the other. My body doesn't do that."

"Riley, do the best you can. Remember, it's not about doing anything perfectly, it's about doing what feels good for you. And this should feel good after everything we've done today."

"I can't…" There was a grunt and a sharp exhale from Riley. "I think I'm levitating. Red, am I levitating? I can't feel the ground under my legs or my arms. How is that possible?"

There was a muffled giggle from somewhere in the room as well as a couple of coughs, most likely covering up more laughing.

"Oh, for crying out loud, Riley, we're almost done. Just do what you can." Shauna had clearly lost some of her patience.

After a few more minutes and a few more gentle stretches, Shauna instructed everyone to lie on their backs in Corpse Pose...arms and legs relaxed and falling open, eyes closed.

"Let everything go," Shauna told them. There were audible sighs from around the room.

Shauna put a hand on Cassie's arm to stop her. They were all making their way out of the school and into the warm evening. Shauna waited until the rest were out of earshot.

"How do you think it went?"

"I think it went well. You were organized, you seemed very sure of yourself, and the class was ideal for beginners. Your modifications for Sam and your suggestions on trying more difficult poses for those comfortable were perfect."

"Then I'm a better actress than I knew. I was so nervous. Even though it was my family, I couldn't get over my jitters. I don't know if I can do this, Cassie. What's going to happen when it's strangers...or worse yet, people I've known my entire life?"

Cassie was grateful for the shade the school building cast over them. The evening was warm and she had worked up a sweat during class. How much of it was due to the workout and how much of it was due to her own nerves at being out of practice, Cassie couldn't be sure.

"You can do it. I don't doubt it for a minute. You handled yourself like a seasoned veteran in there. When half the class came crashing down on top of one another? You held it together. When Sam gave that little yelp and everyone panicked thinking she'd hurt herself, you stayed calm. And when Riley was convinced he was levitating? Well, you mostly kept your cool then too."

"Riley is such a dork. I knew he'd be the one to give me the most trouble." Shauna scowled in Riley's direction. "Do you think they all hated it? My brothers, I mean?"

"No, I really don't. I think they were surprised at how difficult it was at times, and I think they were maybe a little disappointed that they couldn't turn it into more of a contest to see which one of them was the best, but no. I don't think they hated it at all."

"Hmmm…"

"Shauna, you did a great job. I know you're going to do well. It was obvious you love yoga, believe in it, and want to help others through it. Anyone who takes your class is going to feel comfortable and leave wanting to come back for more."

Frank waved at Cassie and Shauna and called across the parking lot, "Hurry up, you two. I'm trying to make plans for the evening."

By the time Cassie and Shauna had crossed the parking lot and Shauna had dumped her gear in the trunk of her car, it was clear Frank's plan wasn't coming together as he hoped. Joe and Karen were already driving off. Karen stuck her hand out the window and gave a wave. "Thanks, Shauna, it was a great class."

"I can't, Frank, I have to get back to the inn. I

told Molly I'd be a few hours, not all night," Susan said.

"And I'm going with her," Riley said. "It's a perfect evening to sit out by the lake."

"Jake? Sam?"

"Sorry, Frank, I'm beat. It's been a long week. I think I just need to sit and put my feet up for a while."

"Are you sure you're okay? You didn't hurt yourself in class?" Jake seemed nearly distraught.

"I told you, I'm fine. It was just a little twinge, nothing to worry about."

Jake didn't seem convinced. He put his hand under Sam's arm and started to guide her to the car. Sam appeared ready to resist, but then relented as if sensing Jake needed to nurture.

"You were great, Shauna, thanks for the class," Sam said.

"Yeah, way to go, Sis. I was impressed."

"Thanks, guys," Shauna answered with a genuine smile.

"Well, Shauna, that leaves you. You're not going to wuss out on me too, are you?"

"I need to get home. I want to make some notes about the class...about what worked, what didn't work, what I want to change or add. I have to be ready when I have someone other than you guys in my class." Shauna hesitated a moment and then added, "Speaking of my class...will you come back? Would you consider signing up for a class and coming every week?"

Frank hesitated for just a moment and Shauna looked devastated. Cassie jumped in.

"I will. I can't wait to have a class in town. When do you think you'll start?"

Shauna stole a glance at Frank out of the corner of her eye before turning to Cassie. "Soon. I have an ad ready to go in the paper next week. I just hadn't given them the final go-ahead yet. I wanted to see how today went. But unless I talk myself out of it this weekend, I'll call next week and finalize the ad. The classes will start in September. I didn't think it made much sense to start when everyone is on vacation. Once school starts again people will be ready for routine."

"You already put an ad together? You didn't tell me."

Shauna gave a dramatic sigh, lifting her arms and letting them drop. "I don't tell you everything, Frank."

"I know, but…well, you'd kind of been running things by me about your yoga teaching idea. I just thought…I mean, I would have helped…"

"I know you would have, and I appreciate it. I'm thinking about doing some more advertising, maybe something a little more involved with some photos. I was hoping you'd help me with that."

Frank brightened. "Sure, be happy to."

"Okay, now I really need to get going. Have a good night, you two," Shauna said with a wink. "And thanks again for your help, Cass."

"No problem. See you later.

Shauna was climbing into her car when Frank called after her. "Hey, Shauna! I'll take your class."

Shauna gave him an enormous smile before darting out of the parking lot.

24

"I guess it's just you and me tonight," Frank said as he opened the car door for Cassie.

"I guess so."

"What do you feel like doing?"

"I don't know, want to get a pizza? You probably worked up an appetite."

"Actually, I did. That was kind of hard. I didn't expect it to be hard."

"It was just new. Everything seems hard when it's new. Give it a little time." Cassie turned to him as he put the car in reverse. She placed her hand over his. "You made Shauna happy tonight. It was sweet."

Frank lifted a shoulder in a half shrug. "I have a hard time telling her no. Those other idiots can be a little clueless sometimes. She spent so long trying to act like one of the boys, to fit in with us, but she's not a little kid any longer. I don't think they always realize that. They still think of her as the tomboy chasing us around on the baseball field or the hockey rink, doing whatever she could to show us she should be included. She's paid her dues. She's more than earned our support."

"Do you think the others will take her class?" Cassie was skeptical.

"Once I'm done with them they will."

Cassie grinned at him. "Aw, her knight in shining armor."

"If she needs one, it will be me."

Frank stopped at a red light and turned to study Cassie. His eyes seemed to bore right into her. After a minute she squirmed. "What?"

"I think tonight calls for something other than pizza. I have an idea. Let's go home, get changed, and then let me surprise you."

It was Cassie's turn to study him. "I guess I can do that."

Frank was sitting on the sofa, idly flipping through a seemingly infinite number of channels when Cassie emerged from her room and did a twirl. Frank dropped the remote. He wanted to stand but didn't think he could.

Cassie had put on some sort of strappy bright pink dress. Frank briefly wondered how she'd figured out how to put the thing on with all the straps that crisscrossed on her otherwise bare back, then he realized he didn't care. He just thanked God that someone had made the dress, that Cassie had purchased it, and that she somehow knew how all those straps worked.

The skirt stopped just above Cassie's knees and when she twirled, it swirled and billowed around her legs.

A-line skirt, Frank thought, as an afternoon he had spent with Shauna—when she had gotten into a fight with her best friend and had begged Frank to go homecoming dress shopping with her—flashed through his mind. But he promptly forgot Shauna and that never-ending day at the mall when his eyes traveled down Cassie's endless legs. At the end of those legs were sandals, equally pink and equally strappy.

She had put her hair up and her long, graceful neck and smooth shoulders begged to be touched. His fingers, and his lips, tingled.

He wanted to take her picture, wanted to make sure he never forgot exactly how she looked at that very moment. Beautiful, stunning, sexy…but, above all, happy. Happy as he hadn't seen her since their days in Chicago. Happy as he'd longed to see her again.

"So? Do I look okay? You didn't tell me where we're going. I wasn't sure how to dress."

Okay? What was the word for okay to the billionth degree, he wondered? And were they going somewhere? He couldn't remember.

"You look fantastic, amazing, perfect. There's probably another adjective, a better one, but I'm having trouble thinking right now."

Cassie just laughed at him.

"Shall we?"

"Do we have to?"

"Yes. You promised me a surprise."

"That may have been my single greatest mistake in life."

The drive was magnificent. Cassie still didn't know

where they were going, but she leaned back and soaked in the view. The air had cooled, the humidity had gone down, and the evening was about as perfect as any she could remember.

They drove along winding roads, through thick forests, lush green at the height of their summer grandeur. They passed lakes, some big, some hardly more than ponds. Boats dotted the surfaces and the sun, slowly beginning to sink to the west, sparkled on barely rippling water. They rolled down the windows, turned up the music, and enjoyed.

If the drive was magnificent, the restaurant was doubly so. Tucked away in a towering pine forest, the exterior of Secrets was all rough-hewn logs and glass. The stone path that led to the front door and then wound around to the back was lined with trees set aglow with thousands of little white lights. Flowers bloomed riotously and the air smelled heavenly.

Frank led Cassie around to the back where a deck spanned the entire length of the restaurant and offered spectacular views of the lake. More twinkle lights were strung over and around the deck. Tables were set with crisp white linens and, Cassie noticed, were scattered with enough space between them to offer the diners privacy. Waiters dressed in formal black and white made their way from table to table, lighting candles and turning the scene magical.

"Oh, Frank," Cassie breathed.
"Do you like it?"
"I love it."
"Inside or out?"
"Outside, don't you think? It's a beautiful

evening."

"Yes, yes it is."

They were seated at a quiet table along the edge of the deck. Frank ordered a bottle of wine and raised his glass.

"To tonight, to whoever designed that dress, but mostly to you, looking happy."

Cassie blushed and clinked her glass to Frank's.

They sipped their wine, placed their orders, and let their conversation flow from one comfortable topic to the next.

"I'm glad the rest of them decided they were busy tonight," Frank said. "This wouldn't be nearly as much fun with Riley sitting next to me."

Cassie laughed. "I guess I have to agree." Then she grew serious. "Don't say anything to anyone, but I'm pretty sure Karen is pregnant and that's why they backed out."

"What? How? I mean, not how, but…really?"

"I caught her a couple of times during class looking a little queasy, a little off balance. She didn't have much to say after class, seemed in a hurry to leave, and Joe didn't argue. I can't claim to have personal experience, but I've worked with enough women to recognize the signs."

"Wow. Another kid. Huh. I'm going to have nieces and nephews all over the place before long." Frank leaned back in his chair, a mixture of amazement and pride on his face.

"Don't say anything, though. If I know one thing, it's that a woman doesn't want people to know until she's ready for them to know. They'll make an announcement when the time is right."

Frank nodded. "I hope it's a girl this time," he said with certainty. "I need to see Joe with a daughter. He'll never be able to handle it."

"He'll figure it out. I think dads just figure it out." She heard the sadness creep into her voice and knew the moment Frank heard it, too.

"Cassie?"

"Sorry, didn't mean to put a damper on things." She was quiet for a moment, lost in her thoughts. "Sometimes I can't help but wonder...wonder what it would have been like."

"If you'd known your dad?"

"If I'd known him, if he'd been there when I was growing up, if he'd been there for my mom..."

"What was it like for you? Growing up, I mean. You've never told me much other than it was just you and your mom."

His voice was so gentle, his eyes so tender and caring, Cassie couldn't refuse him.

"It was good sometimes, not so good other times. My mom always struggled. She never got over losing my dad. She tried hard to make a good life for me, but she didn't know how. She was lost without him."

"Did she ever consider going home? Back to Greece? Did she say?"

"I asked her about it once, about why she didn't. She said there was no life for her there. Her family had turned their backs on her when she married my dad, she said, and she couldn't—wouldn't—go back to them. There were times when I wished she would have. I used to think it would have made things better. But it all worked out."

"You told me once you lived with an uncle."

Had she? That surprised Cassie, she rarely mentioned Dimitris.

"He wasn't actually my uncle, it was just easier to call him that. He was some distant cousin of my dad's who had moved to America, opened a restaurant, and offered my dad a job when my parents wanted to leave Greece. My parents moved in with him, it was going to be only temporary until they could get settled, but then my dad was killed by a hit-and-run driver one day on the way home from work, my mom stayed, I was born, and she never left."

It sounded simple, but it hadn't been.

"And you stayed with him after your mother died?"

"Yes. My mother had made him my guardian. I was only sixteen at the time. So I stayed. For a while."

"And that worked out?"

Worked out? Cassie wanted to laugh. Or maybe cry. "We never got along particularly well. After my mother died, it was worse. He disappeared after her funeral. For a week, I had no idea where he was or if he was coming back." Cassie remembered how terrified she'd been. Not because he was gone, that had been more of a relief than anything, but terrified of what would happen when—because it would be when, not if—someone found out she was alone.

"But he came back?"

"Yes, he came back. Without a word as to where he'd been. Since I didn't know what was happening, I had already gotten a job. A small hotel I passed every day on my way to school was hiring maids. I got the job, and about six months later, after I'd been promoted to the front desk, a guy came in, said he was a talent scout, and gave me his card. Told me to call him if I wanted to give modeling a try. I was lucky, he turned out to be a good guy. It easily could have gone another way. I was naïve and didn't know any better, just showed up at his office one day. But he was a really good guy, took me under his wing, showed me the ropes, helped me build a career."

She hoped Frank had heard enough, that he'd let it drop, but deep down she knew he was as desperate to know more about her as she was to keep things hidden.

"Did things get better between you and Dimitris?"

Cassie sighed. "No, he just tolerated me. Mostly ignored me."

"And then you left when you started college?"

The question she'd been dreading. Cassie could tell by Frank's voice he was afraid he was pushing too hard, afraid of hurting her or upsetting her. It would be easy to tell him she'd had enough. Easy, but not fair.

"I left before that. One night I had a nightmare. A terrible nightmare. It was about my mother, something about her, but I can't remember any details. I just remember waking up scared nearly to death and thinking I had to get out of my room. For some reason, I needed to get out of my room. Almost like in order to escape the dream, or maybe in order to help my mother, I needed to escape my room. Kind of like the dream you told me about with the factory and the alphabet? Scary, more than scary, but you don't really know why."

Frank nodded and Cassie continued.

"I ran to the bathroom and locked myself in. The next thing I knew, Dimitris was pounding on the door and demanding that I come out. He was angry, so angry, and was calling me all kinds of names, talking about the past, nothing much made any sense. I guess I must have woken him when I screamed and slammed the bathroom door. I don't know. I remember I still hadn't really sorted out the dream, so I didn't know if I'd said something in my sleep, something he'd heard that made him mad? He made threats, it got ugly. Finally, when I wouldn't open the door, he slammed out of the house and I heard him drive away. I didn't waste any time. I braced myself, grabbed a few things from my room, threw them in my car, and left."

Frank stared. "You just left? Where did you go?"

"I had a few friends, they worked for the same modeling agency. They shared an apartment not far away. I knocked on their door in the middle of the night, they took me in, no questions asked." And that had been a blessing, Cassie thought. She hadn't been prepared to give any answers.

Cassie could almost see Frank's mind working. "Was that the dream you had at the inn? The one that scared you so badly?"

The dream had been frequent for a while then had become less so until… "Yes," she said. She remembered that night at the inn, remembered again that feeling that she needed to get out of the room, but still didn't know why.

"So then the dream you had at the inn, it didn't have anything to do with that man, with that day in your apartment…"

It had gotten more frequent after that day, she'd even had the dream once in the hospital, but the therapist there had told her nightmares were common after a traumatic experience. The therapist had told her it was likely the dreams were related to losing her mother, those feelings of helplessness, then a similar feeling of helplessness when she was attacked in her apartment brought the dreams to the surface again.

"No, the nightmare didn't have anything to do with that."

Frank seemed relieved. It's what Cassie had wanted.

"Let's dance," Frank said.

"Dance? No one is dancing."

"That doesn't mean we can't."

Frank took Cassie's hand and led her down to the lake and out onto the dock. Then he took her in his arms and began to hum.

The stars had come out and their brilliant twinkling overhead reflected on the lake. It reminded Cassie of the Fourth of July. She melted against Frank and closed her eyes.

They swayed to Frank's humming. Cassie felt Frank's hand on the small of her back, firm, solid, and sure. She knew he wanted to be all those things for her and she wanted to let him. Yet, something niggled at her mind. She couldn't put a finger on it and it drove her crazy. It was the same feeling that had been popping up, unwelcomed, for the past few weeks. How long? She tried to calculate. Six weeks or so, she guessed. What had happened six weeks ago to trigger it? She tried to concentrate, but Frank leaned closer. His lips brushed her cheek and his fingers played lightly over her bare shoulder. He pressed his lips to her forehead and then to her lips.

The feeling was becoming familiar, almost as it had been years ago, and she knew she was lucky. Lucky to have Frank in her life, lucky that he had given her—given them—another chance, and lucky that he was the most patient man she had ever known.

Frank took the kiss deeper and his arms held her closer. Cassie met him move for move. Neither noticed the looks from those still seated on the deck. The looks that said, 'I remember when that was us,' or 'Why can't that be us?' Because at that moment, nothing else, no one else, mattered.

"Cassie, I don't know if I'll ever be able to tell you how happy you've made me. For so long I dreamed of this, but eventually I convinced myself it would never happen. Then I saw you again and I started to dream again. I love you, Cassie, I've always loved you."

"Mmmm," Cassie murmured into his shoulder. But before she could form a thought, before she could answer him the way she wanted to answer him, Frank spoke again.

"Don't leave me. You can't leave me again."

Everything changed in an instant. Cassie tensed. She felt herself go almost rigid, but didn't know why. She felt herself start to fall, felt Frank catch her, and then stopped feeling anything at all. She struggled for balance and when she had her footing, she started to run.

25

The tears, and the humiliation, seemed to have no limit. Cassie barely recognized herself. But Dr. Willard sat across the desk, calm and unwavering in the face of Cassie's breakdown. It helped. Kind of. Just as knowing she had an appointment scheduled with him for that afternoon had helped her get through the weekend. Kind of.

"I don't know what happened," Cassie said between sobs. "The night was perfect. I felt happier than I'd felt in years. Ever, maybe. Frank was sweet, we had dinner, we danced…and then I, I just don't know. I don't know what happened. I hardly remember getting home."

"What happened when you got home?"

Cassie dropped her head into her hands. It had been awful, and she had to order herself to rehash the details for Dr. Willard.

"Frank was so worried, he wanted to take me to the hospital. He was desperate to help in some way. I refused. I didn't know what was going on, but I knew it wasn't something a hospital was going to fix. We went home, I just wanted to go to bed. To hide, really. Frank tried to talk, but I couldn't. Partly I was too embarrassed, but partly I didn't know what to say."

"Were you able to sleep?"

"No. I didn't sleep much all weekend."

Cassie felt as though she'd been run over by a truck. And she knew she looked worse. In an effort to hide the dark circles and mask the sickly complexion, she had employed every make-up trick she'd ever learned. The result was, in her opinion, barely passable.

"What about nightmares? Did they come back?"

"Yes. It seemed like every time I closed my eyes they would start. I don't think Frank slept much more than I did. I woke up screaming or crying every time." Cassie rested her elbow on the arm of the chair and leaned her forehead into her hand to cover her eyes. "I think I have to move out of his house. I can't keep putting him through this." Her shoulders shook as the sobs started again.

"I would advise you not to make that decision quite yet. Let's talk this through, look at other options, and see how you feel when we're done today."

Cassie gave a half-hearted nod as she swiped at her eyes with the handful of tissues she grabbed from the box Dr. Willard had at the ready.

"Try to think back to what you were doing right before you started to feel that loss of control. Did you hear something? See something? Feel something?"

Cassie tried again to remember. She'd been trying to remember for three days. "I don't know. We were dancing and Frank told me he loved me. I wanted to answer him, I wanted to tell him how much I love him, but I couldn't."

"Do you think his words frightened you? Maybe hearing them had you thinking about the future and you felt overwhelmed or pressured?"

Cassie was frustrated. "That's not it. His words made me feel good, not frightened. I was surprised by what he said, but then at the same time, not surprised at all. It just seemed right. And I wanted to answer him. Does that even make sense?"

"Yes, it makes sense." He nodded reassuringly. "Okay, so you weren't feeling frightened or pressured by what Frank said. Do you recall hearing anything else? Was there music in the background? Did you see someone you recognized or who looked familiar? Sometimes a very small, seemingly insignificant event can trigger incredibly strong emotions."

Cassie searched her mind. The events of the evening were so clear to her from the yoga class to the drive to arriving at the restaurant, then enjoying dinner, wine, and dancing. And then it got fuzzy. Maybe there had been something and she couldn't remember. It was beyond maddening.

"I'm sorry, I can't remember anything like that."

"Don't be sorry, Cassie. It's certainly possible there's nothing for you to remember."

Dr. Willard slipped on his glasses and glanced at his notes. Cassie tensed. After a minute, he removed his glasses and spoke gently.

"At our last session we discussed trying some techniques to look a little deeper into the events in your past. Did you give that any more thought?"

Cassie took a deep breath. "I did. I think I had myself convinced to give it a try before this, but now I'm sure. I want to do it. I want to figure out what's wrong with me." Slow tears continued to trickle from her eyes.

"It's important you believe me when I tell you that there's nothing wrong with you. You've made a tremendous amount of progress already. You need to be a little easier on yourself and not look at this past weekend as a setback. There isn't a person around who doesn't have moments when they feel out of control or overwhelmed."

"Not like this."

"Not everyone is the same."

Cassie wasn't convinced, but she didn't argue.

"As I explained before, we may find something, we may not. You'll know what's happening the entire time. If you're uncomfortable at any time, we'll stop."

"Okay."

"Then let's get started."

Cassie left on shaky legs. The remainder of the session had been tension-filled for her, but she'd gone along with Dr. Willard's requests. She knew she'd been completely lucid during his gentle questioning, but already when she thought back on it, things seemed a little fuzzy, as if she'd merely observed someone else and it hadn't been her answering his questions and reacting to his prompts.

They hadn't uncovered anything earth-shattering, but Dr. Willard told her to expect that. He wasn't going to go too deep the first time, he'd just give her an idea of what to expect so she could decide whether she wanted to try again at the next session.

That didn't stop the shaky legs, though. The idea that there was something buried somewhere in her mind was more than unsettling. It was downright terrifying.

They'd also discussed Cassie's fear of trusting those close to her...trusting them enough to confide in them. Dr. Willard had asked specifically about Susan and why Cassie had never talked with Susan about her past. Cassie hadn't been able to give a good answer. She'd tried to explain that she'd never had close friends, that even as a child she'd pulled away when people got too close. Back then it had been her reluctance to bring anyone to her house and to have them meet what passed for her family. The best she could come up with was that it had gotten to be a habit, a way of life for her.

As Cassie drove, she let her mind wander to what it had really been like growing up with her mother and Dimitris and, for the first time in a very long time, let herself dream of what it may have been like had her father not died. When talking with Frank, Cassie had skipped over most of the details about how miserable things had been at times. That didn't mean she'd forgotten.

Cassie had still been young when she realized how unhappy her mother was and tried to convince her the two of them should move away and start over. Her mother had refused, claiming she didn't have any skills other than working in a restaurant, and she'd never be able to support the two of them without Dimitris' help. And Dimitris had done nothing to build the woman's confidence. Cassie could still hear him, in his patronizing voice, telling her mother, 'Oh, Maria, you need to watch your pronunciation. No one will understand you at the market and you'll come home with pecans and honeys instead of bacon and mayonnaise for my BLT.'

Cassie couldn't stop the scowl when she remembered how her mother had always insisted Cassie be respectful and polite to Dimitris. Cassie had tried, but he'd never shown her the same courtesy. It hadn't taken long to learn he barely tolerated her. When the two of them were alone, Dimitris had insulted, criticized, and belittled. Cassie had tried talking to her mother, but she'd been told that Dimitris wasn't hurting her and that she needed to be extra nice to him. He may not have hurt her physically, but the emotional hurt had been crippling. Her mother had never understood. She had insisted Dimitris cared for Cassie and that he was someone Cassie could trust. Cassie hadn't believed any of it, but hadn't argued with her mother.

So, she justified, it made sense she'd never trusted anyone or made any friendships close enough to warrant inviting a friend over to her house. It wasn't a happy place to be.

She smiled a little as she thought back to her friend Kelly. For a while, Cassie had let Kelly get close…well, closer than she'd ever let someone before. Cassie and Kelly, Kelly and Cassie. They'd been a team. Once, when her mother had been in a particularly fun mood, she had decided they needed to go to the lake for the day. Her mother had always loved the water. In the summer, when it was hot, it had reminded her of being a girl in Greece. And in the fall, when the leaves changed, she'd loved to be by the water and take in the colors, so different than in Greece. That day, Cassie worked up the nerve to ask if Kelly could come along. Her mother had happily agreed, and the three of them spent a delightful day frolicking on the beach and eating ice cream.

Everything changed when they got home. Dimitris had flown into a rage, saying there hadn't been a note, he hadn't known where they were, and he'd been worried sick. And there hadn't been any dinner waiting for him. Cassie's mother had apologized and immediately made him dinner. Cassie had first been frightened, then angry, and then ashamed of her mother.

From that day, Cassie started to pull away from Kelly. She knew she could never invite Kelly over to her house. She didn't want anyone to meet her family, nor did she want to answer any questions about them. To a ten-year-old, the answer had seemed clear…no close friends.

But she wasn't that little girl anymore. Why couldn't she trust now? Susan had been nothing but honest, open, and caring from the time they'd met. Yet Cassie had never confided in her. She knew it hurt Susan. Dr. Willard had suggested she make an effort to talk with Susan during the coming week. Cassie wasn't sure she could do it.

And then there was Frank. She'd been trying, but she was still holding back. He deserved so much more.

An overwhelming feeling of sadness engulfed Cassie. It didn't matter what Dr. Willard said. In her heart, she knew there was something very wrong with her.

26

Cassie's mind was still on her session with Dr. Willard as she eased down the gravel road toward the inn. She was met with chaos.

A car was stopped in the middle of the road, still running and the door standing open. A man she assumed was the driver was crouched near the side of the road and appeared to be examining something.

Movement in the yard forced her attention away from the stranger and his car. Tyrell was running. That in itself was enough to put Cassie on high alert, but he was also yelling and waving his arms. Matt was in the yard too, standing frozen in place and clutching Gusto's collar. Since Matt usually gave the boisterous lab a wide berth, Cassie's heart began to thud.

She jumped from her car to hear Tyrell shout, "Don't touch her!"

Don't touch who? Kendra? Where was Kendra?

Cassie began running, too.

It took only a fraction of a second for Cassie to realize Tyrell was headed for the man alongside the road. It didn't take much longer for her to see why, but it did take longer for it to register.

For a moment, Cassie was paralyzed. Trixie was lying motionless in front of the man who seemed at a loss as far as what to do. Tyrell beat Cassie to the dog and as she watched, he pushed the man aside and leaned over Trixie.

"What happened? Did you hit her?"

It came out sounding much harsher and accusing than Cassie intended, and the man balked.

"I'm so sorry, I didn't see her. I wasn't going fast, I swear. All of a sudden she was just there. I tried to stop, but…" He lifted his hands helplessly.

Cassie barely heard him. She crouched down next to Tyrell and reached for her dog.

"Don't," Tyrell said as he grabbed Cassie's arm and stopped her. "She's hurt bad. Her instincts are going to tell her to try to protect herself. She'll bite if she feels threatened."

"But I—"

"It doesn't matter that she knows you. She's scared. We need a blanket or a big towel or something."

Trixie was panting, her eyes wild, but other than her front paws twitching a little, she wasn't moving. Cassie felt completely helpless.

The man started for his car. "I have a blanket."

He was back in a moment and while Cassie murmured reassurances to Trixie, Tyrell covered the dog with the blanket, eased it underneath her, and wrapped her in it. The dog's eyes darted, following Tyrell's movements, but not fighting them. Very gently, Tyrell slid his hands under the blanket and stood, cradling the dog in his arms.

"She needs to get to the vet."

"What happened?"

Cassie hadn't noticed Susan come up alongside her.

"She was hit by a car. I don't know what's wrong, but I think she's hurt pretty badly. I need to take her—"

"Go, go!" Susan answered.

"Um, I'm not sure how I'll drive and hold her…" Cassie jerked her head from side to side as if the answer would be there somewhere.

"I'll take you, it's the least I can do," the driver of the car offered.

Cassie had forgotten he was there. "I just need to go," she said, nearing panic. She reached for Trixie and the dog began to whine. Cassie stroked her head. "I need to go now."

"I can ride with you and hold her, Ms. P," Tyrell said with a hostile glance at the car's driver.

"I don't think we can do that, you need to stay here…" Cassie looked to Susan who shrugged quickly before pulling her phone from her pocket.

"Tom," Susan began as she stepped away from the group.

Cassie led Tyrell to her car and as he was climbing in the back seat, Susan jogged up next to them.

"It's okay with Tom if Tyrell rides with you. Go, I'll take care of the details with Tom and with everything here. Go." Susan pushed Cassie toward the car.

The man seemed desperate to make things better.

"I can follow you, cover the vet expenses. I'm so sorry."

Susan spoke up. "Why don't you come inside with me? Get things figured out?"

With a quick nod of gratitude, Cassie jumped back in the car. She could hear Tyrell from the backseat.

"It's going to be okay, you're going to be just fine, Miss Trixie." He repeated the words over and over.

Five long hours later, Cassie slumped into a chair, leaned her head back, and closed her eyes.

"Dr. Fischer's sure she's going to be okay?" Susan asked.

Cassie didn't lift her head. "That's what he said. All fifty times I asked him. She's got a broken pelvis, but thankfully no other internal injuries. I don't understand how a broken pelvis heals without surgery, but he said surgery is uncommon in these cases, it heals better on its own. She'll just need to stay quiet for a few weeks."

"And how are you?"

Cassie struggled to sit up. She sighed. "I'm fine. What a day though."

"I know. I'm sorry. No problems getting Tyrell back to camp?"

Cassie shook her head. "He waited with me while Dr. Fischer was examining Trixie, then I drove him back while Trixie was sleeping off the sedative. He was incredible today. You know, he knew more about how to care for Trixie than I did. A lot more. Dr. Fischer said he did all the right things."

"He is full of surprises, isn't he?"

Cassie's brow creased and she leaned forward in her chair. "We talked while we were waiting. He told me he volunteered for a time at an animal shelter. I must have looked surprised because his words to me were, 'You know, Ms. P, I haven't always been a screw-up.' Broke my heart a little when he said that. The kid knows so much about animals and is truly passionate about them. Much more so than he is about things around here."

"When I called Tom Lindahl back to explain more about what was going on and what you had told me about getting Tyrell back to camp, Tom told me something. Apparently Dr. Fischer wanted to be a volunteer for the camp, to have kids work with him over the summer, but Project Strong Start had to turn him down because of the easy access to drugs in his office. It's one of the hard and fast rules. Too bad. It sounds like it would have been the perfect place for Tyrell."

"Definitely. We had a lot of time to talk in the waiting room. I asked Tyrell what he's thinking about for the future. He started to slip back into his usual 'who cares' kind of attitude, but I specifically asked him about a career working with animals. He hinted around that with his past, he didn't think he'd ever qualify for something like that."

"A juvenile record shouldn't affect things, should it? If he finishes school and stays out of trouble, he should be okay. Don't you think?"

"I think so. I don't know everything in his past, but I don't recall anything extremely serious. A few shoplifting citations, disorderly conduct, but I think that was about it. Seems like with him it's mostly been an issue of just not caring, not bothering to put in much effort. If it was something he finally cared about that could be altogether different."

"Did you have a chance to talk to Tom when you drove Tyrell back to camp?"

"I didn't. I dropped off Tyrell and got back to Dr. Fischer's office."

"You should give Tom a call, let him know how Tyrell handled things today. Maybe Tom can do something for him."

Cassie nodded. "I will." Then she leaned her head back again and closed her eyes.

"The driver of the car insisted I give you this." Susan handed Cassie a business card. "He wrote his cell number on the back and made me swear I'd have you call him to let him know what he can do. He really was a good guy, and he felt awful about what happened."

Cassie opened an eye as she took the card. "I almost forgot about him. I'll call him tomorrow, but it was an accident. Chasing cars seems to be my goofy dog's favorite pastime. It's just as much my fault for not insisting she be tied up all the time. I guess I've just gotten complacent here with so little traffic." Cassie's voice hitched and she folded her arm across her eyes.

"It's no one's fault. Accidents happen."

"I suppose."

"Do you know what he was doing here?"

"Who? The guy in the car? Was he lost?"

"No, he was looking for the inn because he saw the article in Country Chic and wanted to check out the real thing."

Cassie rolled her head along the back of the chair to face Susan. She smiled for the first time in days.

"Really?"

"Yes, really. That makes twenty-seven…that we

know of. He didn't make a reservation, said he needs to check dates with his wife, but he was still here because of the article."

Cassie grabbed the armrest and pulled herself up. "I knew the article would create interest, but twenty-seven reservations in just a couple months? That's crazy."

"Crazy good. We need to make up the brochures we've been talking about. Having something guests can take home with them, something that tells the history of the inn, will be good advertising."

"I started on it. I've been meaning to show my ideas to Frank to see what he suggests for photos, but I haven't gotten to it. Sorry, I'll try…I'll do it soon…"

Susan was studying her, and Cassie knew the look. Questions were coming. Wanting to avoid them, she rubbed at her eyes, sat up straighter, and changed the subject.

"How did things go here today? I'm sorry I left you alone all day."

Susan waved aside Cassie's concern. "It was no problem. Matt went back in the van, Kendra stayed and helped out, Jordyn and Jennica were here, everything was fine. Our guests have all been self-sufficient, out and about doing things on their own, so it's been an easy afternoon and evening."

"I'm glad to hear that, but I'll make it up to you. Let me know when you want to get out of here for a while and I'll handle things."

Susan grinned. "Sure, I'll do that. If you tell me what's wrong."

"It's been a long day. I'm worried about my dog."

"It's more than that. Something else happened."

"No, nothing, everything is fine. It was just hard today, seeing Trixie like that." Then Cassie caught herself. She was doing it again, shutting out one of the few people she could turn to who really cared.

"Okay."

Cassie heard the hurt in Susan's voice and hated being responsible for it. Summoning every ounce of courage she could find, she turned to Susan and looked her in the eyes.

"Actually, if you have some time, there is something. I wonder if we could talk?"

"Really? I mean, of course I have time. As much time as you need."

So they talked. And talked. Cassie told Susan about growing up, about losing her mother, about meeting Frank in Chicago, about the man waiting for her in her apartment after Frank left, about running away to New York, about finding the nerve to come back to Chicago, about the shock at learning Frank was Riley's twin brother, and about the struggles since Frank had been back in town.

Susan listened. And for that, Cassie was grateful. Susan asked questions at times, shared in Cassie's pain, and expressed horror and shock at some of the things she heard, but for the most part, she just listened. Cassie was nearly as grateful when Susan ordered pizza and opened a bottle of wine. Cassie felt herself start to relax. When Dr. Fischer called to reassure Cassie that Trixie was doing well and should be able to go home the next day, Cassie relaxed even more.

"Cassie, I feel just awful that you've been dealing with all of this by yourself. Please don't let that happen again. You know I'm here whenever you need me."

"I know that. And I knew it before. I just wasn't ready to talk, I guess. Or I didn't know how to start."

"What made you change your mind."

"That's one more thing I haven't been completely honest about. I've been seeing someone…" At Susan's shocked expression, Cassie rushed to explain. "Someone as in a therapist. I've been talking to a doctor, an out of town doctor, for a while now. Instead of the yoga classes I told you I was taking."

"Oh." Slowly, Susan nodded and she looked at Cassie as though things were falling into place. "Okay, that's good. That's really good."

"It has been good. Mostly, anyway. It's hard sometimes talking about things, but it's getting easier."

"And you're feeling better about those things? The doctor is helping you?"

"He is. There are times when it's hard to be patient. Even though going in I knew it didn't work that way, I guess a part of me was hoping I'd go meet with him and be magically cured." Cassie shrugged. "It takes a little more time than that. I'm trying to be patient."

"Everything worthwhile takes time. Everything. This inn took time, figuring out Riley took time, friendships take time." Gusto chose that moment to snore and roll over on his back, legs up in the air. Susan nudged him with her foot. "And this one takes a lot of time. You're making the effort. That's ninety percent of the battle right there."

"Maybe you should consider a second career in your spare time."

"Yeah, my spare time. What's that?" Then Susan

grew serious. "Does Frank know you're seeing a therapist? I won't say anything, of course, but I'm curious about what you've told him, and if he talks to me, what you want me to tell him."

Cassie dropped her eyes. "He doesn't know. I've started to tell him a couple of times, but I've never quite gotten all the way there. Do you think that's horrible of me?"

"Absolutely not. Since I'm practically a therapist, I can tell you that you need to do things in your own time, when it feels right to you, not when someone else thinks it's the right time."

"Such wise words."

Susan laughed and sipped at her wine. "Can I ask what made you go to a therapist? If that's too personal, I get it, but I'm curious. Why now?"

"That's hard to answer. I guess I always thought I was fine, that I had come to terms with everything that happened. Mostly, that I didn't need anyone. Then I came to Misty Lake, I saw Frank again, you and I spend so much time together talking, Frank's family is great, but full of questions. So many things. It seemed like the life I'd been living, just the dog and me, wasn't going to work here. But I didn't know how to change. I didn't like thinking about the past, I still don't, but I finally decided in order to move beyond all the bad stuff and get on with the good stuff, I had to deal with it. Frank tried so many times to get me to talk. I did, a little, but I kept so much from him and avoided so many topics. I realized that was never going to change until I learned how to stop blocking things out. And blocking people out."

"And why me? Why tonight?"

"Because I know I've hurt you and I hate that. And because I need some advice."

"Don't worry about hurting me, I can take it. I grew up with a bunch of brothers so I have thick skin. But now you have me curious. Advice about what?"

"Frank."

"Oooh, I was hoping that's what it was."

Cassie eyed Susan over the top of her wine glass. She took a gulp followed by a deep breath.

"I don't know how to be in a relationship. I'm afraid I'm going to lose him because I'm such a mess. Last weekend, after Shauna's yoga class, we went out to dinner. He took me to this incredible place on the lake, a different lake, where we ate outside on the deck overlooking the water."

"Secrets?" Susan interrupted with a sigh.

"Yes. You've been there?"

"Riley took me once. It's magical, isn't it? I remember that night…" Susan quieted as she looked out the darkened windows.

"That good?"

"What?" Susan looked embarrassed. "Oh, geez, I'm sorry. You were saying?"

Cassie laughed before continuing. "I was saying, we were having the best night. We even danced on the dock and everything was about as perfect as it could be until I freaked out."

"What do you mean, you freaked out?"

"Just that. Frank told me he loved me and I freaked out."

"Because you don't feel that way yet?"

Cassie shook her head and in barely more than a

whisper, said, "I've loved him since the day I met him."

Susan looked shocked. "You have? But then…why? Why aren't you together? And why did you freak out?"

"That's just it. I don't know. My therapist said it's possible I panicked at hearing the words, that I felt like I was being pressured, but I don't think that's it. I don't remember feeling that way. Just the opposite. I remember wanting to tell him that I loved him too. But then things get fuzzy and I don't really remember what happened."

"You mean you can't remember anything? Or you don't remember everything you said?"

"I don't remember much of anything, about getting home or about the rest of the night, except that Frank tried to talk to me and I wouldn't—or couldn't—talk to him. I keep hurting him, and I'm afraid he's not going to stick around for much more."

"If he loves you, he'll stick around."

"But should he? It's not fair to him. No one should have to put up with the kind of stuff I'm making him put up with."

"You're worth it, Cass, you have to believe that. And you're working to try to figure things out. I think you should talk to him, even if it's hard at first. Frank is a good listener. Tell him what's going on, what you're feeling, and maybe even tell him you've been seeing a therapist. Knowing you're working at it will be all he needs to hear. Unless you're ready to tell him you love him," Susan added with a wide grin. "If I know Frank, that will be all he *ever* needs to hear."

27

It was time to check up on her again. Since his visit, he'd been driven. Obsessed. He wanted to know every move she made. It was impossible, of course, given the distance, but that didn't stop him from trying. He scoured the internet reading the local newspaper, checking websites, and now that he had more names, scrolling through various social media sites, searching for anything he could find about her or those he knew she was surrounding herself with.

As he flipped through the Misty Lake Herald, an ad caught his eye. It was just a small thing in the corner of the page, but there was no missing the name. McCabe. A yoga class starting in town and being taught by Shauna McCabe. He'd have to keep an eye on that. She used to take yoga classes.

He did some more searches, but didn't find more information on the yoga class or anything else of any interest. He went to the website for The Inn at Misty Lake. It drove him crazy to look at the photos, but he ordered himself to do so. She may have tried to keep her back to the camera, but he'd known after one glance that it was her.

He started breathing faster and ordered himself to calm down. He couldn't risk another episode. Not now. Just when he felt his pulse slowing, he discovered a new tab on the website's home page. 'Get Cozy with Us.' A fall/winter promotion page, it appeared.

Curious, he clicked. And there she was. This photo was even more provocative than the others. The hint of her profile was visible as she tilted her head back and looked up as if greeting someone. A wine glass hung almost carelessly in her hand as if whatever had caught her attention was far more important than something as trivial as a glass of wine.

The scene was hazy, taken in low light. He examined everything…what she was wearing, how her hair curled, the curve of her fingers on the stem of the wineglass. He studied the furniture, the rug, the fire blazing in the oversized fireplace, and the artwork on the walls. It wasn't until he turned his attention to a book lying on the floor next to her chair that he noticed it.

A name. Right there, as if teasing him. Andrew Coughlin. Had it been on all the photos and he'd missed it? Furiously he clicked through one after the other without spotting the name. He was relieved he hadn't overlooked something in plain sight, but the photo itself enraged him. It was too personal, too intimate.

He ran a search on Andrew Coughlin and in moments was looking at a website. It wasn't much, probably a new photographer or at least new to using a website to promote his business. There were photos he recognized as having been taken in and around Misty Lake. A particularly stunning photo of the park on a summer's evening caught his attention, but he couldn't let himself get distracted.

Then he saw it.

It was her. With him. Another photo taken in the parlor at the inn, but this time it was different. There was no mistaking the feelings they had for one another.

He was dizzy. He closed his eyes and slapped his hands against his head in an attempt to stay focused.

Of course he knew they had been together. Before. And of course he knew she was living with him. But it had seemed platonic. From everything he'd seen and heard and read, he hadn't picked up on any hint of their previous relationship. He'd let himself believe that. Now he wondered if he'd just wanted to believe it.

He got up and paced. He had to go back. Clearly he couldn't leave her there alone any longer. But he'd have to leave without telling anyone. He had already used the excuse of visiting his sick friend, so wouldn't be able to use that one again. But if he simply left, and they found out, it would be a problem. He glanced at his calendar and counted the days. He needed to check in the next morning. If he left right after his meeting, he would have a couple of days until his absence aroused any suspicion.

He sat lost in his thoughts. How quickly could he accomplish everything he had to do? He tried to calculate travel time, how many hours he'd need to sleep, and when and where he should do all he knew he needed to do. He longed for time to plan, but knew he didn't have that luxury. He'd have to leave in the morning.

Just as he was heading to grab a duffel bag to pack what he'd need for the trip, his phone rang. Annoyed, he glanced at the caller ID. Not recognizing the number, he ignored the call and went to the closet in search of a bag.

He was on his way to his bedroom when he heard his phone ping with a voicemail message. Huffing out an angry breath, he doubled back and grabbed the phone, listening as he once again stomped toward his room.

He froze in his tracks as the ramifications of the message sunk in. The guy died. The guy actually died! He did a little jig right in the hallway. He'd played up his visit after his last trip saying how much he appreciated the chance to visit someone who'd been so important to him for so long. He'd even shed a tear right in the doctor's office. There was no way the doctor could refuse him a trip to the funeral. Oh, it was all going to work out. It was meant to be this way, at this time, all along. He'd tried so hard to be patient, to wait for a sign telling him when to act, and now he had one. He skipped to his room and began to pack.

The next morning, he was early for his appointment. His car was packed and ready to go. He had printed out the obituary and had a copy ready along with an appropriately distressed expression. He didn't shave, thinking a scruffy, tired appearance could only help his cause. He giggled to himself. He'd barely slept all night, but he wasn't tired. He was wired. He had waited so long for this.

Focusing on the doctor's questions proved nearly impossible. He had much more important things to think about. It would only be hours now.

"What's that?" He told himself he needed to pay attention. Grieving could only get him so far. If he didn't pull it together, the doctor might get suspicious.

"I asked if you're okay to drive. It's a long trip."

"I'll be fine. I've never minded driving."

He could feel the doctor's eyes boring into him.

"How do you feel about losing your friend? Have you been sleeping? Any problems since you got the news?"

"I was sad to hear, of course, but I believe he's in a better place. He was suffering terribly the last time I saw him, but he seemed at peace. I have to be, too."

"That's a healthy way of looking at it."

The doctor seemed pleased. Fool.

"Funerals can be difficult, however. Do you feel prepared?"

He wanted to slug the guy. "I'm prepared. I'll use the techniques we've talked about and I'll get through it without a problem. I feel good about it." Just say what he wants to hear.

"Okay. You know you can call if you need to talk. If I'm not available, the service will get you in touch with someone else who can help."

"I know, Doctor, thank you."

The doctor stood and extended a hand. "Have a safe trip, and don't forget about our next appointment."

"I will. And I won't."

He gave the doctor's hand a quick shake then turned for the door. His desire to be out of there was almost more than he could bear. He was forced to turn back around at the doctor's voice.

"I forgot about your journal." The doctor picked

up the notebook from his desk. "My fault. I guess with all the talk of your friend and your upcoming trip, it slipped my mind. We need to take a look at it every time."

"I need to be going, and you probably have someone else waiting. Could I leave it with you, you take a look, and we'll talk about it next time? I can write on something else while I'm away."

"I guess that will work for this time."

The doctor's tone and his condescending smile were like that of a teacher addressing a kindergartener. He felt his face heat and his hand clench into a fist inside his pocket.

"Well then, see you next time," the doctor said.

He waited until he was out the door before muttering, "Wrong. See you never."

28

Cassie walked in the door of Frank's house ready to talk. To really talk to him. Since her conversation with Susan a few days ago, she'd been mulling things over and had decided Susan was right. Frank deserved to hear everything.

Things had been strained between them since the night at Secrets. Every time their paths had crossed they'd made polite conversation, but it hadn't gone any further. Cassie could tell by the look on Frank's face that he wanted to ask questions, but was most likely afraid to…afraid that she would refuse to answer or afraid of what he'd hear, she couldn't be sure.

So today was going to be the day. She'd spent part of the morning at the inn, helping out while the kids were there, but it was her day off. She had moved up her appointment with Dr. Willard so would be seeing him later that afternoon, and Frank had told her he planned to do some work at home before a late afternoon client meeting, so she figured this would be as good a time as any.

But now, as she walked through the house, her shoulders slumped in disappointment. The house was empty. She gently scooped Trixie out of her crate, cradling the still sore dog in her arms as she made her way to the kitchen. There she found a note on the table.

Rain in the forecast for tomorrow, went to check out possible location for shoot today. Be home later.

Defeated, Cassie plopped down in a chair.

"Well, now what?" she asked the dog.

Trixie cocked her head then nudged Cassie's hand.

"Okay," Cassie mumbled as she obliged and began stroking the dog. Trixie melted into Cassie's lap and sighed her contentment.

Frank had told her about his new client, an online sportswear company looking to update its website as well as prepare fresh print ads. He had mentioned a spot he knew of that he thought would be perfect to take outdoor photos of models wearing the client's biking, hiking, and yoga clothes.

Cassie drummed her nails on the table. She had been debating with herself about broaching another subject with Frank. He had been hinting around about Cassie getting back into modeling. Just very casually, and just for a few of his projects. He was convinced the sportswear client would be a perfect fit. While she didn't want to disappoint him, she really wasn't interested. But, she had what she thought was a far better idea.

She'd already mustered her courage and called her former agent back in Chicago. She hadn't even been sure he was still in the business, or if he'd remember her—but he was, and he did—and after she got past the nerves, they'd had a pleasant conversation. And she'd heard exactly what she'd hoped to hear from him. Now she just had to convince Frank.

Kendra could do it, Cassie knew she could, but she worried it might be more difficult to convince Kendra than it would be to convince Frank. Cassie had seen glimpses of Kendra's self-doubt. They didn't come often, and they didn't last long, but they were a factor. Cassie was convinced if Kendra gave modeling a try, starting out slowly and building her confidence as she gained experience, she'd overcome any issues with self-doubt. And it just might be a way out of her current predicament at home.

She'd have to talk to Frank first, of course. The last thing she wanted to do was to make promises to Kendra and then not be able to back them up. She sighed and got to her feet. The afternoon wasn't going to go as planned, that was clear, but she'd make the best of it. She changed into shorts, a tank top, and her running shoes. Since it would be a while yet until Dr. Fischer cleared Trixie for a walk, Cassie carried the dog out into the yard and let her explore while safely on the end of a leash.

"I'm sorry, girl, you're going to have to content yourself with that for the time being," Cassie said as she settled a reluctant Trixie back in her crate. "Follow the doctor's orders and you'll be running again in no time." She patted the dog before securing the latch. Then she stretched and took off for a much-needed run.

Frank maneuvered his car up the narrow dirt road through the dense trees thick with rich, green leaves to the clearing at the top of the hill. He climbed out, grabbed his camera, and as he had done so many times before, took a moment to marvel. From here, most of Misty Lake was visible, and he loved looking at his town.

He let his eyes follow Main Street, past the restaurants and shops, past the post office and the police station, all the way to the church with its steeple stretching toward the sky. The school was on the other end of town and even now, so many years since he'd been a student there, the sight of the empty parking lot brought a smile to his face.

Summer vacation. Those seemingly endless months when school was just a distant memory and the sun-drenched days were filled with bike riding, swimming, and baseball. Of course, he'd gotten older, had juggled summer jobs, and had traded his bike for a car, but by then he'd discovered girls, and those girls liked to go to the beach, and wear bikinis, and summers had gotten even better.

Grinning at the memories, he turned and looked in the opposite direction. The road led out of town and he followed it as far as his eyes could take him. It had been five days since he'd driven Cassie down that road and to Secrets. Five days since what had been a perfect evening had gone so wrong. He still didn't have a clue as to why it had gone wrong. He'd tried to talk to her, but she hadn't been willing and he'd been afraid to push. Was it time to push? He simply didn't know what to do next. He didn't want to lose her, he knew that much, but how to make sure he didn't remained a mystery.

Frustrated, he kicked at a rock and watched it roll down the gentle slope before having its path blocked by a much larger rock. Was that it? Was his path—their path—to happiness blocked by something much larger than the both of them?

Cassie had talked to him at Secrets, she'd told him things she'd never told him before, but he'd gotten the sense that there were still things he didn't know. And one of those things must be what was keeping them apart.

Maybe Cassie didn't realize it herself. Maybe it was something that seemed inconsequential, but that was affecting her deeply. Maybe if she talked to him and told him everything, he could help her realize it and get past it.

He had to help her, he just had to. He couldn't stand to see her unhappy. Because even when she seemed happy, when she was smiling and laughing, he knew there was something that wasn't quite right and that she wasn't truly happy. He'd fix it, he promised himself. Regardless of how long it took, he'd fix it.

With a satisfied nod and with the feeling of an enormous weight lifted off his shoulders, Frank raised his camera and began framing shots.

He worked for over an hour. He found a flat, grassy area that he knew would be the perfect spot to spread out a yoga mat. The backdrop of trees and scattered wildflowers exuded a feeling of serenity. He snapped a few shots as he pictured Cassie in a Warrior II Pose. Then he huffed out a little laugh. He'd have to make sure to tell Shauna he remembered something from her class.

It was near midday, the sun high overhead, so Frank didn't expect the shots to be spectacular. For now, he just needed to scout out locations and gauge angles that would provide the best background. For the actual shoot, he'd come back with his models in the morning or in the evening when the light was at its best.

He moved through the trees to a path worn in the earth from countless mountain bikers. Here, the trees were too thick to get the type of shot he had in mind. He followed the path until he came to an area where the trees thinned enough that there was more room to work with. He could prop a bike in place and use a small fan to give the illusion of movement. But he thought he'd try some action shots, as well. The path would also work for photos showcasing his client's running clothes.

Again, he pictured Cassie. Running on the path, her hair secured in one of the company's headbands, a bright pink tank top, black running shorts with coordinating pink trim…it would be perfect.

He had ideas for a couple of other models he'd like to use, but his intent was to feature Cassie. She was a perfect fit for the company's target audience. He just needed to convince her. But he'd need a younger model, as well. His client had stressed the burgeoning market for teen sportswear and his desire to have his company become a teen's first choice for a trendy, but high-quality, product.

Here, he had another idea. He hadn't mentioned it to Cassie yet, didn't know if it would even be possible, but he knew a model when he saw one, and Kendra was meant to model.

He knew she was only seventeen and that could pose a problem if her parents refused to sign a consent form. Or if she didn't live with her parents. He'd asked a few general questions about the kids Cassie was working with trying to learn a little about Kendra's home life, but Cassie didn't give much information and he knew that she shouldn't. He hadn't pushed. He'd bring up the subject with Cassie, see what her feelings were, and then, if it seemed like it could work, he'd have to get in touch with the director of Project Strong Start. Details, he thought. So many details.

Frank continued searching for possible locations, taking shots from different angles, and envisioning what he could do with props. Then he spent some time taking shots for his stock photos. A single purple flower bursting from a sea of yellow weeds caught his eye. He captured a butterfly balancing delicately on a long blade of grass. He found a mossy tree trunk, a startlingly red cardinal amidst the deep green leaves of an oak tree, and a boulder with enough of an indentation on the top that some dirt and water had settled in it and a small white flower had bloomed.

He spent nearly fifteen minutes snapping pictures of a baby rabbit who happened upon him and seemed unsure of what to do. The rabbit hopped closer, froze in place as if trying to make itself invisible, then when Frank didn't move, ventured even closer, stopped to nibble on some wildflowers and twitch his nose in Frank's direction before finally darting away.

Frank was so focused on the endless choice of subject matter that the rustling and snap of a branch startled him. He whirled around, but didn't spot anything.

"Is someone there?" he called.

He stood and scanned the area. There was another noise. This time he pinpointed a location off to his right where the trees were thickest. A small animal like a squirrel or rabbit wouldn't make so much noise. It could be hikers, but they'd likely answer. It could be teenagers not wanting to be found. Or, he admitted to himself, it could be a bear.

He knew there were occasionally bears in the area. Just last week there had been an article in the paper about a family whose camping trip was rudely interrupted by a bear and her two cubs. While he wasn't one to panic, he didn't feel much like tangling with a mama bear. Besides, he reasoned, he had gotten a good idea of what he wanted to do with the photo shoot, had gotten plenty of material to work for hours on stock photos, and he needed to get ready for his appointment with his client.

He kept an eye out over his shoulder as he made his way back to his car, but never saw a bear. Or anything else, for that matter.

Frank rubbed his eyes as he closed the car door and started the engine. Maybe he'd imagined the noise. Heck, maybe he'd fallen asleep on his feet and had dreamt the noise. With as little sleep as he'd gotten the past week, it was a possibility. He'd woken to Cassie's screams at least once a night since their date at Secrets. He told himself again he was going to help her...and decided if he couldn't, he'd try to convince her to talk to someone who could.

Frank's mind was far away when another noise demanded his full attention. Something with the car, but he didn't know what. He supposed it was due for a once-over at the garage. He tried to remember when he'd last had a tune-up, had the brakes checked, or even had an oil change. No, he knew he'd had the oil changed since he'd returned from his magazine assignment. He felt a little better about himself, thinking maybe he hadn't neglected the car too badly. Truth be told, he didn't know a lot about cars. Joe was the motorhead in the family, although he was more interested in boat motors than car engines.

Frank grinned as his dad's voice sounded in his mind. 'Nowadays no one can fix a car. There are so many gadgets and gizmos and what-have-yous that a guy can hardly change his own oil anymore. I remember the days when just about every guy worth his salt could fix just about whatever was ailing with his car. Now? No way. Those car manufacturers have seen to that.'

That tirade had come after Sean had tried to replace hoses and a thermostat on Anna's car, claiming he had done it as a teenager and he could do it now. The resulting bill had reached into the thousands and it had been the last time his mother had let his dad anywhere near her car.

Frank was still chuckling to himself as well as reminding himself he needed to stop by his parents' house as he moved to the right lane and onto the highway exit ramp. He blinked hard a few times telling himself he needed to focus as he couldn't quite believe he was already at the exit. He really needed some sleep.

He tapped the brakes to slow the car and when the brake pedal met the floor, he was suddenly wide awake.

"What in the—" Frank muttered as he began pumping the brakes. When nothing happened, his mind began to race. His first thought was that it must have been even longer than he remembered since he'd had the brakes checked. His next thought was that Clyde, the mechanic who had serviced every car Frank had ever owned, would chew him out for letting it go so long. Then, in an instant, his only thought was the minivan with the cartoon figures on the back informing the world that the happy family consisted of a father, mother, two kids, two dogs, and a cat. And that the van was in his path and he had no way of stopping.

Everything happened in a matter of seconds. Frantically, Frank slammed his foot on the brake again and again. When the car didn't respond, he pulled on the emergency brake. Nothing. Knowing he'd never slow enough to take the curve, and knowing he'd never avoid the minivan and its occupants, two of which he could see secured in car seats in the back of the van, he said a quick prayer and jerked the wheel to the right.

"Cassie, please, wait!"

Cassie heard Dr. Willard calling after her, but she didn't slow. Although her legs were barely steady enough to support her, she somehow managed to make it to her car, to fumble with the key long enough to push the button to unlock it, and to fall into the seat. She knew Dr. Willard was still calling to her, but it didn't register with her any more than did the honks from angry drivers as she pulled out into traffic, heedless of those around her.

For a long time, she just drove. She absolutely refused to let herself think. She turned up the music as loud as it would go, opened the windows wide, and let herself get lost in the pounding bass and the hair that swirled and whipped around her head. She focused on the white line in front of her. Nothing else.

Detective Zalinski had barely hung up the phone before his feet started moving. No answer. He'd have to try again later. He muttered an oath as he slammed his thigh into the corner of his partner's desk as he zipped around it.

"Hey, Zals, what's up?"

"Pull up everything you can find on an ex-con named Martin Santos. I'll be right back."

While his partner muttered an oath of his own before turning and banging on his computer keyboard, Detective Zalinski hopped down the steps two at a time. When he reached the basement evidence room, he stopped for a moment to catch his breath and to smooth his wavy, chestnut hair. He straightened his tie and, after checking over his shoulder to make sure no one was around, puffed up his chest and plastered a smile on his face. While he didn't like to play the card, he knew with Bitsy the process would be much quicker if he did.

Bitsy had been with the department longer than Zalinski had. She took her job seriously, and she guarded the evidence room with the tenacity of a pit bull. But Zalinski knew Bitsy, knew how to play the game, and knew how to get what he wanted. He was ready to do just that as he pulled the door open.

Eighteen years on the force and eighteen years of dealing with Bitsy still hadn't prepared him for what met him as he caught sight of the evidence room stalwart. Zalinski had witnessed the many reincarnations of Bitsy, but she appeared to have reached a new level.

Every time Bitsy split up with a man—and it was often—she needed a fresh start, as she explained to everyone who would listen. New hair style, new makeup, some kind of crazy clothing choice, you name it, Bitsy was willing to try it. Zalinski had seen her hair go from brunette to blonde to red and just about every shade in between. He'd been there when she'd decided to try jet black hair with matching lipstick, nail polish, and wardrobe. He'd even survived the track suit phase where she'd worn various designer brands with their name proudly scrawled across her ample behind. That had resulted in the Chief having to make an addendum to their dress code to ban casual clothing bearing the name of the manufacturer. It had taken three weeks—and the Chief's desperate pleading with one of the female detectives to wear similar clothing for a week to make it seem as though the decree wasn't aimed solely at Bitsy—before that fiasco had been resolved. The Chief, along with most everyone else in the department, was secretly terrified of Bitsy.

Today, though, Zalinski was at a loss for words. Bitsy stood behind the desk in her usual spot, but there was nothing usual about what met Zalinski's eyes. Her hair was a shade of pink Zalinski would have sworn didn't exist if he hadn't been looking at it. It nearly defied logic, it was so bright. Her lipstick, her nails, her clothing, and the makeup dotting her cheeks were just as pink. She was holding a pink pen complete with pink feathers on the end, had a pink coffee cup on the desk, and her computer had somehow or another turned pink. Zalinski blinked. Then blinked again.

"Hey, gorgeous, it's about time. You haven't been down here to see me in ages. Come tell me what's been keeping you so busy that you can't spare a few minutes for the only person in this place who really loves you."

"Bitsy…how have you been?"

Not how he had planned to begin, but he was in shock. He looked around and marveled at how she had managed to turn just about everything in sight pink.

"How have I been? That's the best you can do? Nuh-uh, that just won't do."

She shook her head and her pink hair floated from side to side like the most intensely pink cotton candy Zalinski'd ever seen. He forced himself to focus.

"Aw, just fooling with you, Bitsy. What I really want to know is what you're doing for the rest of your life." He took her hand and brought it to his lips, his eyes never leaving hers.

Bitsy threw her head back and laughed. "Now that's more like it, sweetie pie. And since I threw that no good, two-timing rat Freddy out on his butt, I'm all yours."

She batted her eyelashes at him and it was all Zalinski could do not to gasp when he realized her eyelashes were also pink. He gave his head a brief shake. Madness, it was sheer madness—Bitsy was nearly sixty—but he stayed focused. He was in a desperate hurry.

"Now that's an offer no sane man could ever refuse. And I guess that makes your no good, two-timing rat Freddy anything but sane." Before she could answer, he turned on all the charm he could muster. "You know how much I'd love to spend the rest of the day hiding out down here with you, but I have a case involving a rat that just may rival yours. It goes back a few years, but I know you can find the evidence box for me." With that he threw her a wink and a smile, making sure she spotted the dimple in his right cheek.

"Anything for you, you devil. You know I can't say no to that dimple."

Six minutes later he was back at his desk, rifling through the box. He didn't know what he was looking for, but he was certain there was something there.

"Zals, what do you want to know about this guy?"

his partner asked. "I see you helped put him away a few years back."

Zalinski had had a different partner back then, the case hadn't been particularly news-worthy, so there really was no reason for Daniels to know anything about it. Zalinski tried to tell himself all of those things in an effort to keep from biting his partner's head off. He gritted his teeth and mumbled, "Yeah, I helped put him away."

"So what are you looking for now? Looks like the guy's been out on parole for a while. You like him for another case?"

Zalinski glanced up at Daniels. He was hardly more than a kid, but roughly the size of a mountain. Zalinski was 6'-3" and Daniels had him by at least four inches. The kid had to weigh over 250, but there wasn't an ounce of fat on him. His dark hair was always kept in a precise crew cut, his clothes always neatly pressed, and he never did a thing that wasn't strictly by the book. His one fault, Zalinski thought.

Rather than answer him, Zalinski asked his own questions. "What can you find out about what he's been doing since his parole? Where he's working, where he's spending his free time, where he's living, that kind of stuff."

"Says here he's been working on a loading dock. Want me to make a few calls?"

"Please. See if he's been missing work or getting into trouble on the job, especially with any female employees. Then see if you can find out anything about family or friends that may live out of town. If you find any connection to Minnesota, let me know where exactly in Minnesota."

Zalinski resumed his examination of the evidence box. Daniels knew when to stop asking questions, and for that, Zalinski was grateful. He wasn't sure how he'd explain his actions. When he'd gotten the call from Santos' parole officer, he'd immediately shoved aside the paperwork he'd been completing and had shifted gears. While the PO didn't think anything was out of the ordinary, he'd done as Zalinski asked and let him know Santos had requested a travel pass to attend a funeral in Minnesota. Santos had already been gone a couple of days. Zalinski had squeezed the living daylights out of the pencil he'd been holding in order to keep from jumping in his car, finding the parole officer, and squeezing the living daylights out of him. He was supposed to keep Zalinski up to date on any happenings with Santos. Up to date, not up to two days ago. Zalinski had managed to keep his cool though. He needed the parole officer on his side.

Zalinski couldn't bring himself to believe it was a coincidence that the funeral just happened to be where Cassandra was living. Cassie, he reminded himself, she'd asked him to call her Cassie. While he'd had to give up on trying to prosecute Santos for the attack on Cassie, he'd never stopped believing Santos was the one responsible. There had to be something they'd overlooked at the time that would tie him to Cassie. He looked at the clock on the wall in front of him. It had been about thirty minutes since he'd tried Cassie. He started dialing as he continued leafing through reports on Santos.

29

Gradually, Cassie came out of her trance-like state and began to notice her surroundings. She didn't know her way around the Twin Cities well, but knew she must be on the outskirts. Traffic had increased significantly, pine trees were fewer, and office buildings were plentiful. She checked the time, tried to remember when her appointment had been, and realized she'd been driving for well over two hours. Shaken, she pulled off at the next exit and found a fast food drive through where she ordered the largest diet soda on the menu.

She eased her car into a shady parking spot far away from anyone else, gulped her drink, then leaned her head back and closed her eyes. She knew she had to think about what she'd learned in Dr. Willard's office no matter how difficult it may be. A low moan came from deep in Cassie's throat as she let herself remember.

Like her previous session with Dr. Willard, the

details seemed a little fuzzy as though everything had happened, but maybe not to her. Maybe she'd sat in on a session, merely observed. But no, it had been her. It had been her learning, remembering, and shattering into a million pieces.

She sat for a long time trying to make sense out of it all, but it didn't make sense. Nothing made sense. How could she have forgotten? How did that even happen? She vaguely recalled Dr. Willard explaining how the brain, in some sort of self-preservation mode, can block out things that are too painful to remember…too painful to relive.

She didn't know what to do next. Run away, maybe. Far away. She looked around her, at how far she'd driven without even being aware of what she was doing. She'd been headed for Chicago, she realized, whether consciously or not. And then what? What did she think she was going to do? Confront him? She didn't even want to lay eyes on him.

Suddenly it was all too much…learning what she'd learned, the years of her life he'd cost her, the nightmares, all of it. Including the soda. She threw open the car door, stumbled for a grassy patch under the trees, doubled over with her hands on her knees, and vomited.

After what seemed like forever to her, Cassie was able to straighten. She swiped a hand across her mouth and looked around, grateful no one seemed to be paying her any attention. She made a quick visit to the restroom where she splashed cold water on her face and then was back in the car with the air conditioning blasting. She forced herself to concentrate. She had to do something. The detective, the one from Chicago…Zalinski. She'd call him.

Cassie dug her phone out of her purse and discovered it was still turned off. She'd turned it off before her session with Dr. Willard, and had been in no condition to worry about turning it back on afterward. She powered it on, and after finding his number on the old receipt she'd tucked in her purse, dialed the detective. As the phone was ringing, she scrolled through her missed calls and her text messages. Eight missed calls from Susan, four from Dr. Willard, and two from a number in Chicago.

Her hand shook as she disconnected from the call to Detective Zalinski. Susan would never have called her so many times if something wasn't really wrong. She opened her text messages and found three from Susan. 'Call ASAP.' Cassie's mind ran wild with possibilities. Susan was sick? Maybe it was Susan's family in Chicago. Someone had an accident? Or Sam. Maybe a problem with the pregnancy? Cassie recalled the incident during the yoga class that Sam had brushed aside as just a twinge. One of the kids?

There was just one voice mail from Susan, and one from the number in Chicago. She listened to the message from Susan first. *Cassie, please call as soon as you can.*

The tone of Susan's voice left no doubt in Cassie's mind that it was something serious. Cassie called Susan's cell phone, then the inn, and was nearly frantic when there wasn't an answer at either number. She slammed the car into gear and tore out of the parking lot. For the second time that day she was on the receiving end of a slew of nasty looks as she barreled into traffic and swerved around a slow-moving truck. Once she was back on the highway, she tried Susan again, but was met with the same result.

Crazed with fear, Cassie began recklessly passing

cars. She noticed the state trooper ahead of her in the shade of an overpass before he noticed her. She slowed to a more reasonable speed and picked up her phone again. The message from the number in Chicago was still there, waiting. Bracing herself, she turned on the speaker and played the message.

She pulled over on the shoulder and flipped on her hazard lights. Although she couldn't claim to know much at the moment, she did know she was in no condition to drive.

She still didn't know why Susan was trying so desperately to get ahold of her. She still didn't know what to do with the information she had after her session with Dr. Willard. But now she did know one thing.

Martin Santos was in Minnesota.

30

Cassie was driving again. Like before, she was barely aware of her surroundings. But unlike before, her mind was intently focused on what she needed to do. First of all, she needed to get back to Misty Lake. She figured she was still close to an hour away. The minutes seemed to drag by.

She still hadn't reached Susan so still didn't know what was going on that had Susan so upset. She hadn't tried Detective Zalinski again, but had decided there likely wasn't much to be learned from him. He'd told her Santos was in Minnesota. That was all she needed to know.

Then, since there was nothing to distract her, and since she knew she had to think about it, she forced herself to review her session with Dr. Willard.

It started out fine. He asked about Cassie's rush to come back so soon and she told him about her evening with Susan and how she'd felt prepared to talk things through with Frank. While she felt like things were moving in the right direction, she also felt like there was still a missing piece. She was ready, with Dr. Willard's help, to delve back into her past in the hopes that they'd find that missing piece.

It hadn't taken long. It was as if the memories were there, just waiting to be set free. Now, even though it had only been a few hours, those memories were already starting to blur. She remembered the outcome, but couldn't remember all that led up to it. And she still couldn't truly believe the words describing the incident had come from her. Until she'd heard herself say them, she'd had no idea she knew any of it.

It took her fingers tingling with numbness for Cassie to realize she was clutching the steering wheel hard enough to crush it. One finger at a time, she loosened her grip and flexed her fingers. She tried to breathe slowly, but it was difficult. Her breath wanted to come in short gasps.

She was certain now she'd been heading for Chicago, but was far from certain what she thought she'd do once she got there. Try to find some sort of closure? It didn't seem right, somehow. If she were being honest with herself, for as shocking, unsettling, and horrifying as it had been, it somehow didn't seem right. It didn't seem like the whole answer, the whole missing piece. Part of it, maybe, but not everything.

She should have stayed at Dr. Willard's office, she knew that now. She should have talked it through with him. Talking may have led to more. Now, she was so embarrassed she didn't know how she was going to face him again.

She was debating calling him, leaving a message at least, trying to apologize somehow, when her phone rang.

She'd been holding it in her hand and it gave her such a shock, she jerked and the phone flew from her grasp. Trying to keep one hand on the wheel and one eye on the road, she leaned and stretched until her fingertips brushed the phone. With a grunt and a final stretch, she was able to grasp the phone before it quit ringing.

"Hello? Hello?" Her caller ID told her it was Susan.

"Cassie." Susan breathed out what seemed like a week's worth of pent up anguish. "Finally. Where are you?"

"Driving. What's wrong? What happened?"

"Oh, it's fine…it will be fine."

It wasn't fine, Cassie could tell. "Tell me what's going on, Susan." Cassie could hear voices in the background, and if she wasn't mistaken, a page over a PA system.

"Um, it's Sam. She had a little scare, but turns out it's nothing to worry about. Where are you? Driving where?"

"I'm on my way back to Misty Lake. It's a long story. Are you sure Sam's okay? The baby's okay?"

"Yeah, she thought she was going into labor, but turns out, it was false contractions. There's a name for it, I can't remember…" Susan's voice grew steadier as she talked, but Cassie still wasn't convinced.

"You tried calling so many times, you had me worried sick."

"I'm sorry. I panicked and wanted to get to the hospital. I was hoping you were at home or nearby and could come over to the inn. I couldn't reach Molly and, well, I didn't think I could just leave…"

"Susan, are you sure you're telling me everything? You sound upset. Are you at the hospital now? Is Molly at the inn?"

Cassie heard Susan take a deep, shaky breath. "Yes, Molly's there."

Not an answer to the important questions. Before Cassie could start again, another voice came on the line.

"Hi, Cassie, it's Joe. Susan's a little shaken up, but everything is going to be all right. Are you close to home?"

"It's about thirty miles yet. Is everyone at the hospital? Sam must be worse than Susan told me."

"Sam is going to be just fine. I promise. Why don't you stop by the hospital when you get into town? You can see for yourself."

"So everyone is there?"

"There are a few people here, but you know the McCabes." He gave a weak laugh.

"Then you probably don't need me there. Maybe it's better if I head to the inn, make sure things are running smoothly."

"Susan just checked in with Molly. No problems, Molly has everything under control, no need to worry. You should stop at the hospital. Susan can update you on everything, and I think she wants to apologize again for giving you a scare."

"Okay, I'll stop by. It shouldn't be more than a half hour. Call me if anything changes."

"You can count on it. Drive safely."

With that, Joe disconnected and Cassie was left staring at her phone. She wanted to believe them, but was having a hard time doing so. She took a peek at the speedometer and decided she could risk a few more miles per hour.

"I can't believe you made me lie to her. She's never going to forgive me." Susan yelled through her tears as she looked at the McCabes gathered around her.

Riley grabbed her and held her close. "Red, you did what you had to do. She's driving, you said she's upset about something already. The last thing we need is another accident. She'll be here soon and I'll take the blame. Please don't cry." Riley stroked her hair as Susan sobbed into his shoulder.

Susan felt guilty about that, too. She'd told them she knew Cassie was upset. While she hadn't given any details, she felt as though she'd broken their bond of trust and likely ruined any progress she and Cassie had made.

She still didn't know what to make of the call she'd gotten from Cassie's therapist. The man had sounded positively conflicted on the phone, but at the same time, near sick with worry. He hadn't said much at first, just that he was looking for Cassie because she'd left something behind at his office. She hadn't been answering her cell phone, so he'd tried the work number she'd provided. When Susan told him she didn't know where Cassie was, the doctor had encouraged Susan to try to get in touch with her. Telling her without telling her—that was the only way Susan knew to describe it—that he was worried about Cassie. Very worried.

First Cassie, now Frank…Susan felt her knees giving out. Riley held on and led her to a chair where he sat and deposited her square on his lap, not letting her go for an instant.

Susan knew Riley was sick with worry over Frank,

they all were, so she allowed herself only a couple of minutes longer to draw on his strength before standing and turning to him.

"I'm fine, Riley." She laid a hand on his cheek and studied the worried lines on his forehead. "And Frank is going to be fine, too. I know it."

Then it was Riley's turn to draw on Susan's strength. He stood, leaned his forehead against hers, and squeezed his eyes shut.

31

Justin Patterson wasn't sure any more what he had expected a career as a mental health expert would be like. He did know that this wasn't it. Most of the people he saw were criminals, forced to see him by a judge who couldn't figure out what else to do with yet another law breaker. His patients didn't want to be there and didn't want to be helped. And they made it abundantly clear they didn't trust a blond-haired, blue-eyed, ivy-league-educated frat boy. They were wrong about the ivy league frat boy, but he'd stopped trying to explain that years ago.

He'd just sent another patient home after another worthless fifty minutes. He'd asked questions and had gotten nothing but lies in return. Sometimes, just sometimes, when he reached the end of his rope, he'd spend a session behaving like one of his patients. He'd hand the man or woman in front of him the same load of crap they handed him. Just to watch their expressions.

Sometimes he needed to do something to try to make it through the endless parade of deviants and derelicts. And sometimes it startled a patient into cooperating.

Usually, though, he tried to help. There was still a glimmer of that bright-eyed, eager kid who'd scratched and clawed his way through school, working three jobs at a time to afford to pay his own way, and who'd wanted nothing but to make a difference in the lives of people who found themselves in the same kind of helpless situation that he'd once found himself.

Though he rarely did so, he took a moment to study the diplomas and degrees neatly framed and hanging on his office wall. Four jobs, he recalled. Once it had been four jobs at a time.

He'd never taken a handout, never accepted a single dollar of financial aid. Scholarships, yes, because he'd earned them, but not a cent he hadn't. After growing up living off food stamps and church ladies' donations of casseroles, he'd told himself he'd do it on his own or not at all. Aid was there for those who needed it. Not for those who were capable of working but chose, instead, to sit on their asses and call occasionally beating up on a wife or a kid a job.

Justin took a deep breath, held it for a moment, then let it whistle out through pursed lips as he tried to tuck away the past. Thinking about it never did him any good. Instead, he tried to tell himself, yet again, that he'd helped some of them. Every once in a while someone came along who truly wanted help. In those cases, he worked tirelessly, putting in hundreds of extra hours researching, studying, and doing whatever he could to help guarantee a positive outcome.

It was lunch time, so he began clearing files and papers off his desk, preparing for a quick break before his afternoon appointments. A flash of red appeared in the midst of his yellow legal pads and manila folders and he looked at it questioningly. He opened the notebook and remembered. The journal. He'd been going to read it, but hadn't found time. It must have gotten mixed up with his other paperwork. Good thing he didn't mistakenly file it away and forget about it, he thought.

But he reprimanded himself. He was getting careless. The journal had been in his possession for a couple of days already and it was possible he'd left it out where someone could have seen it. A stickler for patient privacy, he made it a point to lock up all of their files, but now he wondered if, being that it didn't look like the typical patient file, he'd left it lying on his desk. Inexcusable. He tried to remember if he'd left a client alone in his office, even for a minute, and if that client would have had a chance to open the notebook. He didn't think so, but it nagged at him nonetheless.

At times, this patient was one he thought he may be helping. There were times when the man was responsive, engaged, and seemed to try. Then there were times when he barely grunted an answer or flat-out lied. It was like working with two different people.

Promising himself he wouldn't make another mistake with patient data, and promising himself he'd read the journal by the end of the day, he tucked it in his briefcase and headed out for lunch.

Tad Zalinski was rarely frustrated, but today he most definitely was. Usually he knew it was just a matter of time until he found what he was looking for, whether he knew exactly what that was, or not. But today, he'd spent the better part of his shift looking through evidence and case notes from the Martin Santos investigation as well as everything he could find on Cassie's case. Unsolved cases did not sit well with him. There hadn't been many over the course of his career, but of those he'd endured, hers had been one of the worst.

He'd told himself then, and he told himself now, that it had nothing to do with the fact that she was beautiful. Or that she looked so much like his wife. He treated all cases, and all victims, the same. But as he studied her photos, he felt the same rage and desire to protect that he'd felt years ago. The creep had bruised and battered her face, and worse, had left her bruised and battered on the inside. And she'd seemed to be all alone in the world. Not one visitor during her hospital stay.

Granted, he hadn't known her before, but the woman he'd interviewed in the hospital, the woman he'd had to calm when she'd nearly jumped out of bed after a tray clattered outside her door, was a far cry from a woman who could stand in front of a camera for a living. She'd been scared and broken and he hadn't been able to prove who was responsible. It still ate at him.

He hadn't ever seen her again, didn't know how she'd healed—or if she had—but he wanted to think she had. Almost as much as he wanted to find proof Santos was responsible. But for as sure as he was that the proof was there somewhere, he couldn't find it.

Zalinski reviewed what he knew. Nothing had been stolen or disrupted, so robbery wasn't the motive. The attacker had been inside her apartment. That meant he knew her, knew her schedule. It wasn't a random attack. Santos admitted he'd worked with Cassie, that he'd found her beautiful, but had claimed it ended there. The pictures he had of her in his apartment were just pictures he'd been proud of, nothing more.

Cassie had been away from her apartment for nearly two weeks. The attacker would have known this, and would have known she was coming home that day. He had to have been following her. He'd been at the hotel where she was staying, maybe even staying with her?

Zalinski thought back to his initial theory that the guy she'd met was the one responsible. Cassie had fiercely defended the guy and had begged Zalinski not to question him. Zalinski hadn't questioned him, but he had done some checking.

He reviewed his notes. Frank McCabe had no history of trouble with the law, not even a speeding ticket. Zalinski'd even searched juvenile records and hadn't come up with anything. While it was no guarantee of innocence, his years on the force had taught him such a serious crime typically wasn't a first crime. And he'd confirmed McCabe had been on a flight back to Minneapolis at the time of the attack on Cassie.

That brought him to another fact that had always bothered him. Cassie had told him, once she'd been able to talk, that she'd screamed and fought off her attacker. Zalinski had let her think that was the case, but deep down, he had his doubts. Most men, especially in the act of committing a crime, could overpower a woman, no matter how hard that woman fought. No, the more likely scenario was that the attacker hadn't wanted to hurt her.

Zalinski wasn't a shrink, but what he'd learned

over the years led him to believe that this guy had expected Cassie to be happy to see him. However screwed up that might seem, Zalinski had seen it many times before. A guy was convinced a woman loved him and wanted to be with him, just needed a little push in the right direction. If that guy wasn't exactly stable to begin with, that little push too often escalated.

Likely, when Cassie had screamed and fought, the guy had become enraged and had tried to overpower her. But, he'd stopped short of raping her, or killing her, because even in his deranged state, he hadn't really wanted to hurt her.

And the other woman, the one they'd tied to Santos, she'd been his neighbor, someone he knew. It fit. Santos fit. He'd worked with Cassie in the past, finding out her current work schedule wouldn't have been difficult. Tailing her at the hotel wouldn't have been difficult. And now he was in Minnesota. Where Cassie was. It was more than a coincidence.

Zalinski leaned back in his chair and closed his eyes to think. What was wrong with people? A rhetorical question, but one he found himself asking all too often.

His partner hadn't had much luck either. Since Santos' parole, it seemed he showed up to work on time, stayed out of trouble, and attended his scheduled meetings with his parole officer. Daniels had learned that Santos was also required to attend meetings with a therapist as part of his parole, but it appeared he made it to those meetings, as well. Daniels hadn't been able to reach the therapist yet, so they didn't have too many details. All Daniels knew was that Santos had suffered a breakdown early in his incarceration and that therapy in prison had uncovered an abusive childhood. That abuse had apparently been found to be the cause of his actions later in life. Prison documents made it seem as if any past issues were well under control long before his release.

That was about all the new information they'd found and that led to Zalinski's increasing frustration. When he heard his dispatcher's voice ring across the room, "Zalinski and Daniels, you guys are up," he groaned.

He'd already convinced his lieutenant to let him pass the previous two calls on to another team so he could continue digging. He knew he wouldn't be able to work a third. With one last look at the papers and evidence scattered over his desk, he begrudgingly stood and scrubbed a hand over his face, then straightened his tie and grabbed his jacket.

Nodding to Daniels, he grumbled, "I guess we better go."

It was going to be a long shift.

Cassie made it to the hospital in twenty-five minutes. She had considered veering off and taking the turn for the lake, thinking she'd do more good at the inn than at the hospital, but she still had a nagging feeling she hadn't gotten the whole story. Or the real story.

She spotted Susan's car in the parking lot. And Riley's truck, Joe's car, Shauna's car, a patrol car she had to assume brought Jake, and a blue sedan she was fairly certain belonged to Sean and Anna. She quickened her pace.

It took only a minute to find them, all huddled together except for Riley, who was pacing. And Sam was there. Sitting in the cluster of chairs with the rest of them, looking perfectly healthy. Cassie narrowed her eyes and looked closer. Something…

"Cassie. You're here." Susan rushed to her and took her by the hands.

"What's going on, Susan? Sam is right there, she looks fine. Where's—"

"Sit." Susan guided Cassie to a chair and pushed her into it.

"Where's Frank?" It didn't sound like her voice, sounded more like a far-off echoing as if she were in a deep cave.

Susan's eyes darted around the group before she answered. "There's been an accident. It's Frank. He had a car accident."

"When? How? Is he okay? He's okay, isn't he?"

"He's still in there." Susan tipped her head toward the swinging doors leading to the trauma center. "We haven't heard much, but what we've heard has been good news."

Cassie leaned her head into her hands. The roaring started slowly, but quickly built steam. She couldn't hear or focus on anything around her with the roaring in her ears. It was as loud as a train and it was bearing down on her.

Not now. Not Frank. She was going to talk with him. Today. They were going to make things work, one way or another. She'd put him through so much and he'd been nothing but patient and kind. So much more so than she'd deserved.

Her hands shook, saliva pooled in her mouth, and she was certain she was going to be sick again. She dropped her head lower between her knees and fought back the nausea.

Gradually, she began to hear those around her.

"Cassie, are you okay?" Karen was kneeling next to Cassie's chair with her hand on Cassie's wrist. Checking her pulse, no doubt.

"Um, yeah, I think so. I just, I've been driving. I need something to drink."

The words were barely out before Susan was shoving a paper cup of water into Cassie's hands. Grateful for both the water and for the distraction, she took a tentative sip. No repeat of the incident in the parking lot, she promised herself.

A little steadier, she looked around at the concerned faces. She pulled herself together. That concern needed to be directed at Frank, not at her.

"Tell me what you know."

Jake took over. Business-like, monotone, and, Cassie could tell, struggling against emotion.

"We got the call at the station around three thirty. A single car accident. Frank's car rolled coming off the highway exit into town. We had to cut him out of the car. It took a while."

At this, Jake's voice shook, and Cassie saw Anna bury her face in Sean's shoulder. Shauna and Sam were blinking back tears. Riley had stopped his pacing and was staring, stony-faced.

"When we got him out, he was unconscious. But the ambulance was waiting and the paramedics took control. They had him here in under ten minutes."

"And? What's happening?"

"Like Susan said, we haven't heard much. He regained consciousness and was able to answer the simple questions the doctors asked him. That's a good sign. He's got a few broken bones and is having some trouble breathing, so they have him hooked up to machines and are running tests. We should know more soon."

It was Karen's turn. "It's all standard procedure. They want to be sure they don't miss anything."

Cassie latched on to Karen. "You must know what all of this means. Can't you go back there and check? Get some real answers?"

"There isn't anything else to report right now. The doctors will learn a great deal from the test results and they'll let us know more as soon as they know more."

"Jake said broken bones. Where?"

"One wrist is in pretty bad shape. A couple ribs are fractured and, while they don't think it's broken, one ankle is swelling so they're keeping an eye on that."

"No internal injuries?"

"That's what the tests will determine."

Cassie didn't know what else to say so she just nodded. Karen, apparently assured Cassie wasn't going to pass out, patted her arm and moved back beside Joe.

The McCabes were the only ones in the waiting room. Once they got done explaining what they knew to Cassie, the room fell into a deafening silence.

Cassie spotted the sign for the restrooms and made her way there. She was bent over, elbows resting on the sink when Susan came in behind her.

"Are you doing okay, Cass?"

"I guess so. It's a lot to take in."

"I know."

They stood in silence for a few minutes. Cassie studied their reflections in the mirror and couldn't decide who looked worse.

"So I assume Sam's okay? There wasn't a scare with the baby?"

Susan's head dropped. "No. I'm sorry, Cass. We just decided that it would be best not to worry you any more than necessary when you had so far to drive. I knew you were upset already, and—"

"Wait. You knew I was upset already?"

Susan grimaced. "Well, you disappeared, I couldn't reach you, I just thought…"

"It's my day off. Why would it be so strange for me to go somewhere?"

Susan hesitated before seeming to deflate in front of Cassie's eyes. Then Susan began talking so fast it was all Cassie could do to keep up.

"Your doctor called. Your therapist. He was worried. He didn't tell me anything, I swear, but he was clearly worried. He said you left something at his office and he was trying to reach you. After a minute, I figured out that was probably just a reason to call the inn. He asked me to try to get in touch with you. I promise he didn't tell me any details but, well, I could tell he was concerned and I just assumed something must have happened…happened at your therapy session…"

Cassie went numb. She felt an odd tingling in her fingers that started to make its way up her arms. She wanted to move, wanted to shake her arms, but she seemed incapable of doing anything.

"Cass?"

Cassie turned and marched into a stall. She unrolled a long length of toilet paper and blew her nose. She kept her back to Susan as she flushed the paper down the toilet. At length, she turned.

"It was a rough session."

"I'm sorry, Cassie. I'm so sorry. It's private, it's your business, and I'm not even going to ask what happened. If you want to talk, you know I'm here, but I won't ask you any questions."

"What did you tell the rest?"

Susan cringed. "As little as possible. As soon as I found out about Frank's accident, I tried calling you. When you didn't answer, and when I got the call from the doctor, I...I guess with everything happening at once, I sort of lost it. I told Riley you were gone somewhere, that I couldn't find you, and that I thought you were upset about something. I was worried about you driving. Somehow it was decided that we needed to get you back here, but after one accident, no one wanted to risk a second. They figured the less you knew, the better."

"So, Sam? That seemed like a good way to get me back? You didn't think I'd be worried about Sam?"

The tears started to roll down Susan's cheeks. "No, it's not like that. Someone just said, 'Tell her Sam had a complication and needed to go to the hospital.' I know it was a horrible thing to do. Sam didn't know about it until after the fact. I really tried to make you believe Sam was fine, though. I just wanted you back here, back here safe and sound."

Cassie collapsed against the wall. "Oh, God. This day. Just make it stop."

She leaned her head back and pressed the heels of her hands into her eyes. When she opened her eyes again, Susan was anxiously studying her, tears still wet on her cheeks. Cassie pushed away from the wall and went to Susan. The two held onto one another and cried together.

32

It had been a long night. An incredibly long night. Once the doctors had assured them Frank was going to be okay, and once they'd all had a chance to sneak in, just for a moment, to see for themselves, Frank's family had trickled out of the hospital and headed for home.

Cassie had stayed all night. She'd left briefly, had rushed home to clean up and tend to Trixie, and to give Joey Rafferty instructions to care for the dog while she was gone, but had returned and hadn't budged from her chair next to Frank's bed until just before Anna and Sean were due to return.

Because, at some point during the night, she'd started to feel a little uncomfortable. Uncomfortable that she'd barged her way into a very private, very family sort of situation. A situation in which she really had no business. Officially.

She felt fairly certain Frank's family liked her. No,

she knew they did. But, still, she and Frank weren't a couple. They were friends, they dated, there were feelings there, but as far as his family was concerned, she wasn't much more than just a friend.

And why should a friend be the one to hear the doctor's reports first? Why should a friend be the one to stay home from work to sit next to Frank's bedside? No, that was Frank's family's place. Not hers.

So she chugged coffee as she drove. She'd told Susan, insisted really, that she'd handle everything at the inn for the day. She felt far from up to the task, but it was only right. Susan needed a break and needed to be with Riley and the rest of the McCabes as they got more information on Frank's condition and his prognosis.

Cassie knew wrist surgery was in his immediate future. Most likely, some time that day. Provided the orthopedic surgeon could fit it in his schedule. If not, the next day. Frank wouldn't be leaving the hospital for a couple of days, anyway. The concussion was serious, and with the fractured ribs, he was still having trouble breathing. They wanted to monitor him for at least forty-eight hours.

So Cassie would work and rely on phone calls and texts to keep her updated. She hoped it would be a busy day or she'd likely lose her mind.

The previous day's guests had all checked out and all three of the girls were hard at work. It was Friday, so Matt and Tyrell were at camp. Kendra, though, had somehow talked everyone into not only working on Fridays, but working a longer shift. It was fine with Cassie. She wanted the company. So once she'd done all the paperwork she could find to do, she headed upstairs in search of the girls.

Detective Zalinski was waiting when Judge Keller arrived for work. Zalinski needed a search warrant, needed it like he needed to breathe, but knew he had to tread carefully. Judge Keller wasn't one to be screwed with.

Zalinski avoided eye contact and drank more coffee as the judge headed into his chambers. Zalinski knew he'd have to allow at least twenty minutes for the judge to complete his morning routine. If Zalinski interrupted, it would take twice as long to get the warrant. If he got it at all.

So he sat, reviewed his notes, and replayed the previous afternoon and evening in his mind.

He and Daniels hadn't thought much of the call as they headed out to meet with Dr. Patterson. A doctor worried about a patient. He'd seen it before. And he knew what to expect. He and Daniels would get there, the doctor would beat around the bush, asking them roundabout questions regarding statutes of limitations, maybe give them a snippet or two, but be so worried about crossing a confidentiality line that he wouldn't give them anything useful. They'd leave, maybe pull the guy, or gal, up to see if there was anything interesting, but then wind up filing it away. Just more paperwork.

Yesterday had been different. They'd barely gotten into his office before Dr. Patterson started blurting out details. Specific details. It had taken a while for Zalinski and Daniels to calm the guy down enough for it all to start making sense.

The doctor had a journal. A journal that, he claimed, outlined an impending abduction, perhaps a murder. When they'd asked how he'd come across the journal, the story had gotten even weirder.

Good news had come when the doctor uttered the words, 'court-ordered therapy.' Court ordered. Music to Zalinski's ears. Anything the patient said during therapy was fair game. That made things infinitely easier, and once they'd explained it to the doctor, they'd had trouble getting him to quit talking.

The patient had been arrested and convicted of assault after the third time police were called by his employees who claimed he was out of control. He'd wound up losing his business and being sentenced to an extended probationary period with the stipulation he attend therapy. And as part of that therapy, Dr. Patterson required him to keep a journal.

Dr. Patterson had outlined a history of instability and periods where his patient seemed to black out and was then unable to account for his actions or whereabouts. The journal was meant to help account for his actions and to help avoid any more blackouts.

Usually, the guy brought the journal to each session and they'd discuss how the previous days had gone. This time, though, Patterson and his patient hadn't gotten to the journal so the guy had left it, telling the doctor to review it and they would discuss it the next time. He'd been in a hurry, their session had ended abruptly, and the guy hadn't wanted to stick around.

The doctor didn't get to the journal for a few days, he'd claimed. Zalinski remembered how Dr. Patterson had averted his eyes and become twitchy when he'd gone over that detail. Zalinski was still curious, but other information had taken precedence.

When the doctor finally did take a look, he'd been stunned. It wasn't the journal the guy brought to every session. Not by a long shot. Apparently, he'd kept two. This journal was filled with fantasies, research on a wide range of disturbing topics, and a very detailed, precise account of what his plans were for the next few days.

The doctor had started to outline some of those plans, and he and Daniels had started to pay attention. When he'd finally given them names and places, Zalinski thought he just might have gotten the break he'd spent his day, and the past seven years, hoping for.

When enough time had passed, Zalinski went to see the judge. He got the warrant. He and Daniels searched the guy's place. It was a little confusing, a lot disturbing, and confirmed what he had already worked out in his mind the night before. Once he was back at his desk, Zalinski started making phone calls.

Later that morning, Frank's brothers gathered outside his hospital room door, talking in hushed tones. Frank was better, much better, but there was still concern.

"We're sure he's okay, right? The knock on the head isn't too serious?" Jake was the most hesitant of the group, being he'd been at the accident scene.

"He's going to be fine. He's got a concussion, but all the scans came back negative so he should be released tomorrow. Just needs that wrist surgery."

When his brothers gave him curious looks, Joe shrugged. "I asked Karen."

Jake and Riley both nodded, accepting the explanation and looking relieved.

"Dad said he was doing well this morning. More

pissed off than anything," Riley said. "So…" He grinned and pushed open the door to Frank's room. "Let's let him have it."

"Hey, guys." Frank blinked as all three of his brothers poured into his room. He'd been dozing, the painkillers making him not want to do much but sleep. Seeing them all at once had him wiggling to sit a little straighter in his bed. Then regretting his decision as the movement set his wrist throbbing and his ribs aching.

"How are you feeling?" Riley asked.

"Not bad, considering." Frank looked at Jake. "Any word on the car yet?"

"It's totaled, Frank. I don't know what the techs will be able to find."

"I'm telling you, the brakes failed. And they don't just give out like that with no warning. Something happened. Something…" Frank paused and considered. "Wait, I did tell you that, right? Last night is a little fuzzy."

"Yeah, you told me. And I'm having it checked out, but it will take some time. Try not to worry about it right now."

Riley changed the subject. "I heard Cassie spent the night." He rocked up on the balls of his feet and then back down again, his eyes never leaving Frank's.

"Well, yes…in that chair right there."

Frank used his good hand to point to the chair now occupied by Joe. Since he knew his brother was trying to get under his skin, Frank ignored Riley and instead thought back to the previous night…how Cassie had looked so worried when she'd been awake, but had then fallen asleep for a short time. Frank had watched the worried lines on her face melt away. As the moonlight played over her, he'd been entranced.

Riley tried again. "Wouldn't leave your side, from what I heard."

Frank turned his attention back to his twin. "We're friends, she was concerned. And shouldn't you be at work?"

Riley just lifted a shoulder. "I'm a contractor. I set my own hours."

"Even Mom left," Joe said. "Only Cassie stayed. Karen told me there was no way the nurses could get her to agree to go home for the night. They eventually gave up and brought her a blanket."

"So?"

"So what gives? It's obvious you're nuts for her, but we can't figure out why a smart, drop-dead gorgeous woman like Cassie is wasting her time with you." Jake looked at Riley and Joe, both of whom were grinning and nodding in agreement.

"Nuts for her? What are we, in sixth grade?"

Riley just shook his head sadly and counted off points on his fingers. "Let's see…you haven't had a date since you've been back in town; I've personally witnessed Jessica Fuller practically throw herself at you at least three separate times and you've ignored her; whenever Cassie's around, you can't take your eyes off her; and right now I know you're hoping she'll walk through that door. Face it, bro, you're done for. Oh, and welcome to the club. Glad you could finally join us."

"Shut up."

"Hah!" Joe laughed at his brother. "That's the best you can come up with? Shut up?"

"Get out of my room. How's that?" Frank leaned

his head back into his pillow and looked at the ceiling, hoping that his brothers would take his advice and be gone by the time he lowered his gaze again. It wasn't to be.

"Now, now, be nice," Jake scolded. "You know us well enough to know that we're not going to take it easy on you just because you happen to be in a hospital bed. So, you may as well start spilling the details. You're not getting out of that bed any time soon and we've got hours...and hours."

"What is wrong with you guys? You're acting like a bunch of old ladies. If it's gossip you're looking for, head over to the coffee shop or the hair salon...or Aunt Kate and Aunt Rose's building. You can sit around and gossip to your hearts' content."

"I don't know what you think you said, but here's what I heard." Riley's voice turned high-pitched and whiny. "I'm so in love with Cassie, she's just the most amazing woman I've ever met. She's smart and funny and beautiful and I can't stand it when I'm not with her. But I'm afraid she doesn't like me and I don't know what to do about it." He barely finished before he was doubling over laughing. Jake and Joe joined him.

When Frank didn't laugh, or even respond, Joe's expression grew serious. "Does she like you, Frank? I mean I assume she likes you, but does she *like you*, like you?"

"Again, is this the sixth grade?" Frank wanted to tell his brothers to get lost, to leave him alone, and to stop digging into his private business, but their expressions now were all concerned. He knew that no matter how much grief they might give him, they cared...really cared. He took a painful, labored breath and let his eyes wander from one brother to the next. After a minute he admitted, "I don't know."

It was almost comical watching the three of them shoot glances at one another. Clearly it wasn't the answer they had been expecting. The joking and the teasing were set aside for the moment.

"What do you mean? I thought you guys were getting serious." Jake seemed genuinely confused.

Frank was equally confused. "Why did you think that?"

"Well, you two are together all the time, neither one of you ever dates anyone else, I guess I—we—just assumed…" Jake didn't seem to know how to continue.

Frank hadn't talked to anyone about his relationship with Cassie. He wasn't even sure he could call it a relationship. Things had been getting better, then they'd gotten worse, and, he remembered, he had told himself he was going to get to the bottom of it all. Try to convince her to talk to someone, someone who could help.

Now he weighed his promise to Cassie not to discuss her past with his desire to maybe get some advice. He was quiet so long Riley finally interrupted his thoughts.

"So?"

"So, I told you I just don't know. She's hard to read sometimes."

"Either you're together or you're not. It doesn't seem that complicated," Riley said.

"You wouldn't think so, but with Cassie, things are just that. Complicated."

"You're not making much sense." Joe seemed nearly as frustrated as Frank.

"I know. Let me put it this way. If it were up to me, I'd spend every minute I could with her and the whole town would know about it. Or, to put it in your sixth grade terminology, I'm nuts for her."

"Then she really doesn't like you? I mean, you've always been a pain in the ass, but you're not that bad. I would imagine a woman could find something to like." Despite his teasing words, Joe's expression made it clear he wasn't having nearly as much fun as he had expected.

"How many ways can I say I just don't know? Cassie has some things in her past—things I'm not going to get into so don't bother asking—that make it hard for her to trust, I guess. I'm not sure how I fit into her future, or if I do at all, but I'm not ready to give up. She's worth the wait."

Jake, Joe, and Riley were silent and all looked uncomfortable. Frank started to laugh at them, but thought he did a good job of hiding it when he shifted his wrist and turned the laugh into a grimace. It also gave his brothers something else to focus on.

"Does it hurt a lot?" Riley grimaced along with Frank.

"It doesn't feel good."

"Surgery's first thing tomorrow morning?" Jake asked, clearly grateful to have something else to talk about.

"That's what I've been told. I was hoping for today, but they want to wait. Orthopedic surgeon is supposed to be here bright and early tomorrow. And then I should get out of here."

Joe perked up. "Hey, I hear they're putting a plate and screws and all kinds of stuff in there. You'll probably set off the detectors at the airport now. Do you have to carry a card or something that says you've been rebuilt?"

Frank scowled. "You're the science teacher, you tell me." After a moment, a slow smirk grew. "You know, as long as he's in there, I think I'll see if I can get the doc to put in some extra parts…turn me into the Six Million Dollar Man. Then I'll kick the crap out of all three of you at once."

The tension broken, Frank's brothers began throwing insults and jabs at one another while Frank sat back and listened. His wrist hurt, the temporary splint and bandaging not doing much to ease the discomfort. His ribs made any sort of movement uncomfortable, and even though he'd been told his ankle wasn't broken, just badly sprained, it ached with the slightest movement. He still hadn't figured out how he was supposed to use the crutches the nurse had provided earlier that day with his wrist out of commission. He decided he'd worry about it later.

On the bright side, aside from the athletic wear job, most of the projects he had lined up were fairly tame and wouldn't require any climbing or otherwise getting to remote locations to shoot. He hoped to stay on schedule. And hoped Andrew could help out. He could also spend time at the computer, tweaking some of his stock photos and working on those he was considering selling at the gallery. Jake had told him his camera and equipment in the trunk hadn't been damaged. At least he thought he remembered asking and Jake answering. He was trying to wade through the fog that was the previous evening when Riley got his attention.

"How much of that pain medication are you taking? We've been talking to you and you're totally zoned out."

"I am a little tired…"

Joe seemed almost relieved as he got up from the chair. "We should probably let you rest. I talked to Mom right before I got here and she said she and Dad are coming by again later this evening. Shauna too…she keeps calling Karen with questions as if there's some secret doctor language and they're all keeping the truth to themselves."

"Shauna gave the doctors an earful this morning. She followed one of them right down the hall demanding to know just how serious the concussion was and what they're doing about it. I'm glad she's on my side. She can be scary."

"That's our sister," Jake said. "And now, we should let you get some rest. You know, if you want to talk more about what's going on with Cassie, or if she needs any help, or…well, I'm here."

"Thanks, Jake."

One by one, his brothers shook his good hand or gave him a good-natured punch on his good shoulder before filing out of the room. Frank could hear their mumbling as the door closed behind them. As hard as he tried, he couldn't fight sleep long enough to catch what they were saying.

"Well, crap. That wasn't any fun at all. I've been waiting for over a year to be on the other end of one of these interventions and that's it? Frank didn't squirm at all. We let him off too easy." Riley grumbled all the way down the hall until they reached the doors to the parking lot.

"You were just a much easier target, Riles." Jake patted him on the back.

"Yeah. It only took about two minutes to get you worked up then Jake and I just had to stand back and watch you trip all over yourself. That was a fun day."

"When are we going to try again? There has to be more to this." Riley looked from Jake to Joe, his eyes demanding their agreement.

"I'm afraid that's it, Riles. We gave it our best shot," Jake said.

"Come on! We'll give him a couple of weeks to heal and then we'll ambush him. He won't expect it. We'll plan things out better next time. I know, we can—"

"Face it, Riley, that's it. We came. We tried. We failed," Joe said.

Riley continued to call after them as they climbed into their cars. "Think about it. In a couple of weeks…I'll figure something out."

Jake and Joe both waved as they pulled away, shaking their heads and laughing at their brother.

33

So far, so good, he told himself. Things were going exactly as planned. Not that he had doubted it for a minute. He had waited too long to make a mistake now. And in just a few hours it would all be over and everything he'd wanted for so long would finally be his. He closed the door on his cheap motel room and made his way to his car for his final trip into Misty Lake.

Cassie managed to keep her hands busy and her mind mostly off of the events of the past twenty-four hours. The girls were a great help. As they all worked together to clean guestrooms, gather laundry, stock supplies, and add special touches to each room, the girls chatted. Well, Jennica and Jordyn chatted. Kendra joined in at times, when cajoled, but mostly just focused on her work and scowled at the frivolous conversation.

The twins were busy talking about their

boyfriends and about a big bonfire planned for later that night that absolutely *everyone* would be attending. They asked Cassie questions, or asked her opinion, often enough to have her focusing on them rather than on the dozens of other topics that wanted to demand her attention.

She'd gotten a couple of texts already from Susan who had met up with Riley at the hospital. Frank was doing well…still uncomfortable, but much better. Cassie learned the surgery wouldn't happen until the following day. For as much as she knew Frank had been hoping for that afternoon, she couldn't help but think another day in the hospital would do him good. She had no idea how he was going to manage even the simplest tasks with all of his injuries. Just when she was starting to worry and wonder how much help she could be, Jennica got her attention.

"So what do you think, Ms. Papadakis? Yellow or blue?"

"I'm sorry, yellow or blue what?"

Jennica spun in a dramatic circle. "Argh…I've been talking forever. Tonight. Yellow dress or blue dress?"

"Ah. Okay. Dress."

Cassie studied the petite dynamo. With her yellow-blonde hair, fair complexion, and soft blue eyes, Cassie didn't see yellow as being her color.

"Blue. Definitely blue. Especially if you're talking about that adorable cobalt blue sundress I saw you wear to The Brick a few weeks ago. It's perfect for you. Makes your hair and eyes pop."

"Wow, thanks. Blue it is." Jennica grinned and turned back to the bed she was making.

"What about you, Jordyn, what are you wearing?"

"I think just some jean shorts and a t-shirt. It's a

bonfire, not a dance." She rolled her eyes at her sister.

Yes, Cassie thought, twins but definitely individuals. A lot like Frank and Riley…

Jake was still chuckling to himself about Riley's utter disappointment at their talk with Frank when he walked into work. He started to make his way by his deputy Marc's desk, but Marc held his phone with one hand and used the other to wave down Jake.

"Okay, yes, okay, just one minute. He just walked in. I'll transfer you. Yes, I'll tell him it's urgent."

Marc put the caller on hold.

"I've got a guy on the line, a detective from Chicago. He really wants to talk to you. I'm not sure what's up, he hasn't given me many details, but he did mention Cassie Papadakis. The woman who's working with Susan out at the inn?"

"Yes, I know who Cassie is."

"Right. Well he's worked up about something. Maybe you just want to take it?"

"Sure, put him through."

Jake flung his jacket over the back of his chair then sat down and picked up his ringing phone.

"Sheriff McCabe."

There was an audible sigh of relief.

"Sheriff. I was hoping to talk to you. Detective Tad Zalinski, Chicago P.D."

"Detective. What can I do for you?"

Normally a call from another agency was routine. Jake sensed this one wouldn't be. The mention of Cassie's name had Jake on alert. Hadn't Frank just told them minutes ago that Cassie had things in her past that he wouldn't, or couldn't, discuss?

"It's going to sound crazy, but bear with me…"

For the next two minutes, Jake listened. Then he halted Detective Zalinski mid-sentence so he could call Marc and another deputy, Tim, into his office. He put Zalinski on the speaker phone before asking him to continue. Jake wanted more than one set of ears in on the call.

Ten minutes later, Jake disconnected. Tim was already on his way to the hospital to post guard outside Frank's room. Jake tried Cassie at the inn, but got no answer. He didn't have any better luck with her cell phone.

"Dammit." Jake talked as he ran with Marc to the parking lot. "I'm heading to the lake. I'm almost certain Cassie is there today, but I want you to run by Frank's place and make sure she's not there. If you don't find her, head to the inn."

"Got it."

Jake punched in Frank's cell phone number as he drove, but as expected, did not get an answer. No cell phones in the hospital. He tried Riley's phone as well as Susan's, but didn't have any better luck. Frustrated and increasingly uneasy, he called the hospital and asked the receptionist to try to locate Riley. He gave her instructions to have Riley call.

Then Jake drove faster than he should, even with the lights and siren blaring.

They had moved their focus to the barn. Cassie wanted to be sure things were in place for the group coming over the weekend. It wasn't a big affair, just a family wanting to use the space, so no catering or decorating, but there was still prep work. There was always prep work.

"Let's move another table against the wall here." Cassie pointed. "They asked about bringing in snacks and drinks. It's probably best to keep those things off to the side. Their goal, from what I understand, is to sort through years and years of pictures and home movies. Definitely keep the food and drinks away from that."

They moved tables and arranged chairs. They made sure the bathrooms and the extra rooms in the loft were clean, stocked, and ready to go. Then, because Cassie needed pretty even if it wasn't a formal event, she sent Jennica inside for tablecloths and candles.

They worked a little longer before Cassie checked her phone. She hadn't had a call or text in a while, and she was antsy.

She sighed in frustration. Cell service was spotty, especially inside the barn, and she wasn't able to get a signal. Since they were nearly done, and since Jennica hadn't returned with the tablecloths and candles, she decided to head to the inn.

"I'm going to check on Jennica. She must be having trouble finding what I asked for. Be right back."

She watched her phone as she walked across the yard. She didn't have service until she walked inside the inn.

And by then it was too late.

Barb had been a nurse at the hospital since before the McCabe kids were born. A sturdy woman with graying black hair that curled tightly to her head, she had yet to meet the patient she couldn't handle. She didn't hesitate at poking her head into Frank's room without knocking.

"Frank, I'm going to get you up soon and you're going to walk up and down the hall again. You're no good to anyone lying in that bed and feeling sorry for yourself."

Frank knew better than to argue. "Yes, ma'am."

"And you," she turned and pointed at Riley, "have you gotten that tetanus shot yet? I told you last year when you were in for an x-ray that you'd be due for a booster shot this year."

"Um…"

"Don't um me, Riley McCabe. You take care of that shot or I'm coming to your house to do it myself."

"Okay. Ma'am," he added when she narrowed her eyes at him.

"That's better. Jake is trying to reach you. He wants you to call him."

"What does he want?"

"Now how am I supposed to know the answer to that? I just know he left a message to have you paged. You didn't answer your cell phone."

"You told me I couldn't use my cell phone in here."

"And I was right. But make it snappy and I won't tell if you turn it on now." Barb winked at Susan as she turned and left just as quickly as she'd arrived.

Jake was almost to the lake when his phone rang.

"Riley. Are you still at the hospital? Where's Cassie?"

"What?"

"Pay attention! Where's Cassie?"

"She's at the inn, I suppose. Red is here with me, so—"

"Ask Susan. Now."

"Wow, okay, just a sec."

Riley made a face at the phone when he pulled it away from his ear.

"Hey, Red, is Cassie at the inn? Jake's looking for her."

"Yes, she should be. Why?"

Riley shrugged.

"Red says she should be there. What's the problem?"

"I don't have time to explain everything. I got a call from a detective in Chicago. He's looking for a guy he thinks is tied to Cassie. He was plenty worried. I am too."

"Well, hell. What can we do?"

"Keep trying her phone. She's probably just out of range. I'm almost there, gotta go."

Riley stared at the phone after Jake disconnected.

"What's wrong?" Susan asked. "Why is he looking for Cassie?"

Riley paused a beat, debating.

"Try calling her. Jake said he can't reach her."

"Why? What aren't you telling me?" Susan's voice rose and she was on her feet.

"Riley?" Frank said. "Tell me what's going on."

"I don't know. Not much, anyway. That's the truth," Riley added when Frank opened his mouth to argue. "Jake said he had a call from a detective in Chicago who's looking for a guy who's tied to Cassie in some way. I didn't get any details."

"And he can't find Cassie?"

Frank was struggling to sit up.

"Lie down, you idiot. You can't get out of that bed and you know it." Riley, less gently than he should have, settled Frank back on the pillows.

"If something is wrong with Cassie, I'm will not lie here on my back. You can count on that."

"Cassie isn't answering…her cell or the phone at the inn." Susan's voice was shaking now. "Riley, what's wrong? Tell me what's wrong."

"I don't know. I just don't know."

"We have to go. We have to get over there. Maybe she's hurt. The kids are there. Riley, we have to go!" Susan tugged on Riley's arm.

"Jake said he was just about there. I'm sure nothing's wrong." But Riley sounded far from confident.

"I don't care. Let's go. Please!"

"I'm coming with you." Frank gingerly swung his legs over the side of the bed, using one crutch in his one good hand to boost himself to standing.

"Are you crazy? Get your butt back in that bed!"

Frank's voice turned deadly calm. "Keep your hands off me, Riley, unless you're going to help me put on my pants. I am going. You're not going to stop me. Now help me, or get out of my way."

It was Susan's turn to try. "Frank, you're hurt. You need surgery, for heaven's sake. You can't possibly leave the hospital, they won't let you."

"They don't have to let me." Frank grunted as he struggled into his pants. "Get me my shoes."

"Frank," Susan pleaded.

"We're wasting time. Make sure Barb isn't in the hall. She's probably the only one who could stop me."

Knowing his brother well enough to know that arguing would be a waste of breath, Riley cracked the door and peeked into the hallway.

"I don't see anyone."

"Good. Then let's go."

It wasn't easy, but they got Frank out of the hospital and into the car. It was clear the whole thing hurt a lot more than Frank let on, but he was determined. Susan looked positively terrified by what they were doing.

Just over ten minutes after Riley talked to Jake, Frank, Susan, and Riley were headed for the inn.

Cassie scrolled through her phone as she walked across the parlor. There were no text messages, but there were missed calls. From Susan, from Jake, and from another local number she didn't recognize. Her heart started to beat faster. Just like the day before…everyone trying to reach her. Frank…

Fear had her almost unable to move. She felt faint. Her throat went dry. She half stumbled, half ran to the kitchen, desperately needing water.

She was so focused on getting a glass and filling that glass she didn't notice Jennica. It wasn't until she had a glass in her hand that it registered and she whirled around.

Jennica was seated at the table, gagged and tied to a chair. A man stood next to her, but he was turned enough that Cassie couldn't see his face.

Cassie froze in place, the hand holding the glass still raised. Her mind didn't want to work, so she struggled to process what she was seeing. She ordered herself to focus.

Jennica's eyes were round and filled with fear. She appeared unharmed, but Cassie couldn't be sure. The man turned. It took a moment, but then Cassie recognized him.

Nothing made sense.

"What do you want? Why are you here?"

The man just smiled, looking oddly relaxed and content.

"Let her go."

"I can't do that."

"Why? What could you possibly want with her? You don't even know her."

"She saw me. I didn't want that to happen. It's the only thing that hasn't gone right so far. Such a shame." He shook his head, looking sad.

Trixie, hearing the man's voice, started barking and scratching at her crate in the parlor. The man seemed to debate with himself, then ignored the noise and turned his attention back to Cassie.

"What do you want?" Cassie repeated, this time more forcefully. She wouldn't be afraid. She wouldn't.

"You, of course."

A whimper escaped Jennica. The man's expression changed to one of annoyance and Cassie couldn't hold back her fear.

"Be quiet," he demanded.

Jennica dropped her head, but not before Cassie saw the tears. Ensuring the girl wasn't harmed was her sole focus.

"Just leave her. I'll go with you, but leave her alone."

"Of course, you'll come with me. That's why I'm here, isn't it? But I can't leave her."

Cassie couldn't decide what to do. She didn't see a weapon, but figured it likely he had one. If she just kept talking, trying to convince him, Jordyn and Kendra would show up soon. She couldn't chance it that he got to them too.

"Let's go. Now."

Cassie turned to leave the kitchen, praying he would follow. When she dared a look back over her shoulder, she saw him bent over Jennica.

"No!"

Realizing she still held the glass in her hand, she hurled it at him with all her strength.

He groaned when it struck him in the head. Cassie had hoped it would enrage him or startle him enough that he'd come after her, but he seemed only sad.

"Why would you do that?" He rubbed at his head. His eyes widened in curiosity when his fingers came back bloody.

Out the window, Cassie saw Kendra and Jordyn leaving the barn. No. Please, no. Then, before she could decide what to do, she saw Jake. He got the girls' attention, and within a moment they were running in the opposite direction.

Jake was there. Somehow, he must know what was going on. Cassie breathed a small sigh of relief.

It was short-lived. When Cassie looked back, the man was hacking at the ties on the chair and pulling Jennica to her feet.

"I think we'll leave now. Yes, it is time to leave."

He pushed Jennica in front of him and then took Cassie by the arm, leading them both into the parlor. Trixie was frantic. On top of everything else, Cassie worried the dog would hurt herself.

"That dog is really quite a nuisance. Maybe I shouldn't have let her go. No, no. That would have made her sad. Remember?"

He was mumbling, having a conversation with himself, it seemed. To Cassie, it was more terrifying than if he'd been shouting at her.

And 'that dog?' Trixie? He'd been in Misty Lake before? Cassie tried to concentrate, tried to put things together. Matt had said there'd been a call…the guy talked funny. Cassie recalled a glimpse of something near the side of the house the day Trixie had run away. He'd been there?

He forced an unwilling Jennica across the parlor. Cassie put a hand on the girl's arm, trying to calm her. When they reached the door, he ordered Jennica to open it. When she did, they came face to face with Jake.

"Don't move," Jake said evenly as he trained his gun on the man.

Jennica gave a muffled scream and dropped to her knees. At the same time, the man grabbed Cassie's arm and dragged her with him.

Cassie had enough. Enough of the fear, enough of being a victim, just enough. She spun around, lifted her elbow, and connected with his jaw. Startled, he let go of Cassie's arm and staggered to the wall, trying to keep his balance. He started mumbling.

"Why? Why would you do that? You need to come with me. You want to come with me, I know you do. You've always wanted to be with me." His words came faster and started to slur. His eyes glazed over and he seemed to be far away.

"It's taken so long, Maria, so long, but it's finally our time. I waited, like I know you wanted. I did everything you wanted. We should leave now, the two of us. I love you, Maria. You know how much I love you."

Then, with barely more than a whisper, he added, "Don't leave me. You can't leave me again."

And there it was. Finally. The missing piece.

All at once, things fell into place for Cassie. It had been him that night in her bedroom. It hadn't been a dream about her mother and a dash to the bathroom to hide from that dream. It had been him. She'd known that since making the discovery with Dr. Willard, but now it all fit.

And it had been him in her apartment, years later. She knew that now. That memory was back, too, just like the memory she'd uncovered with Dr. Willard's help. Dimitris had called her Maria then too.

Cassie felt a thousand things all at once. Anger, sadness, regret, relief…so many things. But it was over. It was finally over.

When Jake moved closer, Dimitris began screaming.

"No! Get away! Maria, come with me now. We're leaving, it's all planned. We'll be happy, you and me. I'll make you so happy. Everything is ready, I've taken care of everything. Come with me."

Jake's voice was steady. "I need you to calm down. We're going to take a little walk, and we're going to talk, and we're going to get this figured out."

He didn't seem to hear Jake, just kept yelling and pleading with Cassie.

"You need to stop," Cassie said.

He ignored her. The ranting reached fever pitch. Cassie could tell Jake was ready to make a move. For as much pain as Dimitris had caused her, right now she could only feel pity.

"Dimitris! *Stamata! Akouseme!*"

And that stopped him. He stared at Cassie.

"Dimitris, I'm not Maria. I'm not my mother. It's Cassie. Look at me. I'm Cassandra, not Maria."

Dimitris' eyes darted everywhere. He trembled from head to foot. His faced drained of color, and then he collapsed.

When Jake moved to handcuff Dimitris, Cassie turned. Unexplainably calm, her only thought was making sure the girls were okay.

She looked up and found Riley and Susan watching, mouths agape, from the doorway. Jennica was clinging to Susan, eyes wide in terror, but safe.

And Frank. Frank was there. Somehow, Frank was there. Leaning on a crutch and partially supported by Riley, his eyes were soft and filled with what Cassie could only describe as love. She went to him and they held one another.

The next hour was chaotic. Susan went to retrieve Jordyn and Kendra from the back of Jake's car and to work at calming all three girls. Marc arrived as Jake was getting Dimitris to his feet. Tim arrived just a minute later.

"Sorry, Jake, these guys busted Frank out before I could get past Nurse Ratchet." Tim hooked a thumb toward Riley and Susan.

"Barb?" Riley guessed.

"Yeah, Barb. She wouldn't tell me what room Frank was in until I swore up and down I wasn't there to question him about the accident. She said he was in no shape for it and that I was to let him rest. Threatened me with all sorts of medical procedures if I so much as mentioned the accident. Geez, that woman." Tim shook his head.

"It turned out okay, Tim. Don't worry about it. Guarding Frank was just a precaution."

"You were having me guarded?"

"If you would have heard the story I got from Detective Zalinski, Chicago P.D., you would have asked for a guard."

"Detective Zalinski called you? That's why you knew to come here?" Cassie had settled Frank into a chair and hadn't left his side. Judging by the hold Frank had on her arm, he wouldn't have let her if she'd tried.

"Yes. He had quite the tale to tell. When all this is settled, I'll give you the details. If you want them, that is."

"I'll let you know. Thanks, Jake." Cassie blinked back tears. "Wait, just one thing. How did Detective Zalinski figure it out? He was warning me about a different man, a man who… This is all so confusing."

"Zalinski caught a break from a doctor Dimitris had been seeing. The doctor got suspicious, called the police, Zalinski got a warrant and, well, from there I guess things were easy. Dimitris' house was full of pictures. Of you, of what I now know must have been your mother. And there was detailed information on his plans."

"Oh." Cassie didn't know what else to say.

"Like I said, if you want to know more, we can talk another time. I'll call Zalinski and let him know what happened here. He's very worried about you." Jake turned to his deputies and nodded in Dimitris' direction. "You guys get him back to the station. I'm going to talk to the girls then see they get home. I'll be along shortly."

"Sure, boss."

Jake's deputies led a now docile Dimitris to the back of a squad car. He only looked back once and seemed bewildered as he studied Cassie.

"Like it or not, Frank, we need to get you back to the hospital." Riley held out a hand to his brother.

"Give us a minute, won't you?"

"Yeah, I guess I can do that."

The room cleared out and it was just Cassie and Frank.

"I didn't know what was going on. I'm still not sure I do. But I was scared, Cassie. I was so scared that something was going to happen to you. That I wouldn't be there to do anything about it. Again."

Cassie shook her head. "I'm sorry. There's so much I'm sorry about. I should have told you more, should have figured things out sooner…"

"No. From what I saw, it looks like something no one could have figured out. That was your sort-of-uncle, I assume."

"Yes, that was Dimitris. So much didn't make sense for so long. Now it does. Well, I guess I don't know that it makes sense, but at least things fit. All the pieces finally fell into place."

"Are you okay?"

"I am. I really am. It was always his problem, not mine. I know that now. The dream I told you about wasn't a dream. I'm sure Dr. Willard could explain it better than I can, but I think I must have somehow told myself it was a dream in order to block out the reality. He shattered whatever trust I had. I had just lost my mother, he was all I had left…I couldn't deal with it. And it was him in my apartment. I know that now, as well. Today when he said,

'Don't leave me, you can't leave me again,' it all came back. He said the same thing that night in my bedroom and again that day in my apartment. He convinced himself I was my mother. He called me Maria then, too. I remember it all. It's not pleasant, but I remember."

Frank pulled Cassie close and leaned her head onto his chest. "I wish I could take it all away. I wish I could make it so none of it ever happened."

"I know, but it's going to be okay. For the first time in my life, I know that things are going to be okay. Better than okay."

Frank pulled back. "Dr. Willard?"

"Another thing I didn't tell you. I've been seeing a therapist, Dr. Willard, when I told everyone I was going to yoga. He's been helping me wade through some of this. Yesterday at my appointment he helped me remember that my dream wasn't really a dream. We got through part of it, but not all the way. I was so upset, I left his office and started driving. I think I was headed to Chicago when I got the message that…you…about your accident."

Cassie's hand flew to her mouth. "Oh, Frank, it was him, wasn't it? That's why Jake wanted his deputy outside your room. Dimitris did it, didn't he? He did something to your car."

"I don't know. I suppose that could be what Jake was thinking."

"It's my fault. It's all my fault you're hurt, and you have to have surgery, and you can barely get around, and—"

"It's not your fault. If it's anyone's fault, it's his. You didn't do anything. Please don't think you're responsible. I couldn't live with that."

Cassie wasn't convinced, but didn't want to make things any worse for Frank. She nodded.

They were quiet for a time, holding one another and lost in their thoughts.

"I think I have to continue seeing Dr. Willard, at least for a while. I have some answers now, but I'm not sure I know what to do with them. He was helping me, I think he could help me more. This past week I was trying so hard to figure out what happened when we were dancing at Secrets. I guess I know now."

Frank paused a beat and then jerked. "I said that, didn't I? I said, 'Don't leave me, don't ever leave me,' or something like that."

"I didn't remember before, but yes, I think that's what happened. It's those words…some kind of trigger. I'm afraid I'm still a little messed up."

"Hey, you're not messed up. You're just right. And by all means, continue seeing Dr. Willard. I want you to feel like there's nothing in your past that can ever come back to hurt you. As for the future, I'll make sure nothing there ever hurts you."

Cassie turned to him and smiled. "And you'll never have to say those words again, because, if you'll have me, I'm not going anywhere."

At that, Frank took Cassie's face in his good hand and kissed her. And Cassie kissed him back with all the love she'd been wanting to give for so many years.

Riley poked his head in the door.

"We need to go, Frank."

"Yeah, I suppose."

Riley and Cassie helped Frank to his feet and they started the long, slow walk to Riley's car.

"I didn't know you spoke Greek," Frank said, trying to muffle a yawn as they helped him settle in the back seat.

"You heard that, did you?"

"Got there just in time to hear it. It was kind of sexy."

"Not if you'd have understood what I was saying."

"You'll have to talk Greek to me sometimes… sometimes when…"

Frank's eyes fluttered closed and his head dropped back against the seat. Cassie smoothed the hair back from his forehead, pressed her lips there, and very carefully closed the car door. She turned to Riley.

"I have to stay and figure things out here. You'll see he gets back to the hospital and gets checked out? Make sure he didn't hurt himself more?"

"I'll see to it."

"Thank you, Riley. Thank you."

Cassie watched the car drive away, and for the first time in her life, she looked forward to, rather than feared, the future.

34

Cassie couldn't help but think about the last time she'd been in a hospital waiting room with the McCabe family. That time she'd been scared, first for Sam and then for Frank. And for so many other reasons. Today, she didn't think she could be happier. The past couple of months spent working with Dr. Willard, sharing everything with Frank, and, for the first time ever, having a life she considered normal, had resulted in her finally understanding what it meant to be genuinely happy.

She watched Sean pace and Anna nervously twist the strap of her purse while Shauna looked on. Riley, Joe, and Susan said a few words to one another, but mostly just watch the clock. Karen made the rounds from one family member to the next, offering comfort and reassurance, both as a nurse and as the most recent delivery room veteran.

Frank sat next to Cassie, one hand on her knee and the other twirling his phone. There were nerves, yes, all around, but there was so much to celebrate. A new McCabe, any minute if they could believe Jake's latest update.

"It's Friday night. Do you really think he's going to call?" Cassie asked as Frank continued to play with his phone.

"He said Friday. It's Friday."

"Yes, but it's eight o'clock. Don't you think it's possible he didn't get to it and he's called it a night? You'll hear from him Monday. Just relax."

It felt good, Cassie realized, to be the one trying to reassure rather than the one needing reassuring.

"I don't know…maybe."

Frank barely had the words out before his phone vibrated in his hand. With an 'I told you so' look at Cassie, he whispered a quick hello to the caller and hurried from the waiting room.

It was only a few minutes before Frank returned, his huge grin seeming to enter the waiting room before Frank himself. Cassie smiled along with him.

"Good news, I take it?"

"The best news. He loved it. He loved the whole thing. The pictures, the ideas for the website, the print ads, all of it. But he especially loved the models."

"Oh, stop. Model maybe, I'm sure he loved one of the models."

"He specifically said the models were perfect, exactly what he'd had in mind."

"I can't wait to tell Kendra. She's going to be so excited. I knew it would work out, I knew all along, but I tried to keep my excitement in check…just in case. I still worry about her a little, can't help it."

"I knew she'd be perfect too, almost from the moment I saw her."

"It's all coming together—for everyone—isn't it?"

When Frank merely gave her a mysterious smile and kissed her cheek before turning back to scroll through emails on his phone, Cassie leaned back in her chair.

It all was coming together...for her and for Kendra. It hadn't taken much convincing to get Kendra to give modeling a try. She'd been surprised at first when Cassie and Frank had broached the subject, but had quickly warmed to the idea. With the stipulation that Cassie work with her. Cassie still wondered how Frank had gotten Kendra to insist on that, but Cassie had agreed and once Frank had healed enough, and once they'd gotten the appropriate paperwork signed by Kendra's parents, they'd made the trek back up the hill that Frank had scouted the day of his accident. If it had bothered him being back, he hadn't shown it.

Kendra was a natural, and she'd blossomed in front of their eyes. When she'd left Camp Strong Start a few days after the shoot, she'd done so a new person. She was full of confidence, eager to finish her last year of high school, and excited for what her future would hold.

Cassie had been in touch again with her former agent in Chicago and he'd agreed to meet with Kendra. So in a few weeks when Kendra had a break from school, Cassie would return to Chicago for the first time in over a year and would reunite with someone from her past. She wasn't simply not dreading it, she could hardly wait.

There was nothing to fear in Chicago. Cassie believed that now. Once she'd recovered from the shock of finding Dimitris waiting for her at the inn, she'd asked Jake for all of the details. It had been hard to hear, but Cassie had done it. She'd asked questions and if Jake hadn't known the answer, he'd been more than willing to work with Detective Zalinski to get all the information Cassie wanted.

Dimitris' house had been nothing short of a shrine. The walls, the tabletops, and his computer were filled with images of Maria and of Cassie. At some point he'd fused the two into one, had wiped from his mind the knowledge that Maria had died, and was convinced beyond a doubt that Maria was living in Misty Lake. And that she was waiting for him, as she always had been.

Even if Dimitris hadn't turned up in Misty Lake triggering Cassie's memories, she figured she would have started remembering things on her own. It had been spending time with Kendra, getting to know the girl, and uncovering so many similarities in their lives, that had awakened something in Cassie…that feeling that was always playing in the corners of her mind, but that she hadn't been able to put her finger on for so many weeks.

Over time, and with Dr. Willard's help, Cassie had unraveled her tangled memories. She understood now, and accepted, that when a person experiences a truly traumatic event that triggers a potent stress response, the brain will sometimes repress memories of that event. It may be significant details of the event or it may be the entire event. There wasn't anything wrong with her. Quite the contrary. She had lived through more than one traumatic event and had dealt with them, in her way, in order to survive. She considered herself a fighter. And she could now think back on those events that had caused her anguish, and deal with them rationally.

The night in her room, when Dimitris had pleaded with Maria to come away with him, begged that she never leave him again, and grew angry when he was refused, was now as clear as day to Cassie. She'd been scared, had broken free from Dimitris' grasp, and had locked herself in the bathroom.

The attack in her apartment was still a bit fuzzy, but Dr. Willard felt that it probably always would be. Not so much because Cassie was still blocking it out, but because she'd been physically injured and there were some things she most likely just didn't have the answers to.

At first, she'd spent time wishing she would have sought help earlier, that she would have dealt with her past sooner. It would have saved a lot of heartache and she could have moved ahead with her life sooner.

Now, she realized she couldn't—and wouldn't—deal in what ifs. The past was the past. She couldn't change it. The future, though, was wide open and would be whatever she made of it.

And she was making the best of it. She and Frank were happy. Oh, were they happy. They laughed, they talked, and they loved. Cassie knew it would always be that way. And because of that, she could handle anything.

Just that morning she'd opened the glove compartment in her car looking for the report from the last time she'd had the car serviced. She'd found a picture. It was a picture of Dimitris and her mother and must have been taken soon after Maria and Georgios arrived in America. Maria looked so young...and so much like Cassie.

Cassie had never seen the photo before, certainly hadn't put it in her car, and knew it had to have been left there by Dimitris. He'd been in her car, he'd been at her home, he'd been where she worked. A few months ago the find would have sent Cassie into a panic. Today, she just felt pity. Pity for Dimitris that he had wasted his life on something that was never to be. That he'd never let himself be helped.

Cassie had simply cut the photo in half, saved the half with her mother and tucked it into a frame, and dropped the half with Dimitris in the wastebasket. It had been that easy.

She knew that Dimitris was confined to a mental health facility. She didn't know where. Jake had told her Dimitris had been charged with several crimes, both in Minnesota and back in Chicago, and that his lawyers had worked plea deals. He'd been ordered to the mental health facility in lieu of prison after psychological exams had revealed a host of issues. Cassie hadn't asked for many details. She knew he was far away, that he would be in the facility for many, many years, and that he was no longer a threat. It was all she needed to know.

Cassie had also spoken once with Detective Zalinski. She owed him more thanks than she could ever express, but she'd tried. He'd sounded over-joyed to hear from her and had been willing to answer the one question that still bothered Cassie.

Martin Santos, Zalinski learned, had been in Minnesota legitimately, at the funeral of a relative. The coincidence that had seemed too much of a coincidence to actually be one, had, in the end, turned out to be nothing more. Zalinski had apologized repeatedly for worrying Cassie about Santos. After talking for a while, they'd both agreed that the facts regarding Martin Santos had ultimately led Zalinski to Dimitris so there was nothing to apologize for. On the contrary, Zalinski's dogged determination had been what brought the entire situation to a close.

Cassie smiled at the back of Frank's head, still bent over his phone and pecking at it with one finger, as she thought back over all that had happened. She still struggled with the fact that Dimitris had hurt Frank. And that he'd put Jennica in danger. Jennica was fine, she actually seemed to enjoy the attention the incident brought, Frank had recovered, and everyone, including Dr. Willard, told her she needed to move past the guilt. She was trying.

Cassie looked up as the waiting room door burst open. Jake, wearing scrubs and grinning bigger than Cassie would have thought possible, but at the same time appearing slightly dazed, stood in front of them. He paused a moment, looked around at everyone waiting, then raised his arms in the air. "It's a girl!"

They had a moment to congratulate Sam, to accept cigars from Jake, and to get a peek at the perfectly adorable, adorably perfect Claire Elizabeth before leaving the new family to get acquainted.

When Frank opened the car door for Cassie, she caught sight of the brightly wrapped package on the back seat.

"You forgot the gift you bought."

"I sure did, didn't I? That's okay, I'm sure we'll see them again before the baby can outgrow a teddy bear."

"You bought a teddy bear? All by yourself? That's so sweet."

"Sweet, huh? Let's hope that's how Claire refers to me…her sweet uncle."

"Oh, Frank." Cassie couldn't resist. She grabbed

his face and pulled him in for a kiss before he could close the door.

When they got home, they both fell on the sofa.

"Wow, waiting for a baby is exhausting," Cassie said.

"For sure. I wonder if Sam realizes how hard we worked."

"Ha, ha. Okay, she probably had it a little harder. Don't you just love the name. Claire Elizabeth. Named after Sam's mother and grandmother. It's perfect."

"I think you're perfect." Frank handed her the gift he'd had in the car. "Why don't you open this?"

Cassie stared at him as if he'd lost his mind. "I'm not going to open the baby's gift. Why would you want me to do that?"

"Just open it. I'll get something else for the baby. You can help me, now that we know it's a girl."

"Frank, what are you talking about? This is for the baby."

She couldn't figure him out. He seemed almost giddy. Maybe the combination of waiting at the hospital for the baby and getting good news from his client had been too much for one night. Maybe—

"Do I have to help you? Here." Frank tore at the corner of the wrapping paper.

"Frank!"

"Just open it, Cassie."

"Fine. You'll just have to wrap it again, but if that's what you want…"

Cassie tore the paper off the box then looked at Frank again. He nodded his encouragement, so she lifted the top off the box. Layers of tissue paper covered whatever was inside. Cassie dug down far enough to determine it couldn't be a teddy bear unless it was an awfully flat one.

With one eye on Frank she pulled away the last of the tissue.

It was a picture. No, it was two pictures, framed side by side. The Fourth of July, playing with sparklers…Cassie remembered how she'd drawn a heart in the dark night, how she'd headed back to the inn while Frank was cleaning up…

Her eyes prickled with tears. These, though, were happy tears. The happiest of tears.

Cassie was on one side of the frame, smiling through that heart she'd drawn in the air. Frank was on the other side and he'd drawn in the air too. 'Marry me' was scrawled in the dark…and preserved forever by his handiwork.

Cassie's vision blurred as she looked up at Frank.

"How—"

The words wouldn't come. Frank had dropped to one knee in front of the sofa and in his hand was a velvet box holding a ring that shone as brightly as the sparklers he'd given her that night on the beach.

"Will you, Cassie? Will you marry me?"

Frank's voice hitched, his eyes were a mixture of anticipation, love, and just the slightest bit of nervousness.

Cassie's heart nearly exploded. She could dance on air, she could walk on water, she could do anything, she was certain.

"I will, Frank. Of course I'll marry you."

Frank took her left hand from the picture she was still holding and slid the ring on her finger. Nothing had ever felt more right than the ring felt on her finger.

Frank pulled her into his lap.

"I love you, Cassie. I've loved you since I met you, I'll love you forever."

"And I love you, Frank. I've loved you since I met you, I'll love you forever."

When he kissed her, her heart thudded in her chest and her toes curled into the carpet. The tingling she always felt in her belly when he came near turned into an all-out blitzkrieg. She kissed him back with everything she had.

When they finally drew apart, Frank rested his forehead against Cassie's.

"I have never been happier than I am right now. You know that, don't you?"

"If you feel like I do, then yes, I get it."

"Soon, don't you think? We should get married soon. It seems like we've been getting ready for close to eight years."

"Soon is good. I'm betting there are lots of women who will help me plan and shop."

"That's a pretty safe bet."

They were quiet for a moment before Cassie stood and took Frank's hand.

"Dance with me? Let's finish that dance we started at Secrets."

Frank held her close.

And they danced.

Watch for

Shauna's story in Book Four of

The Misty Lake Series

By Margaret Standafer

Coming Soon

Margaret Standafer lives and writes in the Minneapolis area with the support of her amazing husband and children and in spite of the lack of support from her ever-demanding, but lovable, Golden Retriever. It is her sincere hope that you enjoy her work.

To learn more about Margaret and her books, please visit
www.margaretstandafer.com

Printed in Great Britain
by Amazon